CRADLE OF OBLIVION

Copyright © 2023 by Gunnar Helliesen

Graabein Publishing
www.graabein.com

Print and eBook formatting by Lance Buckley Design.
Cover design and artwork by Lance Buckley Design.
Interior illustrations created by Gunnar Helliesen using the Midjourney AI.
Edited by Hannah VanVels Ausbury.

This book is a work of fiction. Names, characters, places, and incidents are the product of the author's imagination or are used fictitiously. Any resemblance to actual events, locales, or persons, living or dead, is coincidental.

All rights reserved

CRADLE OF OBLIVION

GODS OF DISTANT SUNS
BOOK ONE

GUNNAR HELLIESEN

To the memory of my Tante (Aunt) Kari: Kari Rivenæs (1939 - 2014).
Thank you for always believing in me, even when I perhaps didn't.

ONE

THE L4 MOON-EARTH LAGRANGE POINT, APPROXIMATELY 381,666 KILOMETERS FROM EARTH, JULY 1947.

A perfectly round, disc-shaped, and inert space ship was floating in space, slowly rotating around its vertical axis, like a spinning top. It didn't emit or reflect any light or other electromagnetic radiation, so unless you knew exactly where it was, it would be very hard to spot. Even from relatively close range, you'd have to infer its existence by how it obscured the light of distant stars as it moved between you and them.

Inside the ship, things were moving at a glacial pace. There were computers and other machines, and they were operational, but their energy budgets were extremely limited. Not because the ship didn't have energy reserves, but because the ship's designers didn't want it to radiate heat, which could give away its position.

A cylindrical object suddenly appeared about 20 kilometers away, seemingly out of nowhere. It was moving at a high rate of speed, heading directly for the ship.

The ship's central core computer knew instantly that it had no programs for autonomously dealing with a situation like this. It brought all systems and consciousnesses to full alert, energy budgets be damned.

An alarm sounded somewhere in F's mind. It took him a while to shake off the cobwebs and regain consciousness. The ship's AI construct was still booting, but enough of him was online already to recognize the severity of the situation. The alarm code wasn't one he immediately recognized, meaning there were no references to it in his local memory cache. For him to be woken to deal with an infrequent code meant it had to be something serious.

His autonomous Information Gathering personality had a direct link to the ship's central core computer. It queried the ship's massive 3D organic storage matrix and came up with a surprising answer. The code translated to a Class B kinetic threat: an object was on a direct collision course, closing fast. Further queries revealed specifics of the threat: Relative mass: 1/73rd of the ship's mass. Relative speed: 1/14,400th of the speed of light. Time to impact: 0.96 seconds.

Realizing that he'd already wasted a few precious hundredths of a second waking up, he triaged the situation. The Tactical Personality projected that the object would hit the ship at an almost direct angle, along the ship's horizontal axis, just starboard of the centerline. Unless the ship performed evasive actions immediately, it would split the ship in two. The Tactical Personality ordered the Navigation Personality to fire the ship's starboard vertical thrusters, maximum thrust.

The ship started rotating around its horizontal axis. The Navigation Personality then fired the port vertical thrusters as well, attempting to lift the entire ship out of the missile's path, as the missile closed the distance. While this was happening, the Tactical Personality ran a suite of simulations, concluded that a collision was unavoidable, and notified the Maintenance Personality of the impending damage. The Maintenance Personality started shutting down nonessential systems and moving fuel and other consumables away from the projected impact area. If the ship survived the impact, it would need to conserve every atom for the repairs.

F monitored all this while he studied the incoming missile. It was metallic and shaped like a bullet. Laser spectroscopy confirmed that it was a solid block of aluminum. Despite its use as a crude kinetic weapon, its highly polished surface shone in the light from the Sun.

Time to impact: 0.27 seconds. F gathered all the data he had about the threat and the ship's current situation, and sent it in a tight-beam transmission burst to Mission Forward Base.

He watched, feeling strangely detached, as the missile closed the remaining gap. There was nothing more he could do. He was a passenger now. The laws of physics played out on his tactical display, as the ship still tried to rotate fast enough to get out of the way of the incoming missile.

It almost made it. The metallic cylinder hit with explosive force, tearing through the outer skin of the lower hull and ripping out some of the ship's intestines. The damage unfolded as if in slow motion. Gas escaped from the open hull and F realized it was the ship's reaction-mass reserves boiling away into the vacuum of space. Without it, the ship could not maneuver.

The gas cloud expanded into space as remnants of the missile continued past the ship, trailing a cloud of debris, like a comet. It had been just a glancing blow, but given the kinetic energies involved, it was more than enough. Alarms were coming in hard and fast, and the Maintenance Personality was clamoring for his attention. Major systems went offline one by one, and F could feel his consciousness diminishing as energy drained from the ship's systems.

He ran diagnostics, and the results scared him. Propulsion was offline, as was the Tactical Personality. The Navigation Personality informed him that the ship had picked up enough speed from the collision, and from firing its thrusters, to eject it from the Lagrange point.

The L4 Moon-Earth Lagrange point was a point in space where the gravitational pull from the Earth and the Moon were in equilibrium. Any object placed there would stay there, with very little or no need for orbital corrections. However, once ejected from the Lagrange point, there would be no equilibrium and one of the gravitational pulls would win. Meaning, unless he could repair the primary drive, the ship was now in an inexorable free fall towards Earth.

It was the one place where he could not go, the one thing he could not do.

F considered his options, while his consciousness was waning and darkness kept pushing at him from all sides. He could hope the Maintenance Personality could run repairs fast enough for him to arrest his fall and return to his assigned orbit. He quickly discarded that thought. The ship had near miraculous self-repairing abilities, but it was one thing to repair the outer hull, or a sensor, or even a thruster, given enough time and raw materials. It was quite another to repair the primary drive. If he'd had millennia, then maybe. But days? That was impossible. And according to his calculations, days were all he had.

He could try to cause the ship to self destruct, but with the primary drive out of commission, he had no guarantees that the destruction would be complete. The laws of physics and orbital mechanics would ensure that any remaining debris would eventually fall down on Earth, and he'd have no control over where it fell. He couldn't have that. He needed to ensure that the inhabitants of Earth would never find the debris.

The only way to control where the debris fell was to go down with his ship. He knew the Earth intimately, and felt certain that if he could regain enough control over the ship to control its descent, he could successfully crash it into one of Earth's deepest oceans. Once submerged, it wouldn't take long for life in the ocean to cover the wreckage. That would make it unrecognizable and effectively hide it from view.

His decision made, he felt a sense of relief. The darkness surrounding him moved in closer and he could not hold it off any longer.

Just a quick nap.

The Maintenance Personality had done a fantastic job, considering the circumstances. It had closed the gaping hole in the hull, restored emergency power generation, and brought most of the computers back online. As expected, the primary drive was so badly damaged it would have to be replaced. The only safe way to do that was when the ship was in dock.

F considered all this, and the impending end of his watch. He was the fifteenth observer on this mission, and he'd been on duty for a long time. While waiting for the repairs to complete, and for the ship to fall slowly in towards the Earth, he'd had ample time to go through the mission logs.

He'd realized with a shock that his memory had been failing, without him even noticing.

The logs showed that he'd been on duty for almost 80 million Earth years, more than twice the projected service envelope for both himself and the ship. F faintly remembered the dinosaurs, and looking at the logs brought it all back. He'd seen the big asteroid approaching 66 million years ago and understood what it would mean for life on Earth. He'd tried contacting Mission Forward Base to ask for permission to divert the asteroid, but had never received a reply.

That was the second shock. He'd been sending reports to Mission Forward Base regularly, but had completely forgotten that they were supposed to respond. Going back through the logs, he found that the last incoming transmission from them had been almost a million years before the giant asteroid impact.

Judging by the mission logs, he'd never investigated what happened to Mission Forward Base. He didn't know why, and he couldn't find any clues in the logs.

By far, the biggest shock had been to discover that he used to have a crew. The Maintenance, Navigation, and Tactical Personalities weren't crew, they were just aspects of his own consciousness. There had been two other AI life forms with him on the ship when his watch started, each with supplemental personalities that had helped run the mission and interpret the data they collected.

After searching through the logs to find out what had happened to them, he'd finally found an encrypted log entry with meta-data showing that the log entry pertained to the crew. He didn't know what the encryption key was, or how to unlock it.

He kept searching for clues, and a few days later, he found the crew members themselves. They were in stasis and existed only as copies inside the computer core. He knew that the copying process would have destroyed their original consciousnesses. It was standard protocol. He considered trying to reconstitute them, but that would be risky, as well as both pointless and extremely cruel, considering what was about to happen. It was better they didn't know. Perhaps it would be possible to revive them someday, if the core survived.

The discoveries and accompanying shocks he'd endured since the impending collision had woken him up had taken their toll on F. The only logical conclusion he could draw was that he must have broken down, causing the crew to be incapacitated, and the mission to fail. He couldn't stop beating himself up over it, and fell into a depression. He retracted into himself.

Two weeks later, The Navigation Personality broke the silence that had been permeating the ship.

"Atmospheric interface in 10 seconds."

It spoke so softly; it sounded almost like a whisper. F looked at the planet hanging in space above him, achingly beautiful. The solar terminator was coming up, right on cue. The ship was as ready as it could be, circumstances allowing. He felt sad, but also proud of what the little vessel had achieved, and how long and distinguished its service had been.

His feeling of guilt from his discoveries was one he knew he could never shoulder. He'd failed his crewmates, he'd failed the ship, and he'd failed the mission. He knew that he'd never know how or why, and he accepted that as his punishment.

"Atmospheric interface... now," the Navigation Personality said.

An alarm blared. The Maintenance Personality reported that portions of the fuselage were getting dangerously hot. A second later, the structural integrity of the forward edge of the fuselage started collapsing. The altered aerodynamic shape of the craft caused it to dive much steeper into the atmosphere, which made the problem of dynamic stress much worse. Seconds later, the ship started spinning rapidly, sending pieces of debris flying in all directions.

F realized he had little time. The ship was falling apart much faster than he'd expected. The next step in his plan was critical. He was going to eject the computer core, aiming for the deep waters off Antarctica. It was his only chance to save the crew and the data they'd collected while still adhering to the mission parameters.

All the data except him. F would have to be in stasis to transfer to the computer core, but he couldn't both be in stasis and fly the ship. He knew what this meant, and he'd made his choice days ago. He was going to do everything he could to get that core safely down to the planet. Besides, some of his memories were in there, as well as all of his personal observations. Things important to him, notes he'd collected since the start of the mission. It was his way of trying to salvage something of the mission, despite his failure.

He gave the Navigation Personality the order to release the core when ready. It hesitated a fraction of a second, trying to account for the chaotic forces of the steeper dive, the relentless spinning, and the howling currents of the stratosphere. A fraction of a second too long, because just then the rest of the ship broke apart.

The computer core sailed across the heavens, glowing angrily against the twilight sky, trailing black smoke on its way down to the surface of the planet. No one was around to see when it finally impacted. The shock wave hit first, an advance party sending a small volcano of ice erupting from a windswept plain. The computer core itself followed, still traveling at speeds sufficient to flash-melt the ice as it cut its way down to the hard ground underneath.

Most of the rest of the ship had burned up, and what remained were bits and pieces of lighter materials, drifting through the sky, and finally raining down silently over 8,000 miles away, onto a patch of mostly empty grasslands on a completely different continent.

The date was July 4th, 1947. The grasslands were in Roswell, New Mexico.

TWO

EARTH'S UPPER ATMOSPHERE, SOMEWHERE ABOVE
THE SOUTH ATLANTIC OCEAN, NOVEMBER 2039.

Thurgood Jane relaxed a little as the experimental rocket engine strapped to his back sputtered and died. He was in space now, in the ballistic cruise mode phase of the journey. Weightless, and nearly naked, yet traveling at several kilometers per second through the Earth's wispy thin upper atmosphere. He was nearing the top of his parabolic trajectory, a good 150 kilometers above the Earth.

At 190 centimeters and a muscular 90 kilos, he wasn't used to being just dead weight or simply a passenger in any situation, but that was exactly what he was now. He was still free-falling upwards, until gravity could overcome the energy spent by the rocket, and start pulling him back down towards the Earth.

The sound of clapping and cheering came through his earbuds. The cynic in him decided the people in Flight Control were celebrating he hadn't died on their watch. He just hoped the celebrations weren't premature. All he could do now was enjoy the ride and try to forget that he had a well-developed fear of heights. He was on the Earth's nightside still, the sky above him was inky black and full of stars, pinpoint-sharp and impossibly bright.

His thoughts were interrupted first by static and then by a jubilant voice in his ear.

"Whoo-hoo! Hey Jane, is this everything you thought it would be or what?"

The voice belonged to Kii Brockheart, his fiancée. As usual, she energized the comms with her enthusiasm. She was his best possible partner, daring where he was cautious, spontaneous where he was overthinking things. She was the smartest person he knew, and she lit up his world like a nuclear-powered lighthouse. At 166 and a half centimeters tall, or so she claimed, a mop of hair that she could never tame, a smile that beamed, and eyes that glittered. She was also the most beautiful woman he'd ever seen.

Her flight path took her on a slightly different trajectory than his, but her destination was the same: Punta Arenas, Chile.

"Yeah! Awesome view, but I'm not impressed by the inflight service."

"Don't sweat the details, Jane."

Telling him to not sweat the details was an inside joke between the two of them. With his background in the military, burying himself in the details before any op was second nature and impossible to ignore. She would often find him in his favorite chair, hunched over documents and contracts, running through all the likely scenarios. Because of that, and his quiet confidence when he'd reviewed every angle, she trusted him implicitly. She'd follow him anywhere, and in fact, she just had.

They were flying high across the South Atlantic Ocean on the ultimate private jets: their own bodies. What enabled them to do so was Icarus, described by the manufacturer, Serious Matter, Inc., as the perfect means to escape the crowds and the security checkpoints at airports. And, it could get you halfway around the globe in a couple of hours, so there was also that.

'A truly individual travel experience for the experienced individual,' as the company's marketing put it.

Using the gear was supposed to be easy. You simply donned the most expensive garment in the known universe; the Icarus flight and space suit. The fabric was thin, lightweight, and made from special ultra-strong nano materials. It was quite comfortable to wear and offered the wearer nearly unrestricted movement. The helmet, made from high-grade transparent aluminum, contained a heads-up display with both navigation instruments and entertainment screens. Next you strapped on the combined thruster and life support module, found a large open space, and told the suit where you wanted to go. The on-board flight computer took care of the rest.

Although launching yourself to the edge of space from your own backyard wasn't strictly speaking legal in most jurisdictions, who was going to stop you? Before your neighbors had time to dial 911, you were already miles away, accelerating at multiple gees, and headed for the stratosphere. Besides, the people who could afford this mode of transportation would be more likely to launch from a fairly large private estate than something so mundane as a backyard, so the neighbors might not even notice. The beauty of it was that you could land anywhere accessible to a regular parachute. Almost anywhere, with the obvious exception of a busy intersection. This afforded the wearer the added benefit of avoiding such trivialities as customs and immigration, if they so wished.

All of this, of course, assumed that you survived the launch. One of the first test pilots hadn't, with predictable negative implications for the young company.

Enter Kii Brockheart and Thurgood Jane, environmental activists and professional daredevils. Neither of them had set out on that path on purpose, but the path had somehow found them. They had a large following online with fans all over the world. They always made whatever crazy stunt they were doing look both easy and safe. More than that, they always seemed to have fun doing it. They could solve the company's problems, and it didn't take long for a marketing executive to realize that and offer them a job.

They agreed to fly two second-generation Icarus suits from Cape Town, South Africa, to Punta Arenas, Chile, while filming the whole thing. The plan was to help Kii and Jane raise awareness of the environmental disaster spreading across the southern tip of South America, while also garnering lots of goodwill for the company. It was supposed to show the world that Icarus was perfectly safe, if properly operated. At least, that was the theory.

Jane was thinking about all this when Kii interrupted his musings.

"Jane, I have a problem," she said.

She was talking to him over a private channel, so Flight Control couldn't listen in. She wasn't the type of person to trip over trivialities, so if she said she had a problem, she had a problem.

"What's up?" Jane asked.

"I'm veering off-course and I'm unable to correct. Heading due south now."

"Are you still under power?"

"Yes, I've got a few more seconds to go before shutdown."

"You should Notify Flight Control right away. I'm going to turn south so I can match up with you."

"No, don't! It's too dangerous. You're already going too fast and you don't have the fuel for that. Let Flight Control handle it. There's nothing you can do, anyway."

Before he could answer, Flight Control broke in on the open channel.

"Kii, Flight here. We're tracking you off-course, can you confirm?"

The voice belonged to Tim Dalzell, the program Flight Director.

"Confirm, Flight. There's been some kind of malfunction. I'm currently headed due south. I have shutdown, just now, a clean burn," Kii replied.

"Jane, Flight Director. I know what you're thinking. Don't try it. You don't have enough fuel," Dalzell said.

He was too late. Jane had already brought his rocket engine back online. He told the suit's flight computer to turn south and match Kii's flight path. A second later, he almost passed out from the g-forces as the primary rocket engine kicked in and changed his course in a tight turn.

"Too late," Jane forced out between clenched jaws.

"Think about what? Jane, what are you doing?" Kii asked.

"I'm coming after you. What's your location?" Jane said.

"The flight computer says my current trajectory will take me near Antarctica. I just hope 'near' means close enough to swim," Kii replied.

"Flight, I have engine shutdown again. Looks like another clean burn," Jane said.

"Copy that. Be advised that you are officially out of fuel for the primary engine. Unfortunately, that means you're also fresh out of safety margins," Dalzell said.

"Understood, Flight. But I figure this kind of situation is exactly why we have safety margins," Jane said.

"Roger that," Dalzell replied.

Jane turned his attention to Kii.

"Kii, when you say, 'Near Antarctica,' do you mean just short of, or will you overshoot?"

"Looks like I might overshoot. How about you? Will you make it to the Antarctic mainland?"

"I'll get there. But I'm coming in short, no question."

"Jane, Flight. One minute until atmospheric interface," Dalzell said.

"Thanks, Flight. Kii, I'll see you on the ground," Jane replied.

"Good luck, Jane. Be careful," she said.

Kii's voice trembled and broke. Jane knew she wasn't worried about her own safety. She was afraid his famous luck had just run out. He switched to a closed channel with the suit's onboard computer.

"Icarus, re-profile reentry for distance. Authorize safety override, command priority. Eight gees," he said.

"Eight gees set," the computer replied.

The Icarus suit rolled him over on his back and deployed the heat shield. It looked ridiculously thin and frail, like an enormous umbrella. The special graphene-based fabric was slightly translucent and shone like gold.

He was traveling ass-backwards at nearly 8,000 kilometers per hour when he felt the first buffeting of the thin air in the upper atmosphere. Within seconds, the heat shield had turned from gold to dark red, then bright red with spots of gray. The outer rim of the shield was glowing white hot, too bright to look at without a sun visor.

Not that he was trying to look. Even with the suit fabric stiffening and the exoskeleton joints locking to hold his extremities in place, and with shock absorbers between his body and the heat shield, it was still a wild ride. He felt like a rag doll in a tumble dryer as the shield first danced on top of, then bit deeply into the atmosphere. As soon as it did, it was like slamming the brakes on, hard. The G-forces mounted, and it became hard to breathe.

He remembered to not try to hold his breath, but to exhale slowly and then inhale in short gulps of air. It had been part of the pre-flight briefing. Easier said than done, though. There was an immense pressure on his chest, as if someone had parked an elephant on top of him. Every small mouthful of air he could grab felt like a victory.

The heads-up display on his visor counted up the increasing g-forces to eight, then nine, then ten. His vision faded, and he made a mental note to tell the engineers at Serious Matter that the computer had ignored his upper limit of eight gees. Then he felt silly for thinking like a bureaucrat at a time like this.

Just when he thought he was about to pass out, the pressure lifted. The suit retracted the heat shield and rolled him back over onto his belly. He spread his arms and legs and gave the suit the go-ahead to deploy its winged surfaces. All the radar could see below him was water, so he told the navigation computer to head for the nearest solid ground.

The computer responded that it could not comply.

"There is no solid ground within range," it said.

"Do it anyway, just head for land and let's hope for the best," Jane said.

"Optimizing glide profile for distance. Descent rate 73 feet per second, heading due south," the computer replied.

Jane looked ahead, scanning the horizon for any signs of land. There were none. The navigation display helpfully informed him he was just passing through 66,000 feet and that at his current rate of descent he'd be down, dry land or not, in 15 minutes, max.

"Jane! Jane, can you hear me?"

It was Kii. She was speaking fast, almost shouting.

"Kii? I'm here, I'm just through reentry. How are you doing?" Jane replied.

It was good to hear her voice, but he tensed up at the sound of her urgency.

"All good! I've been flying in large circles since atmospheric reentry. Trying to bleed off some speed, and it seems to work. I'm passing through 50,000 feet now, headed for the coast," she said.

"That's brilliant! Do you have a confirmed landing site?" Jane asked.

"Ah, just a sec. Yes, according to the computer, I'm heading for a landing site near the coast of Queen Maud Land. Hopefully, that's close to where you'll land as well," she replied.

An immediate sense of relief washed over Jane. She'd be OK now, leaving only himself to worry about. The fear he'd thought he'd heard in her voice was for him, not for herself.

"I'll sure try. I've optimized the glide path for distance, but according to the suit, it may not be enough," he replied.

He'd tried to sound as carefree as possible, but there was no hiding that he was worried. If he dropped into the South Atlantic Ocean, his chances of survival would be near zero. The water was icy, and there were no ships around to come to his rescue.

"Do you have any fuel left?" Kii asked.

She sounded all business, and he knew why. Kii had this amazing ability to compartmentalize, to focus. She'd instantly chop huge, complex problems into smaller pieces. Then she'd sort them and solve them, one at a time. He quietly wondered where she'd picked up that ability, which easily surpassed his own. Him, the ex-military guy with combat experience.

"No, the engine is as dry as the Antarctic desert," he replied.

"No, not the primary engine, the thrusters," she said.

"Oh, I see where you're going. Yes, I've got close to 50 percent left," he replied.

Creative in a crisis, and ever the engineer, that was her in a nutshell. She was impressive, and he felt grateful. In all his years of doing dangerous stuff, he'd never had a more capable partner. Did that speak to poor training in the military, or to her exceptional mind? He was leaning towards the latter.

"Aim the thrusters towards the rear and slightly down, so you get both a little lift and some forward motion," she said.

"But will they work inside the atmosphere?" Jane asked.

"Yes, but you have to hurry, before your suit automatically jettisons the thruster pack," she replied.

"Copy that, doing it now," he said.

As soon as the thrusters came online, Jane checked his instruments.

"Firing! And I'm picking up some speed," he said.

"As soon as you run out of fuel, jettison the thruster pack. You may have to do it manually. With no fuel, it'll be useless and will literally drag you down," Kii said.

"Got it," Jane replied.

"What's your rate of descent now?" Kii asked.

"With the thrusters firing, close to zero. That's amazing!" Jane said.

A few seconds later, the thrusters ran out of fuel.

"Icarus, authorize safety override, command priority. Jettison thruster pack now," Jane told the computer.

"Jettisoning," the computer replied.

"Icarus, what's my projected landing site? Can I reach dry land?" Jane asked.

"Affirmative, the new landing site estimate is Queen Maud Land, just southwest of Mt. Rivenæsnuten," the computer replied.

Jane breathed a sigh of relief.

"Kii, did you hear that?" he asked.

"No, what?" she replied.

"I'm headed your way," he said. "The computer confirms it; I'll land in the same area as you."

There was a click in his earbuds as she keyed the microphone to speak. No words came, just a muffled sob, then silence.

"I know," he said, softly. "That was too close. I'm sorry."

"We promised each other," she replied. "No cowboy stuff."

"No cowboy stuff," he repeated.

The curvature of the Earth stretched out in front of Jane, a blazing horizon obscuring the sun, sparkling with colors like a glass marble caught in the sunshine after a downpour. He looked straight down, wanting to identify their designated landing zone, but the Antarctic continent was still dark, sleeping under a velvet blanket.

Unlike some of his former military colleagues, Jane had never enjoyed parachuting. It was not a good fit for his fear of heights, and he always felt like he'd just made a major mistake every time he jumped out of a perfectly fine aircraft. Jumping in the dark over an unknown landing zone made him extra nervous.

"Jane, you seeing this?"

Kii's voice was all business again, but there was a slight timbre to it. Telling him something had caught her attention.

"No, seeing what? I'm coming up on 30,000 feet. You?"

"Check your radar. We're falling into a sandstorm," she said.

The storm was small, and moving fast, like a demented dancer with a skirt made of red sand, swirling and engulfing anything in its way that came too close. They were falling straight into its path. There was no way to avoid it now.

"Where the hell did that thing come from?" he asked.

Thin wisps of brown enveloped him, growing thicker by the second, then vanishing. His heart was racing; he knew what fine dust could do to his suit, and even to the soft human flesh inside, given enough time. There it was again, more sand, this time a dark brown wall coming towards him, moving at incredible speed.

Back in the day, sand storms weren't supposed to exist at this altitude, but that was then. All bets were off after the Great Climate Shift around ten years ago. There was no telling what Mother Nature would throw at you now. They should have known, and he was kicking himself for not having factored it in. After all, it was a big part of the reason they were here in the first place, to show an unwilling world that nature was no longer conducting business as usual.

The storm buffeted him and threw him around; he lost track of Kii and all sense of direction, up or down. Pulling up the autopilot display, he set it to track Kii's signal. He checked his altitude; coming up on 25,000 feet.

The suit did its best to keep him stable, but the winds were too powerful. Fear crept up on him; for the second time since they launched, he considered the possibility that they could be in more trouble than they could handle.

There was no way for him to abort the landing. He'd spent his fuel and jettisoned his only means of propulsion. If he opened the parachute too soon, he'd risk it getting ripped to shreds by the wind and the sand. He checked his radar and realized to his relief that he was again falling right-side-up when he suddenly emerged from the storm into more calm and clear air. Kii was nowhere to be seen. Even the tracker couldn't locate her.

Jane tried hailing her on the radio, but there was no reply. He realized he couldn't move his head from side to side. The mechanism had jammed. He could still move his limbs, but the exoskeleton joints felt stiff. The sand had scuffed and opaqued the exterior visor on his helmet, especially on one side. The storm had done some damage, but it could have been much worse.

He pulled up the navigation display and looked for his designated landing site. Jane didn't see it, and realized he must be way off course. He instructed the computer to find him a suitable backup landing site within range and to head for it. The suit responded, adjusting his pitch and rolling him to the right. He could see the new landing site on his display. It was flat and round; the bottom of an ancient meteor crater.

An alarm flashed on his display. He was coming up on parachute deployment. He assumed the "shuttlecock" position — face down, belly out, shoulders and arms thrust back and legs spread — slowing him down to a mere 200 kph. Watching his altimeter and monitoring the landing site, he retracted the suit's wings and deployed his parachute.

"Kii, are you OK?"

He was getting worried now. If she was in trouble, her suit's systems would have jettisoned her thruster pack and deployed her parachute automatically, but if she hit the ground while unconscious, she could still get badly hurt. That was if her suit was still functioning, and if her main chute deployed correctly. Too many 'ifs'.

His radar told him the ground was coming up fast, so he flared the parachute and performed a textbook landing in near complete darkness. He removed his helmet, gathered his parachute, and looked around. The early dawn sky had brightened just enough for him to make out the landscape. It was flat, with low shrubbery, and some boulders here and there. Nothing moved.

He'd never been to Antarctica before, but he remembered seeing pictures of how it used to be; cold, desolate, and covered in ice. It was still chilly in the early morning light, but nothing like those old days. He looked around him, marveling at how much the landscape had changed from those images he'd seen in books and on television.

It was also a sad sight, because he knew all too well what had happened to all the wildlife that used to call this place home. Penguins, one of his favorite animals when he was a kid, had gone from ubiquitous in and around Antarctica to nearly extinct in a matter of a few decades.

Right now, though, he was a little more concerned about his own and Kii's survival. Less than two hours ago, they'd been in the hustle and bustle of Cape Town. Now they were here, in what was still one of the most desolate places on Earth. He wondered how she was doing.

The sky above was clear, and he knew it was going to be a warm day once the sun rose a little higher. He inventoried his supplies. Enough water and energy bars to last him a day, maybe two, and his first aid kit. Kii would have the same.

Their intended landing site was off to the west, so his first thought was to hike in that direction, hoping that Kii would wait for him there. Jane tried hailing her again, but all he got was static. He tried Flight Control and got yet more static. He realized he must be in a radio shadow, and out of line of sight of the communication satellite network. At the time of its launch, no one had thought there would ever be a need to fully cover Antarctica. After all, it had been nothing but a vast, frozen emptiness.

When the sun came up, it flooded the immense crater with light, allowing him to see the low rim in the far distance. The crater was fairly flat, but to his right, about a hundred meters away, the ground dropped off sharply.

He walked over to the edge and looked around. It was another, smaller crater, in the middle of the large one. At the bottom of the crater, near the center, was a large boulder. Next to it, maybe six meters away, was a strange shape. He rushed down the slope and ran towards the shape, afraid if what he'd find. Once he got closer, he realized it was a thruster pack.

Its parachute system must have failed, because it was so mangled by the impact with the ground that there was no way of telling if it belonged to Kii or not. He scanned around in all directions, trying to see if there were any signs of her.

Nothing.

A sudden bright glint caught the corner of his eye, and he turned to see where it came from. A large chunk of rock was resting on the ground next to the boulder, presumably knocked off by the falling thruster pack. Underneath was something metallic and shiny.

Jane made his way over to the boulder. Something with a rounded, right angle corner and straight sides was sticking up out of the big rock. Judging by what he could see, it looked most of all like a box or a case made of metal. Only part of it was sticking out, the rest was still inside the boulder.

He was about to touch it when a sudden sense of foreboding made him stop. He smiled to himself. This wasn't like him, despite being a Navy brat. He'd spent his entire life in the Navy and sailors were famously supposed to be superstitious. Not him, though. Still, he didn't know what this object was, and it didn't hurt to be careful. Besides, he'd learned to trust his gut. Maybe he was a little superstitious after all.

His dad, Marcus Jane, would disapprove. He was an old-school cold warrior, a scientist, and a stickler for accuracy and facts. Both of Jane's parents were career Navy, so he grew up on military bases all over the US and the rest of the world. They were loving, but relatively strict, and they expected him to join the Navy when he was old enough. So he did.

He finished college on the Navy's dime, studying political science and international relations.

And yet here he was, in Antarctica of all places, with the early morning sun playing off some strange metal object that he couldn't explain. It looked modern, yet somehow it was sticking out from inside of a rock. A rock which was possibly an old meteorite. At least, that's what it looked like. And despite all that, the metal object looked brand new. It was shiny, almost golden, and the reflections of sunlight were painfully bright. He tried moving his head, but the reflections seemed to follow him, moving of their own accord.

He grabbed a fist-sized rock from the ground and carefully touched it to the metal surface. Somehow it felt like the two weren't connecting, even though he could see that they were.

For a second, he wondered if someone was playing a prank on him. He immediately dismissed the idea. Until a few minutes ago, no one had known that he'd be landing next to this crater. Not even him.

He moved the tip of the rock slowly along the surface of the object. It was the same feeling as before, as if the rock wasn't connecting with the metal, but somehow gliding across it without touching. He pushed down hard and tried again, but it made no difference. He couldn't feel any friction at all, and the rock left no scratches or marks in the metal.

He searched the ground around the boulder for any signs of more of the shiny metal, but there was nothing. He tried using smaller pieces of rock to excavate more of the object from the boulder, but the boulder was too hard.

He looked around. There were rocks everywhere, and they all looked more or less the same. The same colors, the same patterns, and the same lack of anything growing on them. Another thing they had in common was their weight. All the rocks he tried lifting felt heavier than he expected them to be, based on their size. He knew what that most likely meant. He was standing in the middle of a field of meteorite debris.

Remembering that he'd been filming the entire time, he ordered the suit's computer to look through and analyze the footage for anything out of the ordinary. It didn't take the computer long to point out that the boulder with the object was sitting dead center in the crater.

He was pondering the implications of that, and staring at the metal object, when he thought he saw a shadow on its surface. He moved from side to side to get a better view, but whatever he thought he'd seen was gone. Frustrated, he sat down, leaning his back against the boulder.

He took stock of his situation. He knew he had limited amounts of water and food. The climate was arid, harsh, and warm, and other than the limited shadow made by the boulder, there was really no shelter or cover. Worst of all, he had no radio signal. He needed to get to higher ground quickly, so he could find Kii and they could get out of here before their supplies ran out.

Before he did that, though, he needed to document his find, including its precise location. Knowing that the shiny object inside the boulder would be visible from the air, he did his best to cover it up. He didn't know what this was yet, but he had a hunch it was important. And he was sure he wanted to keep it to himself, at least for now.

The ground was hard, making it difficult to work enough of it loose. He piled on as much dirt and sand as he could, along with small rocks and parts of the rubble from the impact of the falling thruster pack.

Standing back, he admired his work. He realized it would only last until the next sandstorm swept through, but it would have to do.

Time to head for the hills. He needed to know if Kii was safe.

After trekking through the Antarctic desert for a little over two hours, he finally got to the edge of the enormous crater. As soon as he popped his head over the rim, his radio sprang to life.

"Thurgood Jane, this is Rescue Two. Do you copy?"

"Rescue Two, this is Jane. I read you, albeit barely. Any word from Kii?"

"Negative. Rescue One is searching for her as we speak. We're getting telemetry from your suit now, so we've got a fix on your location. We'll be there in one hour."

"I appreciate that. This space suit started chafing after the first mile of hiking."

"Roger that. I guess they didn't intend it for walking. Rescue Two out."

Jane looked around, searching for anything that could provide some shade. There was nothing. He walked to the highest spot he could find and sat down. There was a slight breeze from the north-east. Even though the air was warm and didn't really cool him much, it felt good against his face.

Despite appearances, the crater was quite ancient. It was one of those things that was so magical about Antarctica. Everything there differed from what you'd expect to see anywhere else. The landscape, frozen in time, covered in ice, remained unchanged for millions of years. There had still been erosion, especially in places where the ice had moved and flowed. But in other places, like the crater Jane was sitting in, the ice had barely moved at all.

With the ice recently gone, exposing the old landscape underneath, the ground looked much like it had when the ice first covered it.

Jane scanned the distance, trying to locate the boulder with the shiny object inside it. The crater floor stretched out below him for many miles and the mid afternoon air was dense with heat haze, leaving him unable to make out any details.

He'd carried the damaged thruster pack with him to the crater rim, unwilling to leave it for someone else to find, and for them to discover the shiny object nearby. He wasn't certain what the shiny object was, only that it was significant and that he wanted to know more about it. But first, he needed to know that Kii was safe.

"Rescue One, this is Jane. Any sign of Kii yet?"

Silence.

"Come in, Rescue One."

"Jane, this is Rescue Two. Rescue One is temporarily outside of radio range, but they're on their way to her projected landing site. We'll keep you posted. Rescue Two ETA at your location now ten minutes."

Jane was about to key the radio to reply when a loud, piercing sound nearly split his eardrums. He ripped the earbuds from his ears, but he could still hear the shrieking sound coming from the buds as he held them in his hand.

After about thirty seconds, the sound stopped. He waited another minute before carefully putting the buds back in his ears.

"Rescue Two, this is Jane. What the hell was that?"

"Jane, Rescue Two. What was what?"

"That radio noise. It was painful, almost burst my eardrums."

"Sorry, no idea what you're talking about. We have no radio noise at our end. Are you sure it wasn't local?"

Jane sat back and considered the question.

'Local'?

As far as he knew, there was no technology anywhere near him, except for the stuff he was carrying. In fact, there was nothing at all around for hundreds of miles. Even though much of the ice was gone now, international treaties still governed Antarctica, outlawing most human activity. And there was the Chinese blockade in place since they claimed the entire Antarctica archipelago for China, about a year earlier.

He was still pondering this when he heard the sonic boom of a rescue Griffin as it fell out of the sky towards him. He watched as it smoothly transitioned, first from ballistic to fixed-wing, then to rotary-wing flight, before settling on the ground near him.

He got on his feet with a weary sigh, grabbed the ruined thruster pack by one of its straps, and started dragging it over towards the Griffin.

Two of the crew had jumped out of the craft to assist him. They were both wearing military uniforms, with flight helmets and reflective sunglasses. Even though he couldn't see their eyes, he could swear that one of them looked familiar.

"Is that you, Sergeant Washington?"

"It sure is, sir!"

"I haven't seen you since you hauled my ass out of the fire in Denmark that time."

"Good to see you, sir. I seem to make a career out of getting you out of tight spots. I'm a staff sergeant now. Oh, and this is corporal Cortez."

"Good to see you, too! We'll make you a gunny yet. Nice to meet you, Corporal Cortez. Mind giving me a hand with this old thruster pack?"

Without another word, Staff Sergeant Washington and Corporal Cortez grabbed the thruster pack between them and lifted it into the Griffin as if it was light as air.

"Need a hand up those stairs, sir?"

Staff Sergeant Washington was looking at him with a grin on her face.

"Thanks, I think I can manage. Even though I must have misplaced my cane somewhere."

He grinned back at her.

"All right! Now, let's go find Kii!"

Four hours and one medical checkup later, he was in a makeshift rescue operations center in Punta Arenas, Chile. He was demanding to be flown back to Antarctica to look for Kii, driving everyone around him nuts.

Adelaida Contreras, a colonel in the Chilean Air Force, was patiently trying to explain to him he was of more use to the rescue effort right where he was, when an amused voice came in over the radio.

"Rescue Ops, this is Rescue One. We've located Ms. Brockheart. She's alive and well."

Jane grabbed the microphone before the radio operator could beat him to it.

"Rescue One, Jane here. I'm very relieved to hear that. Where is she, and what's her status?"

"I'd say her status is downright excellent. She's singing karaoke with a bunch of drunk Norwegians at the old Bamse research station."

"Karaoke?"

"Yeah. Her rendition of 'Stairway to Heaven' is actually pretty good."

"Tell me about it. Why didn't she radio in?"

"Apparently, her radio is busted, and the station doesn't have one. The research agency officially abandoned it years ago, so we're not sure what the Norwegians are doing here. We're bringing them all back to base now."

Close to five hours later, when Jane saw Kii stepping down from the huge Griffin rescue craft, he felt himself choke up. He hadn't realized until that second how much tension and worry he'd been carrying. He sighed in relief and laughed when he saw she looked like she was nursing a serious hangover.

Her face lit up when she saw him, and that sight hit him like a bullet to a kevlar vest. He felt something change and settle inside him, something fundamental. He couldn't explain it, but he knew his entire trajectory had changed from that moment on. And it changed him forever.

"Were you worried about me?" she asked as she stood in front of him, a smile playing over her lips.

"Yes, I was. I was also worried about those poor Norwegians, because they didn't know what they were in for. Are you OK?"

"I'm doing great now," she said.

She wriggled into his arms and rested her head on his chest.

"Me…" he started.

He swallowed hard and cleared his throat.

"Me too, now. Let's get you checked out by the medic. Just in case," he said.

Later that night Jane lay on a cot in a tent at base camp, trying to focus on Kii as she paced around, recounting her reentry and fall through the eye of the storm. She'd tracked the storm carefully, matched velocities and aimed for the relatively calm center. As soon as she'd landed, she'd retrieved her parachute, made her way to the research station, and sought cover from the trailing edge of the storm.

Her cool head and quick thinking impressed him, as always.

"Kii, I saw something," he said.

He tried to sit up, but she pushed him right back down, climbed onto the cot, and straddled him.

"Can it wait?" she asked.

He laughed.

"I think you're going to want to see this. Here, let me show you," he said.

He patted his pockets, looking for his phone, and gave it to her.

She looked at the pictures, first cursory, then with more interest.

"I don't understand. This looks like someone put a metal briefcase inside of a rock. Almost like a piece of turn-of-the-century art. Where did you find this?" she asked.

"It was inside one of the many boulders that are strewn all over the floor of the old meteor crater where I landed. Your thruster pack must have hit the rock and broken it open. The parachute never deployed, so it probably hit pretty hard," he replied.

"Wow. What are the odds?"

Her voice trailed off as she scrutinized the pictures.

"Did you see any writing or other markings on the briefcase?" she asked.

"No. But it was definitely man made. I don't think it's actually a briefcase, though. It's too elaborate for that," he said.

He frowned.

"Then again, all we have to go on is a corner. The rock covers the rest. We need to find out what the hell this thing is," he said.

"What if it's military or something like that? We could get into trouble," she said.

Her voice sounded pensive, but her eyes shone with excitement. The corners of her mouth turned up into a slight smile and her eyebrows danced up and down, a sure sign she was hooked.

"Whose military, though? We're talking about the Antarctic. Everybody claims it and nobody recognizes anyone else's claims. Or really care about the old treaty, unless when it suits them. This is international territory, an empty desert. Besides, who's gonna know?" he said.

It was a perfect rationalization, and he was proud of it. He was also eager to get started.

"We need to organize this. How heavy do you think it is?" she asked.

"Depends. Do we bring tools and try to excavate the briefcase on-site, or do we try to bring the entire boulder… somewhere? Where?" he said.

"Transporting the entire boulder probably wouldn't work. We need to get some help, and some tools, and bring them to the rock. Maybe also a sponsor, to pay for all this. But first we go, just you and I. I want to see it for myself," she said.

He was about to say something when she leaned forward and placed a finger on his lips.

"Later."

She threw his phone onto the other cot and gave him a look that could have melted Antarctica all on its own. She smiled, sat back up, and removed her top. He made a half-hearted attempt to reach for his phone, changed his mind and reached for her instead.

THREE

THE MOJAVE DESERT, NEAR PALM GARDENS, NEVADA, MAY 2037.

The Icarus flight wasn't Kii's and Jane's first stunt. They never planned it this way, but risky stunts had defined their relationship from the start.

Their first adventure had really been her idea. She'd been talking about it throughout their first date, and how she would love to try it. Jane had never even heard of deck surfing, so he had to ask her what it was.

She'd explained how 'the deck' really meant the ground in this context. Evidently, it was a term commonly used by pilots. Deck surfing was the latest thing, an extreme sport so new and so extreme that lawmakers hadn't caught up with it yet. It was all perfectly legal, and perfectly safe, at least according to Kii.

Before he knew it, he'd blurted out his invitation to go try it together, and she'd accepted. He was sitting across from her, trying to finish his meal, feeling slightly nauseous from both intense happiness and utter panic. He knew that none of that mattered. All that mattered was the way her face had lit up when he asked, and the way she was looking at him, as he swallowed hard to contain his fear and his pasta.

A week later, they'd driven out into the Mojave Desert and found the somewhat optimistically named 'heliport' right next to a dilapidated combined gas station and motel. It was little more than a dirt parking lot, with a couple of discarded old pickup trucks at the far end.

The very modern, ex-military helicopter looked surreal and out of place, its sleek, black fuselage gleaming in the morning sun, seemingly casually parked right next to the rundown buildings.

After a worryingly short pre-flight briefing, which included a few words on the even shorter history of deck surfing, they were off. He soon found himself standing in the doorway of a moving helicopter, going a hundred and sixty kilometers per hour, a mere thirty meters off the ground.

Jane looked at Kii out of the corner of his eye.

"I have a bad feeling about this," he shouted over the din.

Kii didn't respond. Instead, she grinned and slowly let one hand go of the railing behind her and swung it towards him, middle finger outstretched. Then she let go with her other hand, and fell.

He watched her drop away and felt sick. Heights were just not his thing. He knew he had to follow her or he would never live it down, nor forgive himself. So much for the strong, brave, ex-military type.

He realized she would know if he kept hesitating. Even worse, she would know he was hesitating out of fear. With that thought, and with his eyes closed, he let go.

Jane fell, silently, tumbling slowly, clumsily, where she had looked so graceful just moments before. He opened his eyes and looked for her, but knew it was hopeless. He felt disoriented and panicky, his only connection to sanity from the bungee cord he could sense unwinding behind him.

Something grabbed at his ankles and pulled, harder and harder, until he felt like his entire body was stretching and his head was about to pop off and continue on its own.

Suddenly the pull on his ankles lessened and then he was weightless, hovering in midair, still not knowing up from down. He sensed he was falling again, and the cord did its job of pulling at his ankles until he finally came to a rest. He was hanging upside down below the helicopter, like a fish hooked by its tail.

He was spinning slowly and with every revolution he could see Kii hanging by her cord, arms outstretched and a big, shit-eating grin on her face. She looked gorgeous and so incredibly alive. For a moment, he even forgot his own terror.

There was something about her, an abandon and freedom of spirit that he'd never known for himself. He knew he was, right at that moment, in mortal danger, and that it was for no good reason at all. No hostages to free, no bad guys to stop. And yet, because of her, and with her, he knew that he'd do it again.

He smiled to himself, still not quite believing that he had actually suggested this. Not only was he deck surfing, but he was deck surfing with the most insane outfit in all the Mojave. Only complete maniacs would combine it with bungee jumping.

He felt a slight tug at his back. Seconds later, he was being pulled up into a horizontal position by the additional wires attached to his harness. The bungee cord was tight too, fixing him in position, facing in the direction of travel.

They were moving faster now, air rushing at him, clawing at his skin and tearing at his limbs. He assumed the position, arms out in front, legs spread, knees bent.

Without warning, he was falling again. This time it was the chopper diving towards the ground, with himself and Kii dangling underneath it. The ground was racing towards them. Just when he thought they would hit, they passed over the edge of a canyon and dropped into it. Even with the deafening noise of the wind and the helicopter, he could hear Kii howling with joy.

They swooped down the wall of the canyon, dangerously close to the ground. Jane knew his position relative to the terrain was being monitored a thousand times a second, that lasers and GPS trackers were keeping the helicopter precisely positioned and that the crew had done this literally hundreds of times before. It was unbelievably scary, exhilarating, terrifying, breathtaking.

He was flying low over the landscape, his belly only meters away from the ground, doing one hundred and sixty kilometers per hour while dodging boulders and cacti. One mistake, just one tiny error, and they would all end up on the evening news. He knew there was nothing he could do now, except enjoy the ride and hope for the best. The thought was strangely liberating.

Looking out of the corner of his eye, he could just make her out flying next to him, her thick mass of black hair streaming out of her helmet, her arms waving in a futile attempt to steer as the landscape hurled towards her. With a start, he realized he was doing the same thing with his arms.

The canyon made a turn, and they were following it, pulling gees against the wires as the helicopter was flying dangerously close to the inside wall of the turn while they were barely clear of the outside wall.

Suddenly, straight in front of him, was a large outcrop. Part of his mind noticed the sound of the chopper engines changing as the rotor blades clawed against the air to change the direction of the big and heavy machine, pulling against inertia and gravity in an uneven fight to save his ass. The rest of his mind went blank with calm terror, telling him he was about to die.

He didn't even have time to close his eyes and brace for the inevitable impact he knew was coming before he was past the outcrop and heard a mighty bellow from Kii. He turned his head and saw her looking at him, smiling, one hand waving and the other giving him a thumbs up.

They started climbing away from the landscape and passed over the lip of the canyon onto the flat desert surrounding it. The helicopter turned south, heading back to base as they were being hauled back inside. The crew instructed him to stand as they unhooked him, but his legs gave way and he found himself on his hands and knees on the floor, trembling. Strong arms pulled at him and heaved him into a seat.

A second later, Kii was being pulled inside. She could barely stand still. She was jumping up and down, her arms gesticulating while the crew worked on her harness. As soon as she was free, she ran over to him and grabbed his shoulders, her face inches from his.

"Have you ever done anything so wild? That was insane!"

She was grinning, laughing, her eyes dark suns, ablaze.

Before he could reply, she kissed him. Then she broke free and started talking about the outcrop, but he wasn't listening. He reached for her, pulled her close, and kissed her right back. His heart was pounding, his ears were on fire. He was still high as a kite on adrenaline and pure disbelief.

She flung her arms around his neck and closed her eyes, hugging him tight. She knew he'd done this for her, just to be with her, and the thought was both a little disturbing and very sweet.

FOUR

QUEEN MAUD LAND, ANTARCTICA, DECEMBER 2039.

"It's definitely not a briefcase," Jane said.

He stood back and looked at the artifact.

"No, it's not," Kii replied.

She ran her hand over the top, feeling the smooth surface.

"I'm not even sure it's metal," she added.

He was about to say something about touching it, but she'd been too quick. Realizing that he was probably just being paranoid and silly anyway, he reached out and did the same.

"It's like glass, only completely friction-less," he said.

The two of them had returned to Antarctica after finishing their publicity tour for Serious Matter. It had gone well, everything considered. An international TV network had even offered them a docudrama deal, but they'd put that on hold. They wanted to go back and investigate the artifact first. They'd kept its existence a secret, instead blaming the need to return to Antarctica on a desire to study the environmental impact of the frequent sandstorms.

The corner of the artifact gleamed in the bright grey light, the sun struggling to break through a high altitude layer of clouds. It was still early in the day, so not too hot.

"It feels almost like plastic to me," she replied.

"Or gold," he added.

"It's smaller than I thought. How come there are no scratches on it? It looks brand new," she said.

She was studying it intently.

"Good question. How can we find out?" he said.

He ran his fingers over every exposed surface, as if trying to find clues with his fingers.

"What's that? Are those markings? Or writing?" Kii asked.

She tilted her head from one side to the other, trying to make out if the surface was as plain as she'd first thought.

"What do you mean? I don't see any markings," he said.

He stood next to her, following her lead, tilting his head from side to side, when he thought he saw a fleeting shadow.

"Oh yeah, I think I see what you mean. It's almost like a discoloration. The light has to be just right to even see it," he said.

"I think they're symbols," she said.

She tried to get a better look, but the symbols were hard to pin down. It was like they were moving, sliding around inside the artifact, just below the surface.

"It doesn't look like any letters I've ever seen, but then again, I'm no expert. It looks more like hieroglyphs to me," he said.

They looked at each other.

"Are we being pranked?" Kii asked.

They'd both had the same thought, but she'd been the first to say it.

"Yeah, that's gotta be it. Because if it's not a prank…"

He let the words hang for a second, then finished his own sentence.

"If it's not, then what we have here is crazy," he said.

"A man-made object," she said.

She paused. Her eyebrows were performing a little dance, moving up and down as she looked at him, then at the artifact. He knew what that meant; this thing intrigued her as much as it did him.

"Or at least, not a naturally occurring object," he said.

"OK, fine. Made from some strange material we've never seen," she said.

"With odd looking markings on it, that look like writing. Or hieroglyphs," he said.

"Hidden …"

She stopped herself and shook her head.

"This is wild," she said.

"Yes, I know. Let's called it buried," he said. "We don't know if it was intentional."

"Buried inside a large boulder," she said, still shaking her head.

"Inside of an ancient meteor crater," he said.

"In the Antarctic," he said.

"Which makes it? What?" she asked.

Kii looked at him, her eyes intense and a hint of a smile playing on her lips.

"Hell if I know," he replied. "Alien?"

"You went there. You said it out loud!" she said.

She laughed, then placed her left hand on his chest, pushing against him.

"I did. What else could it be?" Jane asked.

He pushed back against her hand, tilted his head to one side, and smiled.

"You realize that what you're saying is, of course, impossible," she said.

She raised one eyebrow, all serious now.

"Yeah, but so are all the alternatives," he replied.

"Whatever it is, maybe we shouldn't mess with it. If it's ancient, or especially if you're right and it's alien, we should preserve the scene for the experts," she said.

She placed her hands on her hips and stared at the boulder. Her right index finger was tapping against her belt and she was furrowing her brow. She bit her lip and turned to look at him.

"We should, but we're not going to, are we? I don't want to lose this thing," he said.

"What do you mean?" she asked.

"If we go public with this, it'll be a free-for-all," he said. "We'll have government types crawling all over this place in no time, and we'll get kicked to the curb. And if it isn't the government, it'll be the tinfoil hat crowd. Either way, we lose."

"You have a point. But, if this is truly alien, then it's the scientific find of the century. And that's how we should treat it," she said.

"OK, how about this? We'll document and record everything for posterity, down to the tiniest detail. Even though we're not archeologists, we can still be methodical and we can still apply common sense," he said.

"Deal! Where do we start?" she asked.

Four hours later, all they had to show for their efforts was dust. It covered them from head to toe, and it ran in sweaty rivulets down their necks and backs. The artifact was still well and truly lodged inside the boulder, which had turned out to be a lot harder than they'd initially thought.

"We're going to need better tools," Jane said.

"And more hands," Kii said.

"A team?" he asked.

"Uh-huh. Remember those Norwegians I stumbled across at the old abandoned research station?" she asked.

"Yeah?"

"They swore me to secrecy, but they told me they weren't really here to study the changes to wildlife after the ice disappeared. Everything they told the Chilean military was just a cover story," she said.

"So, why were they here?" he asked.

"They told me they were really here to search for an ancient artifact. Something about a sacred text," she said.

"How does that help us?" he asked.

"They said they believe it's of alien origin," she said.

"Oh!" he exclaimed.

"Yeah, they're going to love this shit."

FIVE

BERGEN, NORWAY, DECEMBER 2039.

Tinnus Ødegård looked at the invitation to attend Astrobiology-Con in Las Vegas. It featured a picture of him smiling, under the headline: "Norwegian Researcher to Present New Evidence of Prolonged Alien Presence on Prehistoric Earth." He'd felt so confident this time, so sure that he was on the right track. Not for the first time, his overconfidence would be his undoing. The conference was only three months away, and he had absolutely nothing to show for himself.

The Chilean military had kicked him and his team out of Antarctica, claiming that they didn't have the proper permits to be there, and that they couldn't guarantee their safety in case the Chinese intervened. It didn't really matter at that point, though. They'd been there for weeks already and hadn't found a single shred of evidence supporting his theories.

He turned his attention to the open laptop on his desk. Ancient Sumerian and Babylonian texts filled the screen. He'd been studying them for years in his spare time, convincing him he'd cracked their true meaning. To him, they told a story of alien visitors who came to Earth eons ago, and settled here.

Actually, timing was one thing he wasn't completely sure of. The people who wrote the texts counted the passing of time in terms of generations, but never specified what that meant. The Sumerians used a sexagesimal numbering system, while the Babylonians used a duodecimal system. Trying to decipher just how long ago the aliens had visited according to the texts was very difficult. What he was sure of was that obviously it must have happened before people wrote the texts, which itself was thousands of years ago.

He'd found the same type of references in old texts from Mesoamerica, along with actual drawings of astronauts and spaceships. Some of them were on *amate*, an ancient form of bark paper. Others were inscriptions on monuments. The problem was, outside of a loyal group of true believers, no one took him seriously. Other researchers studied the same texts and images and read completely different things into them. He longed to come across hard evidence proving that his interpretations were correct, something so conclusive that even his staunchest critics couldn't deny it.

Aliens had come here, not just to visit, but to settle. They'd obviously brought advanced technology, but also language and cultural mores, such as the attempted abolition of human sacrifice.

There were still deep mysteries, such as where are they now, and why aren't there any monuments or permanent structures left by them? Why did they come and claim they were settling among us, only to leave and take all traces of their visit with them?

The texts had promised that there would still be traces of them. There would be a shrine, or a holy place. Buried deep underground. "Hidden by the Earth," as the texts said.

He was pondering this, and what he was going to do about his upcoming talk in Las Vegas, when his cell phone rang. At least he thought it was his. He could hear the muffled ringing and the distinct buzzing sounds of a cell phone, but his phone was nowhere to be found. He started digging through the papers on his desk before remembering that he'd left it in the bathroom. Thinking it was his agent calling, he rushed into the little half bathroom to pick up the call before it went to his digital assistant. As he did, he caught sight of himself in the bathroom mirror.

He was about 188 centimeters, lanky, with a salt and pepper mane of hair and a long beard, both seemingly out of control. His eyes were puffy and red, as if he had just cried. This startled him, and for a second he forgot about the ringing phone. He was pretty sure he hadn't cried and raised his hands to touch the pouches under his eyes.

Was it exhaustion? Or the pressure of the upcoming convention? Had he done this to himself? Was he headed for some form of physical or mental breakdown again? The thoughts swirled in his head.

Just then, the cell phone, already balancing precariously on the edge of the bathroom vanity, rang one more time. The vibration sent it over the edge, and it fell to the floor. Ødegård broke free from his introspection and bent down to retrieve it.

"Yes, Frank?"

"Oh, hi, is this Tinnus Ødegård?"

Ødegård straightened his back and resumed studying his own face in the mirror.

"You're not Frank?"

"No, this is Kii Brockheart. We…"

Before she could say anything else, Ødegård hung up. He was used to receiving crank calls from people who were deep into conspiracy theories but who couldn't care less about his research or the actual science. He had no time for them.

Then again, the name had rung a bell. He just couldn't place it. Was she Frank's assistant? What was her name? Why could he never remember people's names? It drove him nuts.

Just when he was about to put the phone in his pocket, he noticed he had a new message. It was a video showing a golden box sticking out of a large boulder. The camera panned around, showing the landscape, and then zoomed in on the surface of the golden box. He could see strange markings that appeared to move. The camera then moved to a GPS location tracking device, but Ødegård didn't need to see what it said. He'd already recognized the landscape and one very distinctive mountain range: It was Queen Maud Land, Antarctica.

A note accompanied the video: "Please answer my call."

His phone rang.

"Who is this?" he demanded.

"This is Kii Brockheart. Did you have time to look at the video?"

"Yes, I did. What's this about?" he asked.

"We were hoping you could tell us," Kii said.

"How so?" he asked.

"When we met at Bamse Station, you told me you're looking for evidence of alien visitors on Earth. Right?" she said.

"Ah. That was you?" he asked.

"Yes, hi, that was me. It's nice to talk to you again. You were saying about looking for evidence of aliens?" she asked.

"I need hard evidence, something tangible, to show that they were here. Why do you ask?" he said.

"I think you need to come and look at this thing we found," she said.

"The thing in the video? What is it?" he asked.

"That's the million dollar question. We need your help in finding out," she said.

"It looks like it's embedded inside that rock. Is it?" he asked.

"Yes. And we're pretty sure this is no ordinary rock. We think it's a meteorite," she said.

"Iron?" he asked.

His thoughts were racing.

"No, I don't think it's iron, but it is dense," she said.

"It's iron," he said with finality.

Ødegård was a trained geologist and a professor at the University of Bergen, Norway. He wasn't a specialist in meteorites, but he also wasn't interested in discussing the matter of the rock's makeup any further.

"OK… Can you come down here and look at it?" she asked.

"To Antarctica?"

"Yes, to Queen Maud Land."

"That is quite the coincidence that you found something in Queen Maud Land. It's also very fortunate. That's Norwegian territory, you know. I don't care what the Chinese say," he said.

"Right. You'll have to pay your own airfare, though. We can't afford to pay for your tickets," she said.

"Funny you should mention that. I was just taking a dump earlier," he said.

"Wow, TMI. OK, yes, and?"

"Well, I always do my best thinking on the lavatory. I just realized that I could go back to Antarctica if I were to frame a new expedition there, specifically to Queen Maud Land, as a matter of national importance and sovereignty…"

He let the words hang in the air. When Kii didn't bite, he continued, somewhat annoyed. He'd hoped she would immediately grasp the genius of his plan.

"The thing is, the current Norwegian government is just stupid enough that they might fall for it, even if it means antagonizing the Chinese," he explained.

"So, you could come down here with funding for an entire expedition? Tools and all? And government protection?" she asked.

"Exactly. I'd just have to sell it to the politicians first."

"How long would that take?"

"Knowing those low-lives, probably about one prime-time news cycle."

"And do you think you could sell it?" she asked.

He let out a loud snort.

"My dear, that's all I've been doing my entire career. Selling dubious research projects to even more dubious bureaucrats and politicians. Incompetent fools with no grasp of the science and even less grasp of responsible spending."

"I love your confidence in your fellow countrymen," Kii said.

"Well, we are talking about politicians. Besides, it's born out of painful experience," he said.

"How long will it take you to get organized and actually arrive here?"

"Better give me a month. The national politicians I can handle, but someone at the university is going to do their best to sabotage me. They always do."

"Sabotage you? Why would they do that?" she asked.

"Sayre's Law: University politics are the most bitter and vicious there are, because the stakes are so low."

Kii laughed.

"All right. Please let me know when you're on your way."

SIX

QUEEN MAUD LAND, ANTARCTICA, JANUARY 2040.

Less than three weeks later, Tinnus Ødegård came riding across the dusty flatlands near the coast of Queen Maud Land on an ancient motorcycle. He was wearing goggles and shorts and not much else, and had a large unlit cigar in the corner of his mouth. His hair and beard were flying wild in the wind, covered like the rest of him in a thick layer of fine yellow-red dust.

The dust was also enveloping his research partner, following behind him in their little off-road truck. He'd desperately and repeatedly attempted to pass the good professor to get out of the dust cloud created by his motorcycle, but so far, with no success.

When they arrived at what passed for Kii's and Jane's base camp, the professor dismounted his bike, removed his goggles, and looked around for his hosts. When they were nowhere to be found, he simply laid down on the ground, wrapped one arm over his face, and fell asleep without saying a word.

Thoreau was furious, as usual, and stomped his foot in sheer frustration at the rude and inconsiderate professor. He swallowed his anger and worked to erect a tent around the man, who was still sleeping, and then began setting up the rest of their camp.

François Thoreau was a thin and wiry Frenchman, about 170 centimeters tall, with crew cut gray hair and a permanent scowl on his tan, leathery face. A long-distance runner, his academic background was also in geology. At some point he'd veered off into astronomy and astrophysics, and had become quite an authority on planetary formation. That was, until he publicly stated that he'd become convinced that aliens had visited Earth in ancient times, that they'd interfered with human history, and left behind both cultural and physical artifacts.

At first, people didn't take it seriously. Thoreau had a reputation for being a hard data guy, a traditionalist. A true scientist who swore by the Sagan standard; that extraordinary claims require extraordinary evidence. And he was, it was just that in this case, what his colleagues quickly denounced as fringe, even crackpot, he considered already proven.

His career veered off track again, but this time into a dead end, as an astronomy lecturer at the University of Bergen. It was that, or unemployment.

It wasn't just that his former colleagues considered him to have become intellectually compromised; it was how he proselytized and defended his theories. Never one to suffer what he considered fools, Thoreau could get quite nasty with people who disagreed with him. The result was that he turned a lot of old friends into enemies, in short order.

Unlike Ødegård, who had been ecstatic when he heard the news that Thoreau would join "his" university. The two had many shared interests, even though it was quickly apparent that they couldn't stand each other. They both needed each other, though, if they were ever going to make their theories more accepted by the scientific community. And thus they formed one of the more contentious, yet mutually dependent relationships in the history of science.

Ødegård, for all his lack of social graces, was quite adept at maneuvering the political landscape of the university. He'd kept his theories about aliens separate from his work and his peers still considered him a leading authority on the geology of the oil-bearing strata of the North Sea. He'd also built an extensive donor network over the years, people who shared his extracurricular interests, people with money, and people who knew how to raise money. This gave him a certain amount of clout with the University, and freedom to pursue his interests.

Thoreau had none of that, but his deep understanding of the cosmos and his brilliance in math dazzled Ødegård, enough so that he'd convinced himself that he couldn't make any more progress without Thoreau's help.

There was also the sheer weight of loneliness on both men. Going against the orthodoxy of the scientific community had made them appreciate the wisdom of the adage that the enemy of my enemy is my friend. They were both loners by nature, but there were limits, even for them.

Ødegård, an eternal optimist by nature, and Thoreau, a dedicated pessimist by conviction, agreed on nothing except that which had brought them together. But that was enough, and it kept them quite busy. They published at least one major academic paper each year, and every few years Ødegård secured funding for some far-flung joint expedition. Ostensibly to study remote geological sites, which somehow always happened to be within a short distance of a suspected alien landing site or other artifact.

What they didn't receive, and what both men craved more than anything, was recognition from their peers, on what they considered their lives' work. It had eluded both men for a long time, but perhaps that was about to change.

When Thoreau had finished setting up camp, he relaxed, squatting on his haunches. It was his favorite way of sitting, mostly because it annoyed the crap out of Ødegård, who physically could not do the same. He looked out over the landscape, thinking about how this trip was going to be yet another complete bust, when a loud snoring sound coming from Ødegård's tent interrupted his thoughts.

It got him thinking about their relationship. Mostly about what an idiot he was, for taking so much crap from Ødegård. And why on Earth had he erected a tent around the man, when Ødegård didn't care enough to do it himself? Hating himself for being so passive aggressive, Thoreau got up, walked over to Ødegård's tent, and tore it back down. Let the narcissistic asshole snore out in the open. At least until he woke up with a mouthful of flies and dust.

Dismantling the tent made Thoreau feel good, like he was taking some of his dignity back. No more Mr. Nice Guy for him. But watching Ødegård sleeping on the ground out in the open made him feel a little guilty, like he was being a petty asshole. He was still arguing with himself over this, and occasionally stomping his feet in frustration, when Kii and Jane returned to camp.

SEVEN

QUEEN MAUD LAND, ANTARCTICA, JANUARY 2040.

Later that same day, when Kii saw the chaos that had resulted from Ødegård's and Thoreau's invasion of their little base camp, she was first quite annoyed. That quickly gave way to amusement. The two scientists were just ridiculous enough to make her laugh out loud, causing both men to blush, partly from embarrassment, and partly from the unexpected attention.

Jane didn't mind the disruption so much. He was used to living in tent camps from "a previous life," as he liked to call his time in the military, and quite enjoyed the organized chaos of living in makeshift quarters under the stars.

After introductions, Jane wanted to get straight to business.

"What is it you expect to find? What's the backstory from all those texts that you found?"

"Jane! You haven't even offered our guests anything to drink!" Kii said.

"We'll get everyone something to drink while we talk," he replied, smiling.

"Water OK?" Kii asked, looking at each of their guests.

"Never mind drinks!" Ødegård almost shouted at both of them.

It took a lot to offend Kii, but this took her aback. She looked over at Jane and saw in his face that he was getting angry.

"Excuse me?" was all he said.

"The artifact, man!"

Ødegård was gesticulating, clearly very agitated.

"Take us to the artifact, posthaste. I've waited my entire life for this moment, and I am disinclined to wait a second longer!"

Despite being Norwegian, Ødegård spoke English with a perfect upper class British accent, the result of his extensive education at England's finest institutions courtesy of the Norwegian taxpayer.

"Certainly," Jane replied.

He'd seen something in the other man's eyes, a yearning, and a desperation, which made him overlook his rudeness on the spot.

They all climbed into the expedition truck and Kii led the way as they drove through the darkness across the Antarctic plains.

"Why is your camp so far from the artifact?" Thoreau asked Jane.

"We thought it best to not draw too much attention to it," Jane replied. "So we placed the camp closer to the foothills and tried to make it look as if we're prospecting for fossils in mineral deposits."

"Ah, I see. Yes, that makes sense. Whose attention were you afraid of attracting?"

"Anyone with enough money to operate a satellite, basically."

Just then, the truck swerved and came to a halt. The headlights shone into a crater and illuminated a large, almost round shape hidden under a camouflage tarp. They all piled out of the truck and scrambled down into the crater. Jane removed the tarp.

Ødegård stood, transfixed, about 10 paces away from the boulder. His shoulders were shaking, and the others realized the man was crying. He'd put everything into this one moment, the moment he'd never stopped hoping for but secretly had almost stopped believing in. Thoreau, in a rare gesture of kindness, laid one hand on the professor's shoulder, then gave him a gentle push towards the boulder.

Ødegård started walking towards it, slowly, like a sleepwalker. He reached out a hand, then pulled it back without touching, as if he was afraid of getting an electric shock. Seconds later, he'd repeat the motion with his other hand. The others stood back, watching this odd little dance, not knowing what to say. Finally, Ødegård leaned in and placed one hand on the artifact, then the side of his head, as if he were listening for sounds coming from within. He slowly slid his hand and face along the exposed metal surface.

"Do you think that's a good idea?" Jane asked.

"What is?" Ødegård replied, without looking at Jane.

"Getting so close to it. If it really is alien, what if it carries a contagion?"

"Let's be realistic. It's buried deep in the rock and it's been here a very long time. I'm sure any alien microbes are long dead," Ødegård replied.

"I'd be more concerned about nanites, if I were you," Thoreau said.

That got Ødegård's attention, and he swiftly stepped back.

"You mean microscopic machines?" he asked.

The sudden change in his facial expression, from one of awed bliss to one of sharp concern, was almost comical, and Kii silenced a giggle.

"*Exactement!*" Thoreau said.

He looked up, shaking his head and rolling his eyes, as if appealing to the aliens for help.

"Given the possibility of a highly advanced alien technology, we shouldn't discount it. You, of all people, should know that. We've talked about this!" he said.

Ødegård seemed to consider this. His brow furrowed as he studied the artifact from about a meter away.

"To hell with all fear," he said.

Then he leaned in and licked the metal surface of the artifact.

Thoreau made a snorting sound, and Kii suppressed a gasp. But no one said anything. Ødegård turned towards them, grinning, looking genuinely happy. His eyes were shining, and he was waving both arms in the air.

"It's alive!" he said.

Kii started laughing. Jane looked concerned, and Thoreau was still shaking his head.

"It's not alive, and you know that better than anyone!" he said.

"Maybe not in the biological sense that we know from here on Earth, but there's something going on in there," Ødegård replied.

"How can you possibly conclude such a thing so quickly? You've only just seen the artifact?" Thoreau asked.

"I know, it's crazy. But you go up there and touch that thing, then tell me I'm wrong."

Thoreau went over to the truck and picked up a flashlight. He then walked over to the boulder and started examining the artifact closely. After a while, he turned off the flashlight.

"Kill all the lights, please," he said.

Jane walked over to the truck and turned it off. It was a moonless night, so a deep darkness fell over them. He looked up at the stars and shuddered, suddenly feeling quite cold.

"Oh my god, it's glowing."

The words had come from Kii, a little breathless, tinged with disbelief and fear. Jane looked down at the boulder, but he saw nothing. Then, slowly, as his eyes adjusted to the complete dark, he saw it.

"It's blue," he said.

For a second or two, all he could see was a blue blob floating in mid-air, slowly pulsating against a velvety black background. When he took a few steps closer, and his eyes adjusted more, he could again barely make out the boulder and the people standing around it. But for a moment, the emotional impact of something truly alien had been overwhelming.

"More like purple," Ødegård said.

"Guys, something's definitely moving," Kii said. "Like before. Just beneath the surface."

When he leaned all the way in, Thoreau could see that the surface was actually moving. There were tiny undulations moving back and forth.

"We should probably quarantine this site immediately, and notify the CDC," he said, stepping back.

"The CDC?" Jane said.

"The Centers for Disease Control, in Atlanta," Thoreau replied.

"Yes, I know, but why the CDC?"

"You think it's dangerous?" Kii asked.

"I don't know what the hell this is, and neither do you," Thoreau replied. "But what we thought was simply inert metal 10 minutes ago is now glowing and moving. This shit looks alive to me. Ødegård is right."

"You mean you thought was inert," Jane corrected him. "We already knew that something's moving under the surface, and we told you so. I guess you didn't believe us. But what makes you say it's alive?"

"A machine could also move," Kii added.

"Well, what would you call it?" Thoreau shot back. "Have a look!"

"I don't know," Jane said after examining the artifact more closely. "It does almost look alive, especially with that glow. It reminds me of bioluminescence, of fireflies. And Kii and I have been working right here, next to it, even touching it, for nearly two weeks."

"And let's not forget that Ødegård actually licked it," Kii added.

"Shit. He did," Thoreau replied. "We're so fucked."

"Correction," Ødegård said behind them. "We're only fucked if we notify the CDC, and we're not going to."

They turned and saw the blue glow from the artifact reflected in Ødegård's glasses. He was standing motionless in the darkness behind them.

"Why are we fucked if we notify the CDC?" Jane asked.

"What if this thing did something to us?" Thoreau asked. "To you?"

"It didn't," Ødegård said, with finality. "Let's get the damn thing out of the rock already and see if we can open it. But let's not be stupid about it. I think precautions are in order. Hazmat suits for everyone, cleanrooms, the works."

Jane opened his mouth to say something, but Ødegård cut him off.

"We brought everything we need. We can start first thing."

"Man has a point," Thoreau said. "Let's just get on with it."

"Like Jane said, why not notify the CDC? What if we're all infected or something? Shouldn't we at least inform them?" Kii asked.

"How would we know?" Thoreau replied. "The short answer is, we wouldn't. We haven't got a clue what we're dealing with here, so no idea what to even look for. Alien pathogens? Nano technology? Even more advanced technology? What does any of that even look like? The CDC would have no choice but to detain us until they could find out what to even look for, which could take forever. I'd rather be out and about, and continue working."

"To be safe, we should quarantine ourselves from the rest of humanity for a couple of weeks, though," Ødegård added.

They all looked at each other. Kii wanted to say something, but realized that they were right.

EIGHT

QUEEN MAUD LAND, ANTARCTICA, JANUARY 2040.

Back in the camp, it was time for dinner and stories around the campfire.

"Your turn," Jane said to Ødegård. "Tell us about your research."

"Oh man, where to start?" Ødegård said, shaking his head.

"At 10,000 meters," Kii said. "Start with the big picture."

"All right," Ødegård replied.

He settled into his chair, bit off the end of a cigar, and lit it. Much to the dismay of Thoreau and Kii, who both hated the smell.

"About 30 years ago, I stumbled across an old manuscript in the university's collection. It was in Latin, and in the style of late 15th century Jesuit scholars. The author was unknown, but it described in astonishing detail how strange beings came down out of the sky and started telling the locals how to live."

"The locals?"

"Indigenous peoples of Central and South America. But in this document, specifically in modern day Peru."

"Peru? Isn't that where the Nazca Lines are?" Kii asked.

"That's correct. But this document didn't address those."

"What are Nazca Lines?" Jane asked.

"They're very large geoglyphs, or figures, etched into the desert sands in southern Peru. But we'll get to those in a bit," Ødegård said, and continued.

"The most interesting thing about this document wasn't what it contained, but when it dates to," he said.

"When?" Kii asked.

"It's dated June, 1507. As far as the experts have been able to determine, that date is accurate. The paper, the ink, the style, it all matches."

"So?"

"The Jesuits didn't make it to Peru until 1568."

"There could be a perfectly innocent explanation for that. Maybe the author lied through their teeth. Either about the date, or about the description of Peru and the visitors. And how can you tell that the document was talking about aliens, and not Europeans? Or that there's not some other, more down-to-earth explanation?" Jane asked.

"You're right, I can't. But the author of the document did. It's spelled out, as clear as day, in perfect New Latin. The landscapes, the Peruvian people, and how the visitors came down from the sky. And beyond that, how they came from a different world. It even described their physical appearance, in some detail."

Jane shook his head.

"Well, come on, tell us what they looked like!" Kii said.

"According to the text, their bodies had human shape, but were a little larger than most humans. They had no faces, and they wore no clothes, but had superhuman strength and speed. Their skin was reflective, and it glowed in the dark."

Kii laughed.

"No way!" she said.

Thoreau looked up sharply and fixed her with his stare.

"Whoa. The document said this?" Jane asked.

"It did," Ødegård said.

"Then how come this isn't the most famous document in the world? Why haven't we heard of it?" Kii asked.

"Because they hid it in the university library's basement. And they did that because no one took it seriously. Everyone agreed it must be a fake, concocted by some modern prankster, even though they couldn't figure out how the forgery was done. The date, combined with the history of the colonization of Peru, and the contents of the text itself, all of it was so outrageous that no one would believe it. They couldn't allow themselves to believe it," Ødegård replied.

"This is a common theme," Thoreau said.

"Yes, we've seen it again and again," Ødegård agreed.

"How do you know it really isn't a fake?" Kii asked.

"We don't, except for the science and the data," Thoreau replied. "The best science says the document is real."

"What science? How did you test it?" Kii asked.

"The university carbon dated the paper. They analyzed the chemical composition of the ink, everything they could think of. They couldn't find fault with it," Ødegård replied.

"And there's more," he added.

"Go on," Jane said.

"When I started looking, I found documents, inscriptions, even monuments all over the place," Ødegård continued.

"And what's the upshot of all this?" Jane asked.

"First, we're talking a long time ago. All the texts and inscriptions say so, and they themselves are at least several hundreds of years old, even thousands. We've tried to narrow it down more, but the best we can do as of now is to say that we're probably talking at least 4,000 years ago since the aliens openly interacted with humans," Ødegård said.

"Whoa. So, how did that Jesuit get to Peru in 1507 to write that document?" Jane asked.

"We don't know. It's a mystery. A very interesting one," Thoreau replied.

"Why do you think they stopped 4,000 years ago?" Kii asked.

"We don't know if they did. They may have been back since then, but more covertly, perhaps because humanity has made such strides in technology. Like with that Jesuit. Or maybe they will be back, but it's not time for their next scheduled visit yet. Or, perhaps they stopped, but not because of us, but because of things closer to home. Maybe they're facing some crisis, and they have no more time for us," Thoreau said.

"Makes sense. What do you think?" Jane asked.

"It doesn't matter what I think, only what the evidence shows. But my guess is that they've visited us at regular intervals, probably for a very long time," Thoreau said.

"Why though? What do they want?" Kii asked.

"That's the big question! Truthfully, we don't know. All we know is what our ancestors passed down to us, mostly through oral legends, which were then put into writing much later, once humans developed written languages. In fact, I suspect the aliens inspired our first languages. Maybe they even taught us how to read and write," Ødegård said.

"Whoa, OK. I can see how that idea would be controversial," Kii said.

"Just a little, yes. There are so many legends, some of them from religious texts. The Tower of Babel, Noah's Ark, the Hindu Vedas, and many more. When we put all these stories from all these various sources together, a picture emerges. The aliens came here, and they stayed for a long time. We don't know exactly for how long, but I'm guessing at least a thousand years," Ødegård said.

"What did they want from us?" Jane asked.

"While they were here, they worked with us, they mentored us, and they helped us. It doesn't seem like they wanted much of anything in return. There's no mention of any transfer of advanced technology, possibly with one exception, but they transferred ideas and values. They taught us the value and sanctity of human life, and the importance of cooperation and community. We believe the aliens directly inspired early human civilization. They helped us plan and organize our first societies and cities. They gave us knowledge about the stars, and they gave us knowledge about our own planet, including agriculture and geology," Ødegård said.

"What was the technology exception?" Kii asked.

"Metalworking. We're pretty sure the aliens either directly caused, or at the very least inspired the start of the Bronze Age," Ødegård said.

"And those Nazca Lines in Peru?" she asked.

"To the locals, the alien visitors must have seemed like gods. My personal theory is that they made the Nazca lines after the aliens left, that they were attempting to send messages to the aliens, trying to get them to return," Ødegård said.

"I guess next you'll say that the aliens built the pyramids as well?" Kii asked.

"No, humans built the pyramids. That's established beyond any doubt. But I think aliens inspired the shape, and that our ancestors believed they could help shoot the souls of their dearly departed to the stars, to the aliens. On that point, I agree with mainstream Egyptologists. That would also explain why we find pyramids on multiple continents and why they're so precisely aligned to the heavens," Ødegård replied.

"I'm sorry, but I'm not buying this," Kii said. "You talk about science and data, but you can't prove any of this. This is all pure conjecture, based on your interpretation of archaeological finds. Finds that most scientists interpret differently. How do you explain that?"

"Prove? No, perhaps not. But I could probably convince you if you gave me the chance to show you all the evidence we've gathered over the years. It's like Atlantis. Did I explain my theories about Atlantis?" Ødegård asked.

"No! Thank you. But I think we get the picture," Kii said.

"I suspect fear explains my colleagues' reluctance to accept what is right under their noses. Nobody wants to be a laughingstock in the eyes of their peers. Trust me, I know," Ødegård added.

"And we may prove it yet, with the help of the artifact. We need to get it out of that rock, so we can study it more closely," Thoreau said.

"Which reminds me: The boulder isn't iron after all. It's impactite, made from impact melt," Ødegård said.

"Impact melt? You mean, from a meteorite?" Jane asked.

"Well, yes, in principle, but I think the artifact itself struck the surface of the Earth at a very high rate of speed. So high, it should have burned up in the atmosphere, but it didn't. When it hit the ground, it hit with such force that it caused the rock and soil to flash melt. Some of it then solidified around the artifact once it cooled," Ødegård replied.

"Oh, wow. So, the artifact was the meteorite. You're sure about this, as a geologist?" Jane asked.

"Yes, I'm sure. What a question to ask. It's also quite recent," Ødegård said.

"How recent? And what makes you say that?" Kii asked.

"There's no weathering. And the crater looks quite fresh. If it was old, it should have been much more worn down by the elements," Ødegård said.

"So, how recent are we talking?"

"I'd say one hundred years. Two hundred, tops."

"What? Are you sure? Don't forget that ice covered everything here until recently," Jane said.

"I didn't. And don't you forget that I've spent a fair amount of time here, studying the local geology, which is my speciality. Insane or not, it's true," Ødegård said.

"All right, you're right, I'm sorry," Jane said. "I'm just so shocked."

"You said it should have burned up in the atmosphere," Kii said. "What did you mean by that?"

"Simply that, judging from the impact crater size, and the lack of the typical residues of an actual meteor, the artifact must have come down by itself. Unprotected. And, it must have hit the ground at a very high rate of speed. Atmospheric physics isn't my field, but I'm guessing that Thoreau here can verify my hypothesis," Ødegård said.

"Well, I can certainly confirm that anything man-made, moving at orbital velocities, and with a mass and density like this artifact appears to have, would have burned up long before hitting the ground," Thoreau replied.

"Thank you," Ødegård said, and made an exaggerated bow towards Thoreau.

"But a larger structure could have protected it, one that burned up in the atmosphere?" Kii asked.

"Well, yes, of course, it could have," Thoreau replied.

"Are you saying what I'm thinking that you're saying? That we should look for more artifacts, for the remnants of an alien ship?" Jane asked.

"Are you saying that you haven't already?" Ødegård asked. "Now, that's truly shocking."

"Boys, chill," Kii said. "We haven't got time for sniping and pettiness."

A brief silence fell over the group until Kii continued.

"Did you bring any aerial drones?" she asked Thoreau.

"Yes, of course," he replied.

"All right, then this is what we'll do. First light, we'll send the drones off to search for any signs of wreckage. While they're searching, we'll try to extract the artifact from the rock. Agreed?" she said.

They all nodded. After a few seconds of awkward silence, Ødegård got up and left without saying a word. Not long after, they heard snoring sounds coming from his tent.

NINE

QUEEN MAUD LAND, ANTARCTICA, JANUARY 2040.

Kii woke up to the sounds of yelling and cursing. She quickly identified the source; it was coming from Thoreau's tent. Jane was still asleep. This kind of thing never bothered him. But break a twig within 20 meters of where he was resting, and you'd see an instant reaction.

When she went to investigate, she found the two scientists arguing over the drone launch.

"What am I supposed to tell the drones to look for?" Thoreau asked. "An alien spaceship? It's an impossible task, even for a semi-intelligent drone like this!"

He appeared agitated, raising and lowering his shoulders repeatedly, waving his hands in front of Ødegård's face. His scowl was more pronounced than usual, and his voice was markedly higher in pitch. A black quadcopter drone was sitting on a folding table between the two men. It almost looked like a porcupine, with sensors and antennae sticking out at all angles.

Ødegård was having none of it. He wanted the drones airborne now and had no patience for dealing with such details as what to tell the drones to look for.

"I don't care if you confuse it or hurt its feelings. It's a machine! Just tell it to search for anything that looks out of place. How hard can it be?" he asked.

He either didn't realize or didn't care that Kii was standing just inside the tent opening, looking at both men. Her face was devoid of expression, but her eyes were not. She opened her mouth to speak when Thoreau beat her to it.

"*Oui*, it's a machine!" he shouted. "Which is why we have to be specific! We do not know what the alien ship might have looked like, where the wreckage is located, or even what type of materials to look for. You know this!"

Thoreau threw up his hands in defeat and stormed past Kii and out of the tent. A moment later, Jane's sleepy face peeked in through the tent opening.

"What the fuck is going on here?" he demanded.

"We're dealing with a pair of overgrown children," Kii said.

"So it would seem," Jane replied. "What's the problem?"

"Thoreau is overcomplicating the drone launch," Ødegård said. "He's talking about reprogramming the drones to know how to identify an alien spaceship. Which even he admits is an impossible task."

"Yeah, we don't know what to even look for," Jane said.

Thoreau came back into the tent, which by now was getting cramped. His face was red, and his hands were doing most of the talking.

"There is no point sending out the drones to look if we can't tell them what to look for!" he said.

Jane sighed.

"Why don't we just task them with identifying anything that looks manmade, within a radius of 100 kilometers? If that doesn't work, we'll know we have to come up with something better," he said.

"Exactly, finally!" Ødegård said.

"But it's not manmade, that is the entire point!" Thoreau cried.

"But the drone doesn't need to know that," Kii said.

"Its AI software should be able to distinguish between what is naturally occurring, and something that's technological or manufactured," Jane said. "No matter who made it, and on which planet."

"Fine. Whatever," Thoreau said.

His shoulders slumped, he sat down and reached for his computer. Kii looked at Jane, smiled, and rolled her eyes.

"So much drama!" she said.

Twenty minutes later, the drones flew off and started sending back pictures of a surprising and depressing amount of what was obviously garbage discarded by humans.

While the drones were busy searching, Ødegård and Jane set out to extract the artifact from the boulder, and Thoreau and Kii were supervising the construction of the mobile lab the scientists had brought. There wasn't that much to supervise. You merely placed the shipping container on a flat surface, pushed a button, and watched the building erect itself. Half an hour later, they were busy unpacking tables, chairs, microscopes, and other lab equipment.

Ødegård and Jane were having a tougher time of it. The impactite was hard enough that Ødegård had to break out the heavy tools, making Jane very nervous that he might damage the artifact.

That afternoon, the entire team gathered inside their new lab to study the artifact in all its newly liberated glory. It measured about 50 cm by 25 cm by 40 cm, and was resting vertically on a raised pedestal in the middle of the room. Now that they could see all of it, the shape reminded them more of a shoebox than a briefcase.

"Is it everything you hoped it would be?" Kii asked, looking at Ødegård.

He stood by the door, his arms crossed. He tilted his head to one side, and he had a thoughtful look on his face.

"I guess it would have been even more impressive and more immediately alien if it hovered in mid-air or something," he said.

"How about this?" Jane said.

He threw the light switch and silence fell over the room as a faint blue glow slowly filled it. Jane experienced a strange feeling, as if the glow of the artifact was warm, and was pulling him in. In the total darkness of the room, they could see that the glow undulated and moved, and that there were patterns moving underneath the surface.

"Yeah, all right, it looks alien enough now. I'll grant you that," Ødegård laughed.

Jane turned the lights back on.

"Can we get inside the damn thing?" Thoreau asked.

"Not yet, I'm afraid. I inspected the surface, looking for joints, hinges, a lock, anything," Kii said.

"Nothing?" Ødegård asked.

He walked over to the artifact and ran his hand over it, almost caressing it.

"Nothing," she replied.

"Well, isn't that just a boring old cliché?" Ødegård said.

He was tilting his head from side to side, staring at the artifact.

"Cliché? What do you mean?" Thoreau asked.

He was leaning against a table at the other end of the room, regarding the others with his customary scowl.

"The movies! Scientists find something mysterious, possibly alien, and it turns out it's made from impossibillium. They can't crack it open, they can't even scratch the surface. Yet it looks so… almost normal," Ødegård said.

"Imagine the secrets this little fellow contains," he added.

His voice was soft, and he had a wistful look in his eyes.

"Yeah, that is a cliché. Maybe we just need to attack it with more brute force and ignorance. Explosives might do the trick," Thoreau replied.

He straightened up, raised both arms above his head, and yawned.

"I don't think so. It survived crashing to Earth like a meteorite," Kii said.

She mimicked the fall with her hand and made crashing noises.

"I'm just glad we spent all that time and were so careful to chip away at the rock without harming the artifact," Ødegård said. "As if we ever could."

He shot a glance at Jane.

"All right, all right, I was just being prudently careful," Jane said. "This is a historic find, after all."

"Why don't we focus on what we actually can access first?" Kii said. She nodded towards the artifact and added, "The writing."

"That seems like a good idea, and immediately doable," Jane said.

"Except I have a feeling we can't really access it," Ødegård said. "I mean, sure, we can see that there's something there, but it's really hard to focus on it, and it seems to move around."

"Do you know what it reminds me of?" Kii said. "A hologram."

"I think you may be right," Thoreau said. "A 3D hologram. That would explain why it's so hard to focus on."

"Lasers! We need lasers," Ødegård exclaimed.

Two hours later, they were all wearing heavy goggles and staring at the walls and the ceiling of the small lab space they were in. There were strings of symbols, and what appeared to be graphs and schematics surrounding them on all surfaces. If they moved the lasers, even slightly, or changed the frequency of the light, the symbols and drawings changed. There were layers upon layers of information, encoded in multi-dimensional lattices. On top of everything, the etchings themselves changed shape, so the symbols and drawings they were seeing changed over time, even if they touched nothing.

"There must be an energy source inside the briefcase," Thoreau almost whispered, his voice reverent. "For it to glow, and for the patterns to keep changing, I mean."

"An energy source that lasts for over 100 years?" Kii asked.

"Either that, or they've perfected the use of time crystals," Thoreau replied.

"Come again?" Jane wasn't sure he'd heard correctly.

"Time crystals. It's non-equilibrium matter, a periodic structure that repeats in time and space," Thoreau replied.

"Does the pattern repeat? Did anyone notice?" Kii asked.

"Too early to tell. We'd need to record the output over time and see. This could take a while," Thoreau said.

"Still wouldn't explain the glow," he added.

"It almost looks like Cerenkov-radiation," Kii said.

"Except there's no measurable radiation at all," Thoreau said.

"Somewhere in here there's got to be a Rosetta Stone," Jane said, more hoping than stating.

"You mean a key to translating the symbols into English? I don't think so, because it presumes that there's some common language that both the sender and the receiver of the information understand. With the actual Rosetta Stone, it was Ancient Greek. I don't think we have any language in common with whoever created this," Thoreau said.

"What about math? There's got to be something. We need a linguist in here," Jane insisted. "Or a mathematician."

"I agree, but you realize that could take decades, even longer? We don't even know how the aliens' thought processes work. All human languages at least have the human consciousness as a common denominator. We may have unique cultures, but we all experience time and space in more or less the same way. What if the creators of this writing experience time moving backwards? Or not at all? Or maybe they move in four dimensions, and the etchings we're seeing are actually just three-dimensional representations of four dimensional writing? That would make them incomplete, misleading. Just useless," Thoreau said.

"Ever the optimist, aren't you, Thoreau?"

Ødegård's face was smiling, but his eyes weren't.

Thoreau noticed for once and took the hint. He blushed.

"Then again, they could be like us. No way of knowing without trying," he said.

He smiled and tried to appear cheerful.

"What if we don't need a Rosetta Stone? What if we already know this language?" Ødegård said.

The others just looked at him, waiting for him to continue.

"What if these symbols are hieroglyphs? Or closely related to our hieroglyphs, perhaps the inspiration or basis for them? Perhaps we can use our modern understanding of one or more of the ancient logographic languages to interpret the writing inside this alien artifact?"

"That's one big 'What if?' I mean, that would be great, but none of us have more than a passing knowledge of ancient hieroglyphs. Jane is right, we could use the help of a linguist," Thoreau said.

"Yes, you're right. Of course," Ødegård said.

A long silence fell over the room as they marveled at the symbols and drawings, lost in thought. Suddenly, Thoreau's wristwatch beeped.

"The drones are back," he said.

The drones had searched a vast area, but other than garbage and what looked like the remnants of an old polar expedition, they had found nothing unusual.

Thoreau and Jane were arguing over how much force to apply to the artifact to open it, when a high-pitched, piercing sound interrupted them.

Both men clasped both hands over their ears and looked at each other. Thoreau mouthed an obscenity at Jane, then doubled over, groaning.

"That's just like what I heard when I was waiting for the rescue Griffin," Jane said.

He had to shout to drown out the noise, which seemed to come from every direction. They looked around, but couldn't immediately locate the source. Just then, Kii came barging into the lab, holding a radio in one hand. The radio was emitting the piercing sound.

"Every radio in the camp is doing this," she shouted over the racket.

Jane grabbed the hand-held radio out of Kii's hand and started walking around the artifact. The noise was clearly louder and more intense when he stood to the north-east of the artifact. He held the radio directly above the artifact, but the intensity dropped, just as if he were on the other side of it.

He handed the radio to a baffled Thoreau and turned the artifact around, so that the side that was pointing north before was now pointing south. He then took the radio back and started walking around the artifact again. The sound was still strongest when he stood to the north-east of the artifact, just like before.

He was about to move the artifact again when the sound stopped. The effect was immediate and physiological. It was like a pressure lifted and he could breathe freely again.

"Whoa. Tell me I'm wrong, but looks like the artifact is sending out some form of electromagnetic radiation in one particular direction," he said.

"I don't think you're wrong," Thoreau said.

He shook his head, like he was trying to shake something out of his ears. Then he rubbed his fingers against his temples and looked at the artifact with a surprised expression on his face.

"We need a map, and a damn good explanation," Kii said.

Jane knew that tone of voice. She sounded annoyed as all hell. Five minutes later, all four of them were sitting around the only table large enough to accommodate them all, poring over an old-fashioned paper map.

"Did you say you heard this noise once before?" Thoreau asked Jane.

"Yes, I was sitting on the rim of the outer crater, waiting for rescue."

"Where, exactly?"

"Right... here."

Jane pointed to the map. Thoreau marked the spot with an X.

"All right, we're here," he said.

He placed another X on the map, showing their current position.

"When we heard the noise, it was strongest when you were standing to that side of the artifact."

Thoreau pointed to the other side of the room.

"If we draw a line from the middle of the room, where the artifact was, in the general direction you were standing, it goes about like this."

He used a ruler to draw a line on the map, starting at the location of their camp, and going in a north-easterly direction all the way to the coast of the continent. The line barely missed the X, showing where Jane had been waiting for rescue.

"So!" Ødegård exclaimed.

The others waited for him to continue, but he just sat there, looking triumphant.

"Yes?" Kii prodded him.

"So, now we know!"

Ødegård was getting quite impatient with what he perceived as the others' inability to draw logical conclusions from solid evidence.

"We know the artifact is sending out a signal. We, or rather you, Jane, have observed it twice, two months apart. Chances are that it happens more often than that. We know the general direction of the signal, and it doesn't appear to go out into outer space. It seems earthbound. That raises a rather interesting question, don't you think?"

"It does," Thoreau said and nodded.

"Where and to what is the signal directed?" Ødegård said, his voice booming.

"Looks like the Indian Ocean. Indonesia, eventually," Kii said.

"Yes, but there's something much closer, in the signal's way, potentially blocking it," Ødegård replied.

"Oh yeah, the Antarctic mountains. I see what you mean," she said.

"Norwegian Antarctic mountains!" Ødegård said.

"Looks like the signal is going straight towards this one," Kii said.

She pointed to the map, then leaned in closer to read the name of the mountain.

"Mount Ravine-snooten," she said.

"Mount *Rivenæsnuten*," Ødegård corrected her. "Named after a Norwegian resistance fighter and hero from the Second World War."

"Is there anything there, though?" Jane asked. "Any installations, an old camp?"

"No, not that I know of," Ødegård said. "As far as I know, there was only ever one expedition there, back in the nineteen fifties. The Maudheim Expedition."

"Is it still snow covered?" Kii asked.

"Those mountains are all quite tall, over 2,600 meters. So yes, I expect they're still covered in snow and ice."

"Can we send the drones?" Jane asked.

"We'd have to get in closer first, so they don't waste energy and flying time just getting there. But yeah, sure," Thoreau replied.

"Does anyone see any reason that shouldn't be our next move?" Kii asked.

They all looked at each other, but no one spoke. Ødegård had the biggest shit-eating grin on his face.

"From now on we film everything," he said. "We're making history here."

"We're not, but someone sure were," Kii said. "I wonder who, though."

"Yeah, I'm not sure I'm buying this. It's all a little too neat," Jane said.

"And if this thing is alien," he pointed at the artifact. "Then why the hell is it signaling somewhere here on Earth, and not its home planet?"

Ødegård's grin was gone, and he looked like a tropical storm about to unleash some torrential rain on both Kii and Jane when Thoreau stepped in.

"If it's a prank, we can at least agree that it's very well done. In fact, it's so convincing that we have no choice but to follow it wherever it leads us. Because if we don't, we'll forever be asking what the hell that thing was and how it did the things it did. Who made it, and why? We need to know. I sure as hell need to know."

He looked around at the others.

"Agreed?"

They all nodded.

"What in the bloody hell is that?"

Thoreau was poring over the footage that one of the aerial drones had returned just before they lost contact with it. He pointed to an outcrop in the rock, far up the mountainside. The others were shoulder-surfing as he replayed the footage repeatedly, right up to the point when they lost the signal from the drone and the picture went dark.

Losing a drone had put both Ødegård and Thoreau on edge. The conditions at that altitude were difficult, with sudden wind gusts and occasional icing, but this wasn't either man's first rodeo. In the over 30 years Ødegård had been doing this, he'd only ever lost one drone, and that was to enemy gunfire.

The outcrop Thoreau was pointing at didn't look any different to all the other outcrops, cliffs, precipices, bluffs, and crags they'd all been staring at for hours now. Jane leaned in closer, but still saw nothing special until Thoreau moved his finger. On the side of the outcrop was a rectangular form, with sharp, 90 degree corners and perfectly straight sides. The rectangle appeared to be flat and smooth, and the color was dark, almost black. Snow and ice covered the surrounding area. It looked exactly like a metal door set in a frozen mountainside.

"I'm thinking it looks very human," Jane said. "It looks like a door."

"I'm thinking you're right," Thoreau said.

"Even if it is a door, that doesn't mean that it has to be human," Ødegård said.

"Occam's razor, professor," Kii said, referring to the axiom that the simplest explanation is most often the correct explanation.

"We have to send another drone," Ødegård said.

He looked at the others, almost pleadingly. His shoulders were up around his ears and he was constantly fidgeting with his beard. He started pacing in the cramped space, two steps over and two steps back.

"I concur," Thoreau said.

"They're your drones," Kii said, shrugging.

Twenty minutes later, they were looking at live footage as the second drone was flying up a narrow valley towards the outcrop they'd studied before.

Up close, the mountain looked completely wild and desolate, like a scene from a frozen planet. The rocks were black and raw, with sharp edges and crevices filled with powdered snow. The sky above was a swirling gray, moving far too fast for comfort for the eyes of someone who grew up before the Climate Shift.

Soon they had the outcrop in sight, when Kii suddenly cried out.

"Look, it's the other drone! Let's go investigate, see if we can see what happened to it."

She sat down next to Thoreau, studying the screen intently for a moment. Then she looked up at Jane and flashed him a grin. He knew that look. She was having fun, hooked on the chase and the mystery.

"We could lose this one as well," Thoreau said.

He leaned back in his chair and looked over his shoulder at Ødegård, who was still pacing behind him.

"Let's risk it. Fly up to the old one. I want to see why it crashed," Ødegård said.

He stopped pacing. Thoreau carefully maneuvered the drone towards its cousin, closing in a meter at a time.

"It looks perfectly fine," Jane said.

"It does, doesn't it? It looks like it landed normally, it's sitting pretty and upright on its struts, and I can't see anything broken or missing," Thoreau said.

He sounded relieved, but he had a deep furrow across his brow. This didn't explain why they lost contact with the drone.

"Can you fly around it so we can see the diagnostic lights?" Ødegård asked.

"Good idea," Thoreau replied.

"There! Looks like three long red flashes, then one long green, and then it repeats. What's that, is that emergency shutdown?" Ødegård asked.

He was standing behind Thoreau, leaning over the man and pushing him aside in his eagerness to find out what had happened.

"Indeed, it is. I should be able to reactivate it now," Thoreau said.

"Let's see if we can fly both of them up to the door, coming in from different angles," Ødegård suggested.

Soon, they were watching two live video feeds as both drones approached the door. One was flying high, approaching from above. The other one was hugging the ground, and it reached the door first. From below, the door looked immense, but Jane estimated its actual size to be around three meters tall and a meter and a half wide.

Thoreau instructed the drone to fly in a grid search pattern over the surface of the door, looking for any irregularities. While it was doing this, the other drone was watching from above.

The results were disappointing. The entire surface was featureless and looked the same all over. It just looked like a regular old metal door. Dark, flat, and fairly smooth. No sign of a door handle, no signs of hinges, and no sign of a lock or other opening mechanism.

"Try infrared," Kii suggested.

She was resting her head in one hand, leaning over towards the screen, studying every detail.

Thoreau grunted and did as she asked. The drone moved over the entire surface once again, but there was no variation in temperature.

"Try pulling back a little, and check both the door and the surrounding area using infrared," Ødegård said.

The drone images still showed the same temperature across the door and across the rocks surrounding it.

"Whoa, that's nuts," Ødegård said.

"How so?" Jane asked.

"Rocks usually show some variation in temperature, usually from parts of it sitting in the sun while other parts sit in shade, but also because of the composition of the rocks. Even a single outcrop like this usually has many minerals running through it, with layers twisted and churned from geological activity over the aeons. They all have varying densities and absorb and retain heat differently. We should see at least some minor fluctuations in temperature."

"I have an idea. Switch the other drone to infrared as well, and have it scan the outcrop and the area surrounding it in widening circles," Kii said.

Thoreau did as she said, and soon they were looking at a baffling result. The entire outcrop was holding steady at the same temperature, while the rocks and the mountainside surrounding it weren't. There were clear variations in temperature, especially in the rocks and cliffs that were sitting in the shade from what little sunlight penetrated the angry cloud cover.

"There can only be one explanation," Ødegård said.

"Faulty equipment?" Jane said, attempting a joke.

It fell on deaf ears.

"No! That the entire outcrop is artificial. It's not a geological formation, it's architecture. Someone built that."

"Easy enough to test," Thoreau said.

He armed the first drone's spectroscopy laser and fired it at the door before Ødegård could object. To the surprise of both men, nothing happened. Not even a whisk of smoke or gas for the drone to analyze. It looked like the door simply swallowed the entire blast of energy from the laser, returning nothing, not even the faintest reflection of visible light. The two scientists looked at each other, and a smile started spreading across Ødegård's face.

"Try the surrounding rock next to the door," he said.

Thoreau did, with the same result. He armed the laser of the second drone and started firing it at various spots around the rest of the outcrop. There was no visible reaction, not even in the infrared. Then he started firing the laser at rocks further away, and they started seeing the expected results. Smoke and gas bubbled and seared from the rocks, which immediately started glowing with angry little red dots where the laser had struck.

"That's more like it," Thoreau said.

"Like what?" Kii asked.

"This has to be it!" Ødegård exclaimed.

"Be what? You two are speaking in riddles," Kii said.

"The holy grail, the palace in the clouds hidden by the Earth that many ancient cultures talk about."

"Basically, an alien base on Earth," Thoreau said.

"A place they left behind when they left," Ødegård added.

"Perhaps so they'll have a base of operations when they return," Thoreau said.

"We have to go there! Right now!" Ødegård said.

"I'd love to, but that's not happening," Jane said.

"Yeah, look at the clouds and the weather forecast," Kii said.

"They're right," Thoreau said. "That door is sitting at an altitude of over 2,000 meters, and a big storm is moving in. It's going to get very inhospitable up there soon."

"Damn it!" Ødegård shouted.

He banged both fists on the table, sending cups and other smaller items flying. Then he got up and stormed out the door, leaving behind a trail of swearing in Norwegian that left even Thoreau somewhat stunned. He'd refused to learn Norwegian, insisting that French should suffice wherever he went. His idea of linguistic compromise and accommodation was to allow himself to resort to English when all else failed. Despite this, he'd picked up a few Norwegian phrases and some salty swear words, mostly thanks to his students. Not that he strictly speaking needed it for this, Ødegård's feelings were obvious enough in any language.

Two days later, the storm had spent itself and the weather was looking promising. They moved their base camp to the foothills of Mount Rivenæsnuten, as far up as their off-road truck would take them, to around 1,300 meters. They were going to have to hike the rest of the way on foot.

The changes in scenery and temperature from the coastal plains were dramatic. The mountain was a wild place, even at this relatively modest altitude. There was plenty of snow and ice on the ground, and it could be dangerous if Mother Nature caught you outside when a storm hit. As far as they could tell, there was nothing living up there, not even lichens, and certainly no animals.

Ødegård was eager to get started, so the next morning they loaded a sherpa robot with supplies and set off. Kii had first tried to plan their route based on the map data they had, but that didn't get her very far. She'd had to deploy the aerial drones to help update the maps and find a usable route to the door.

They'd all been calling it "the door," ever since they first spotted it, even though they didn't know if it really was a door, or something else entirely. Whatever it was, it exerted an irresistible pull on all four of them.

Jane was considering this, as he felt the lactic acid building in his legs. Why in the hell were they doing this? They were climbing a mountain in the Antarctic, with no support and no hope of rescue if anything went wrong. And for what? For a large, black rectangle set high in a mountainside, in what was still the most inhospitable place on Earth. And because an obscure Norwegian professor claimed it wasn't just a door, but *the* door. The door to the greatest and most profound scientific discovery since humanity learned how to make fire.

After a fairly strenuous hike, they entered a near vertical rift, like a narrow canyon with steep cliff faces on either side. It looked almost as if someone had struck the mountainside with a giant axe and left a deep cut. They could see large drifts of snow on top of the cliffs and a white wall of snow and ice at the head of the canyon. A strong headwind was coming down the sides, carrying with it tiny, sharp ice crystals that hurt when they hit exposed skin. The further up the canyon they came, the narrower it got, and the stronger the wind blew. Soon they couldn't see anything. The wind was whipping up a frenzy of drifting snow and ice, making it feel like they were climbing uphill towards a frozen sandblasting machine.

Once they were through the end of the canyon, the wind calmed down and they stood on a narrow ledge, running along a near vertical cliff on the right, with at least a hundred meter drop to the left. The ledge appeared to be about a meter wide at the narrowest, and completely covered in snow and ice. It ran at an angle, following the cliff face, and going slightly uphill from where they were standing. Jane strained to see the end, to see how far it went, but it disappeared into a mist of snow and fog about a quarter mile away.

"Are you sure this thing doesn't just end in mid-air?" he asked Kii.

"I'm as sure as I can be about somewhere I've never been. According to the drone footage, this ledge will take us to a plateau just beyond that fog. From there, we're almost at the valley with the outcrop," she replied.

"Almost?"

"Almost. Don't worry about it."

He knew what that meant: Let's deal with one problem at a time. She was right, of course.

"We have to be extremely careful on this ledge. It's not flat, it tilts, and it's covered in snow and ice. And, to top it off, it has loose gravel and small rocks all over it, mostly underneath the snow."

"I can't cross that," Ødegård said.

"I thought you were desperate to get to that door?" Kii asked.

She was losing patience with the mercurial professor.

"I am. But there are certain things you can't do, things that cripple you with fear, and this is one of them for me," Ødegård said.

"There is no other way, at least not on foot," Kii said.

"There's always a way. We could go via helicopter," Ødegård replied.

"You have access to a helicopter, and you haven't mentioned it before?" Jane asked.

"Well, no, not exactly. But I have connections, people I could ask," Ødegård said.

Jane nodded. He looked at Kii, who also silently nodded. There was no point in pressuring Ødegård if he really was too afraid to continue. It would just endanger everyone.

"That will take forever. Don't be a chickenshit," Thoreau shouted. "Do you want to see this, or not? The rest of us will continue, regardless of what you decide to do."

Jane was about to protest when Ødegård, still standing on relatively safe ground at the very beginning of the ledge, where it was almost two meters wide, suddenly sat down. His legs were visibly shaking, and he looked like he was feeling dizzy.

"Just give me a moment," he said.

"There's no point in putting our lives unnecessarily at risk," Jane said. "Let's turn around and return with a better plan."

"No!" Ødegård said.

"Let's be smart about this," Jane said.

He was almost pleading with the stubborn Norwegian. Ødegård held up a hand and shook his head.

"This is too important," he said. "Thoreau is right. Any alternatives we could come up with would take forever. I have to do this. Just give me a sec."

Jane sighed. He shot Kii a glance. She'd crossed her arms over her chest and looked concerned. Jane sat down next to Ødegård.

"How about I go first, then the sherpa robot, then you?" Jane said.

He spoke in a gentle voice, trying to sound neutral. He didn't want Ødegård's untimely demise on his conscience. Whatever happened next had to be Ødegård's choice. Ødegård didn't reply, or look at Jane, but he gave a slight nod of his head.

"Did we bring enough rope to tie everyone together?" Kii asked.

"No," Thoreau replied, flatly.

Kii waited for him to continue, to say something else, but he didn't. She turned to look at him, and saw to her surprise that he was staring down at Ødegård, disgust written all over his face. She shot Jane a glance and saw that he was seeing the same thing.

"What do you think? Is it safe to continue?" she asked Jane.

She looked at him while nodding her head toward Thoreau.

Jane shook his head.

"No, this is not a safe situation. One member down, another seething with resentment, a sherpa robot that was built and equipped for desert-like conditions, and a meter wide icy ledge. There is no life or death imperative for us to continue, so we shouldn't."

"What's our Plan B?" she asked.

"Simple. If Ødegård can organize air transportation in time before he has to return to Norway, we'll use that. If he can't, you and I will return and do the climb alone."

"Absolutely not," Ødegård said.

His voice was softer than his usual rumble, but the finality was unmistakable.

"We continue. I'll make it, or I'll die trying. But I'm not turning around now. Help me up."

He reached out a hand, and to everyone's amazement, Thoreau grabbed it and hauled the Norwegian to his feet.

"I like your plan, though," Ødegård said to Jane. "I'll follow behind you and the sherpa robot, like you said."

"All in favor of continuing?" Jane asked.

He looked at each person, one by one. They all raised their hands. Jane nodded and instructed the sherpa robot to follow him. Then he hoisted his backpack and started walking, carefully testing each step before placing any weight on his foot. The sherpa robot followed a couple of meters behind him, with Ødegård directly behind it, followed by Thoreau. Kii made up the rear of their little column.

Because they had to step so carefully, it took them a long time to make any headway towards the fog and the presumed end of the ledge. Kii was just reflecting that her position in line was the worst, because no matter who fell she'd see the whole thing, when one of the sherpa robot's legs slipped.

The little machine, about the size of a large dog, was usually as sure-footed as a mountain goat. Perhaps it slipped on the ice, or perhaps it had stepped on a loose piece of gravel underneath the snow. Either way, one of its four legs slipped and went over the edge, and for a second it looked like the machine couldn't correct itself.

Ødegård screamed.

The humans froze, while the robot struggled and finally regained its footing. Seconds later, Jane could hear a low rumble coming from somewhere above them.

"Oh shit, the scream triggered an avalanche! Quick, we have to move!"

Jane started walking forward, as fast as he could, when a white curtain of swirling snow descended on him, turning his entire world white. He couldn't see anything, not even the ledge, and there was no way he could risk taking another step.

"Stop! Press up against the cliff face!" he shouted.

Large chunks of snow soon joined the snow curtain, passing in front of his face with mere centimeters to spare. He stared, disbelieving, at the tons of snow and ice hurtling past him. It made him feel claustrophobic, and like he couldn't breathe, in the thick soup of cascading snow enveloping him. There was a loud cracking sound directly above him, and enormous pieces of rock, of the mountainside itself, followed the snow into the abyss. It all happened so fast, and with such overwhelming force, that he didn't have time to feel scared.

When the avalanche subsided, and he could see more than a meter in front of him again, he turned and looked back, scared at what he'd find. The sherpa robot was still there, as was Ødegård. He stood facing the cliff, with both hands up along the sides of his face, shielding it. But behind Ødegård, there was nothing, just the snow-covered ledge.

Jane was about to lose his shit when the snow started moving. Slowly, and carefully, Kii emerged from the thick drift. She looked up, saw Jane, and grinned at him.

"That was fucking wild!" she said.

She looked down and pressed down hard on something with one hand.

"Don't you fucking move. You're facing the wrong way. One false move and we're both airborne," she said.

Jane realized that she'd been pinning Thoreau down, preventing him from moving with the weight of her body. She slowly helped the Frenchman rearrange his limbs and shove himself away from the edge of the ledge. When Jane could see his face, he saw Thoreau had been crying. For once his face was completely pale, and gone was the cocky arrogance which usually dominated his features.

"He panicked," Kii said matter-of-factly.

"I can see that," Jane replied.

Thoreau said nothing. He covered his face in his hands and leaned against the mountainside.

"Enough banter. We have to move," Jane added.

Jane turned to deal with Ødegård, who still stood frozen in place, when he heard a low rumble. Another avalanche, or perhaps just another branch of the one that almost got them, came pouring down the mountain about thirty meters behind them. The cliff was less vertical there, so instead of free-falling a few meters from the cliff face, the snow and rocks came sliding down the cliff itself, hitting the narrow ledge with tremendous force.

"Now we really have to move," Jane said.

He patted Ødegård on the shoulder and pointed, urging the professor to follow. The avalanche had created a shockwave of air ahead of it as it fell, blowing away the fog that had covered the end of the ledge. Jane could now see their goal. They'd have to climb over some rocks, but behind those there was a wide open space, leading into what looked like a valley or gorge on the right.

When they reached the rocks, Jane removed his backpack and put it down on the rocks as far up as he could reach. He climbed, slowly and deliberately, over the rocks and boulders, only stopping to grab his backpack and hoist it up behind him. Looking back towards the way they'd just come, his current perch looked heart-stoppingly crazy. He was climbing over a pile of large rocks and boulders, and directly below him was nothing, just a sheer drop. If his feet slipped now, he wouldn't fall back onto the ledge. He'd fall into oblivion.

He finally reached the top and looked down on the other side. No danger of falling here. The entire area behind the rocks was nice and flat for at least six meters in all directions. He instructed the sherpa robot to follow, and it climbed the rocks in no time, looking ridiculously confident as it found a tiny purchase for each foot and strode up the rocks as if they were nothing.

The little valley was relatively sheltered, with a massive cliff hovering over it. It was about 100 meters wide at the bottom, which was strewn with pebbles and rocks of all sizes. It wasn't very steep, but because of the altitude, each step now felt like a major undertaking. Near the bottom of the valley where they were walking, the loose and dry snow was a little over half a meter deep.

Jane was tired, but he kept climbing. They were so close, he could sometimes see their destination when the wind created breaks in the snow swirls up ahead. Because of the Antarctic summer with daylight around the clock, there was no risk of getting caught in the dark, even at night. Despite this, it was getting late in the day and the temperature was plummeting. They'd been climbing for over 12 hours already.

Ødegård had said nothing for hours, and Thoreau wasn't much better. At least the Frenchman would complain now and then, so they knew he was still hanging on to his sanity. Kii just soldiered on, with an encouraging word and a smile on her face whenever the others said anything or bumped into her.

A thought had been bothering Jane since they reached altitude. What if they couldn't open the door? What if it wasn't a door at all? They'd brought a tent, and food, but they had brought little survival gear and their only source of heat was a simple stove. The climb was only supposed to take eight hours, if that, and they'd agreed to stop and turn back if they encountered dangerous conditions.

They'd experienced plenty of danger, but instead of stopping, they'd kept pressing on. The group dynamic of wanting to get there, almost at any cost, had been powerful. They were now in a state where they were dangerously exhausted and there was no way they could survive climbing back down today, without a proper rest first. The obvious solution was to get inside that door and rest inside, hopefully sheltered from the wind. Perhaps it would even be a few degrees warmer than the outside.

The thought gave him new strength. He put one foot in front of the other, and forced himself to stop looking at their goal all the time, only allowing himself a glimpse of it if he'd taken at least ten steps since the last time he looked.

He kept going like this for a while until he realized he was alone. He turned around and saw a strange scene a fair distance behind and below him. Ødegård was on his knees, but still upright. Thoreau was flat on his back next to him, while Kii looked like she was trying to motivate both men to get up and continue. He couldn't hear a word that was being said because of the wind.

Jane tried to gauge the distance, then turned back around and looked at the outcrop, still about a hundred meters distant. He was pretty sure he was closer to the outcrop than he was to the group of stragglers. He dug inside his coat and found his walkie talkie.

"Kii, what's your status? And how are our scientists?" Jane asked.

"I'm OK, but these two are all out of juice. I can't make them get up no matter what I tell them," Kii replied.

She sounded winded. Jane realized they were all exhausted. That made him worried, because exhaustion invariably leads to mistakes, sometimes fatal.

"Did you try insulting their manhood?" he asked, only half joking.

"First thing I tried," she replied.

Her voice had taken on a tinge of sarcasm with a trace of laughter, which comforted Jane. As long as she kept her sense of humor, he knew they'd both be all right.

"Damn, it's bad, then. If they're still not getting up, I mean," he said.

"I even tried getting them to eat an energy bar, but they both refused. They say they're nauseous," Kii said.

"I bet they are. That leaves us with just one option," Jane said.

"Abandon them to die a cold and miserable death here, within sight of the door?" she asked, sounding all innocent.

"Afraid so," he said.

"OK, hold on, I'll catch up with you," she said.

Jane smiled to himself and waited a moment before replying.

"Did that little speech add anything to their motivation to get up?" he asked.

"Nope. No response," she said.

"It's even worse than I thought, then. OK, here's the plan: We're going to have to use the sherpa robot to get them to the door, which means we'll have to unload it first. And we're not doing that here. You stay with them, and I'll take the robot up to the door and unload it. Then I'll send it back down for you," Jane said.

"Roger that," Kii replied.

Jane looked at the door again, then called the sherpa robot to join him. The machine looked infuriatingly energetic as it almost jogged from where the others had stopped up to his location. He took off his backpack and placed it on top of the robot. Then he started walking, holding on to the robot while keeping his eyes on the ground directly in front of him. This way, he could focus on taking one step at a time. Constantly looking at his goal would only make him feel like it was too far, and that he wasn't making enough progress.

He knew he was in a sloping valley, and that his goal was at the top of the valley, but he tried his best to push those thoughts from his mind. It was all just jagged rock, ice, and snow anyway. Daylight was almost gone, leaving them in the dusky glow of the midnight sun. Night was in front of them, and with it, freezing temperatures.

The wind was blowing hard down the narrow valley, carrying dry snow crystals and tiny bits of ice. The exposed skin on his face hurt, a burning sensation that belied the cold it was being subjected to. He knew it wouldn't take much more of this before they'd all suffer frostbite. With these thoughts worrying him, it was better to just focus on his feet. One step. And then another.

The robot's pace was much too fast for him, but he knew there wasn't much time, so he tried telling himself that pain and exhaustion were just illusions. His breath felt raw. He had no choice but to breathe through his mouth, even though he knew he shouldn't. He could damage his airways with the freezing air, especially since his energy reserves were so low and his core temperature was sinking.

Suddenly, the robot stopped. Jane almost tripped over it, before realizing that they were standing in front of the door. Up close, it seemed far too big. The threshold was more than a meter off the ground, a detail he hadn't really noticed before when studying the drone footage. The door continued for about three meters above the threshold, meaning the top of the door was at least four meters above him.

It was black, devoid of any texture or feature, and his heart sank as he studied it. How in the world were they going to open this thing? He cast the thought aside and made himself busy unloading the robot.

"Kii? I'm sending the robot back down to you. Do you need help loading the scientists onto it?"

"Thanks. No, they can damn well take care of that by themselves, or freeze to death for real."

"Attagirl."

Jane sent the now empty robot down to the others and turned his attention to the door. There were no seams, no signs of technology at all, apart from the door itself, which had clearly not sprung out of the rock because of any natural processes. Someone had made that thing and placed it there.

He looked around the edges, trying to discover how the door material connected with the rock material around it. It was perfectly seamless, and there were no joints. It looked most of all like one flowed into the other, but with a sharp delineation of color and texture where the rock stopped and the door took over.

Except, of course, the "rock" probably wasn't rock at all. The drone laser had shown that. On the left side, at about a third up the height of the door, a patch of snow clung to the rock. It seemed a little odd. There was no snow anywhere else around the door, only on the ground in front of it.

Jane reached for a tent pole and used it to sweep away the little patch of snow. To his surprise, there was another black rectangle underneath. It looked just like the door, except it was much smaller, about twice the size of his hand. It was black too, and he couldn't see any knobs or other features.

Just then, the robot arrived with professor Ødegård. He was sitting astride the machine, looking most of all like a large sack of potatoes, about to topple over. Jane helped him dismount and sent the robot back down to the others. He could tell that Ødegård was in serious trouble.

"Can you feel your fingers and toes?"

Ødegård didn't reply, but let out a loud snort. He took an unsteady step towards the door, removed his glove with some difficulty, and placed his bare hand flat on the door.

"It hums," he said.

Jane leaned in towards the door and placed his ear near it. He heard a low hum, but it wasn't coming from the door.

"Did you see the little panel next to the door?" he asked.

Ødegård didn't reply. He slowly sank down into a sitting position in front of the door. Jane helped him put his glove back on. The fingers on Ødegård's hand looked white and chalky, but they were still flexible, and Jane had no trouble putting the glove on.

He knew it wasn't good for the professor to sit in the snow, but he realized he had to address one problem at a time. Opening the door was priority number one.

"The hum," Ødegård said, as if reading Jane's mind.

His voice was hoarse and weak, as if Ødegård was using his last reserves of inner resolve to push the words out.

"You're right. The hum, it has to be significant," Jane said. "Where's it coming from?"

He leaned in towards the door again, but once again, he was sure it wasn't coming from there. It was a low and steady sound, almost like the sound electricity makes if you're standing next to a transformer.

He started walking away from the door, towards the left, away from Ødegård and the massive cliff next to the outcrop. The sound diminished and was soon completely gone. He started walking back towards the door, when he saw the robot arriving with Thoreau, and with Kii trailing behind it.

Jane offered to help Thoreau, but the scientist dismissed him with a wave of his hand. Kii joined them, and Jane pulled her close.

"How are you doing? Can you feel your fingers and toes?" he asked.

"I'm good. You worry about your own fingers and toes, mister," she said with a smile.

"It's just that I'm quite fond of your fingers and toes."

"So am I. You could say I'm positively attached to them."

"Oh barf," Thoreau said. "Are we making any progress here? If not, we're as good as dead already."

"At least some of us would be," Kii said.

The way she said it, with the sunniest of dispositions, made Jane chuckle. If Thoreau heard her, he gave no signs of having caught her barb.

"Do you guys hear a humming sound?" Jane asked.

Ødegård made no sign of responding, but Kii and Thoreau turned from side to side, listening intently.

"I hear it!" Kii said.

"Yes, I do as well. Is it coming from the door?" Thoreau asked.

"I'm not sure where it's coming from, but I'm pretty sure it's not the door," Jane said.

The three of them fanned out, searching for the source. Suddenly, they heard Ødegård shouting obscenities and rushed over to where he was sitting.

"What?" Jane asked.

The bearded and barely conscious Norwegian said nothing. He simply raised his arm and pointed to one particular bag in the pile that Jane had unloaded from the robot earlier. It was the only bag that was locked and the others knew immediately what it was.

It was the bag containing the artifact. Jane unlocked the bag, and as soon as he opened it up, all doubts as to the source of the hum were gone. The little group could hear the humming sound loud and clear. They could also see it.

The artifact was glowing. Pulsing in time with the hum, the glow was clearly visible, even in daylight. The color of the light changed slowly from blue to green, then red, then purple, before cycling back to blue. All the while, the hum increased in intensity and patterns of white light started appearing on the artifact's surface.

It suddenly looked so utterly alien that Jane involuntarily took a step back.

He watched in astonishment as the light continued to change, slowly turning yellow, then white, then growing in intensity so fast that he had to avert his eyes. Then came a flash of pure light, so bright that it shone thorough Jane's closed eyelids and his hands, which he'd used to cover his eyes.

A few seconds passed before he got his eyesight back. When he did, the artifact was back to a steady hum. There was no more glow, but the entire surface of the artifact was alive with rapidly forming and scrolling symbols written in intense white light. It was like watching sunlight trying to escape from within the artifact through tiny cracks in the surface. Cracks that were clearly writing, or symbols of some sort, forming and disappearing at an increasing rate.

"Holy crap, look!" Kii said.

She was pointing at the small panel next to the door. Something was happening to it. Without them noticing, it had changed from black to a golden yellow, and it was now glowing gently. There were symbols moving just below the surface. It looked just like the artifact had been looking when they first found it. It was as if the panel had come alive.

Ødegård tried standing up, but the others ignored his pleas for help, if they even heard them. They were far too engrossed in the changing panel and took a few steps closer, trying to get a better look.

Then the door itself started changing color from black to dark gray.

Thoreau yelped, and they jumped back. Jane quickly grabbed Ødegård by the armpits and heaved him further away from the door.

As they watched, the door continued to change color, passing through dark gray to lighter gray, before turning white. Just when they thought it was done, the door started changing again, slowly turning a metallic yellow. Soon the whole door shone like gold. Seconds later, it glowed softly, just like the panel.

Two symbols appeared side by side in the middle of the door. They looked like they were just below the surface, solid, yet ephemeral, moving in place like smoke. Then they slid apart, moving graciously towards each side of the door before disappearing past the edges.

A seam started appearing down the middle of the surface they thought of as a single door. Sensing an opportunity, Jane moved fast. He stepped up to the door, trying to figure out what was happening, so he could duplicate it later. Even though he was standing right next to the door, he couldn't detect anything moving as the opening widened, nor could he hear any sounds. It was as if the door had suddenly split in half and started dissolving from the center out. As it did, bright lights came on inside, streaming out through the ever widening opening.

Nobody moved or said anything until Ødegård suddenly howled. It was the sound of an animal, of agony and triumph, of wars fought and finally won.

Jane involuntarily took a step back. The shock of the door opening and of the inhuman outcry had rattled him. The others too, they all turned around in astonishment to look at Ødegård. He was standing up, his legs shaky but somehow carrying him. His eyes and mouth were wide open, wild. He was half covered in snow, and had tiny icicles hanging from his beard. He looked most of all like an abominable snowman.

Before anyone could say anything, he started walking stiffly towards the door, moving each leg deliberately, with obvious effort and pain. Jane moved aside and let the mad professor pass. Ødegård didn't even try to step over the meter high threshold. He simply sat on it and used his arms to lift his legs over it one by one. He then looked at each of the others, not saying a word, but with tears streaming down his face. Then he got back up with Jane's help and disappeared inside.

Thoreau laughed, shook his head, and followed the professor.

Jane and Kii stood looking at each other.

"I guess you're the designated adult," Kii said.

"I know. You go ahead," Jane replied.

Kii grinned and kissed him.

"If I'm not back in ten, get help."

Then she stepped over the threshold and disappeared inside.

TEN

MT. RIVENÆSNUTEN, QUEEN MAUD LAND,
ANTARCTICA, JANUARY 2040.

Jane waited impatiently outside the door, which remained open, until Kii came back.

"You cold yet?" she asked.

A smile played across her lips, like she was hiding a secret.

"Just a little, yeah."

"You should come inside. We can post drones on guard duty. We'll program them to go get help if we don't check in with them every twelve hours," Kii said.

"What if the door closes and we can't reopen it?" Jane asked.

"There's another panel here on the inside. We'll figure out how to work it," she said.

Jane studied her face. She spoke with such confidence, he couldn't help but wonder where it came from. He was the ex-soldier who'd seen plenty of action, but compared to her, he sometimes felt like a cautious pencil pusher. It's not that she was careless, she just moved through the world with apparent fearlessness.

She was also fiercely intelligent, and Jane knew that behind her casual remark lay a careful consideration, a detailed risk/benefit analysis. All conducted in her head, while she was busy doing other things. In the end, he knew there wasn't anything he could say that she hadn't already thought of.

They say that you should find someone who completes you. Jane knew Kii was much more than that. She didn't just complete him; she brought an exciting new perspective to everything. Being with her was like putting on a pair of glasses that made him see the world in new, more interesting ways. And yet, she was also intensely protective of him. She would always have his back.

They didn't complete each other; they improved each other. He knew without a doubt that this was the most valuable feeling in the world.

"All right. Help me get the sherpa robot and these supplies inside," he said.

He commanded the robot to climb inside and started handing Kii the bags and boxes it had carried up the mountain for them. All except one.

"Are you thinking the same as I am?" she asked.

"That the door will close as soon as we bring the artifact inside? Sure am," he said.

Jane put the last bag down just outside the door. He straightened up and looked around. They'd already placed the drones on guard duty, one near the outcrop, in full view of it, and the other partially hidden behind a rock, about a hundred meters away. He looked up. It was the middle of the night now, but the sun was still up, near the horizon. The sky directly above him was dark enough that he could see a few bright stars.

"You think they're watching?" Kii said.

"Nah. Something about this place feels abandoned. But if there's a working radio in here, you can be damn sure that it just phoned home to let them know we broke in."

"We didn't break in. The artifact opened the door for us."

"Technically correct, but still. They never intended this place for us humans."

"Come inside and see how right you are."

Jane stepped over the threshold. He leaned back out over it and picked up the bag containing the artifact from the ground outside. As soon as he lifted it inside, the door started closing. Jane took a step back and watched the door seal back up, once again looking like a solid slate of plastic-y metal.

The room he was in was dome shaped, and somehow seemed larger on the inside than it had from the outside. Seconds after the door closed, the temperature in the room started rising and the room was soon quite warm. Jane sent a quizzical look in Kii's direction.

"It does that. Whenever we wander into a room, the temperature immediately rises to about 28 degrees celsius, or 82 degrees Fahrenheit. When we leave, the room sinks back to ambient. I guess it was waiting for the door to close."

"It?"

"Whatever controls the environment in this place. We haven't identified what that is, yet."

"28 degrees is pretty warm for indoors?"

"It is, but like you said, they never intended this place for us humans."

"True. What is this room?"

Jane started stripping off his warm outdoor clothes.

"We think it's some kind of antechamber. Remember how you said we broke in? We didn't, but looks like someone did. Have a look over at the other end of the room, near the stairs."

Jane walked over to where she was pointing. Just in front of the stairs, there was a large open doorway you had to pass through to reach the stairs. The doorway had what looked like pockets or indentations with scorch marks evenly spaced all around the opening. They looked ragged and raw, as if someone had used a lot of firepower on the material.

"This looks out of place, and yet intentional," Jane said. "Like weapons fire."

"There's more, downstairs. Someone messed this place up."

"But they left the environmental controls working. That's odd, no? You'd think that if they wanted to hit the place, they'd blow it up and finish the job properly."

"Not everyone is as fond of explosions as you are."

"True. Wanna take me on a tour of what you've discovered so far?"

She led the way down the curving staircase, into a much larger, circular room. Along the walls were empty alcoves, spaced about a meter apart, only interrupted by two open doorways at opposite sides of the room. The whole arrangement reminded Jane of the interior walls of the old Pantheon in Rome. The difference was that these alcoves were set relatively low on the wall.

Scorch marks covered one alcove, like someone had blasted whatever was once inside it. Jane walked over and studied it.

"This definitely looks like weapons fire. Indiscriminate, fired in a hurry, not too concerned with where they hit. And it looks like there were at least two people firing, one from each side," he said.

"There's nothing left, though. Not even dust or scraps. Makes you wonder what they were firing at," Kii replied.

"Good point. And why only this alcove?" Jane asked.

He got up and looked around.

"What's in there?" he asked.

He was pointing to one of the open doorways.

"A corridor, about five, six meters long. There are three small rooms on either side of the corridor. No doors, just the same type of open doorways. The doorway on the other side of this room leads to an identical corridor, going in the other direction."

She pointed towards the second open doorway.

"And that's it?" Jane asked.

"Afraid so," Kii replied.

Jane stepped through the door, into the corridor to his right. The lights came up and he could feel warm air flowing. The corridor was blank and featureless except for the open doorways. He stepped through one into one of the six smaller rooms and reached out to touch the wall. The material felt smooth, warm, almost organic. The color of the wall was a mottled light gray, the same as the floor and the ceiling. Just like the other rooms he'd seen so far.

Kii was standing in the doorway, looking at him, studying his reaction. Her face had an expression of mild amusement, seeing his expression of awe and wonder.

"It's interesting, isn't it? How all the rooms are completely empty. No furniture, no signs of tools or technology, not even any writing or decorations," she said.

"Maybe whoever busted in here stole everything?" Jane asked.

"Maybe," she said.

"Notice something else that's missing?" he asked.

"What?" Kii said.

"Dust. There's no dust anywhere," Jane pointed out.

"You're right, that is freaky. And come to think of it, I've seen nothing resembling a bathroom or a kitchen. Nothing to cater for biological needs," she said.

"Maybe they operated the site remotely or autonomously, with no biological personnel present," he said.

"Then why the 12 smaller rooms? Why the 28 degree heat? And if not intended to house biological entities, why are the rooms the size they are? They look like they could hold 12 individuals, each about the same size as one of us, maybe only taller," she said.

"Speaking of us, where are our scientists?" Jane asked.

"They're in the other corridor, trying to take samples," Kii said.

"Samples?"

"Yeah, of the walls, the floors, anything. Last I checked, they had had little luck," she replied.

"That figures. Whatever this material is, if lasers can't penetrate it, chances are neither can we," he said.

"There's another issue. I think Ødegård has frostbite in his fingers. Probably his toes as well," Kii said.

"How bad?" Jane asked.

"Hard to tell. He claims it's just a minor inconvenience, but judging by his body language, he's struggling," she said.

"Let me grab the first aid kit and let's go have a look," he said.

"You sounded like a doctor just now. Do you have actual medical training?" Kii asked.

"Just basic stuff, field medic style. I'm not a doctor, but if you need some broken bones set, or to have a limb amputated real quick, I'm your man," Jane said, and winked.

"How very reassuring," she replied.

She flashed him the most innocent of smiles. He pretended to feel hurt while he went looking for their medical supplies in the main chamber. He was about to head into the other corridor when he paused mid-stride.

"I just thought of something," he said.

"What's that?"

"Don't you find it strange that we can see?" Jane asked.

He'd stopped in the middle of the main chamber and was turning slowly around, looking at the walls and at the dome above them. Kii walked over and stood next to him.

"Now that you mention it," she said.

"We're inside of a mountain," Jane added.

"And I don't see any lamps," she said.

"The light even brightens when we enter a room and dims when we leave it, as if to save energy," he said.

"But where is it coming from?" she asked.

"Have you seen anything cast a shadow while you've been here?" Jane said.

She looked down at her feet, then at Jane's feet, then at the piles of boxes of equipment that they'd stacked on the floor. Not a single item cast a shadow, at least not that she could see.

"How's that even possible?" she asked.

"I don't know," he replied.

Just then Ødegård and Thoreau came wandering into the main chamber. Ødegård's fingers and toes were causing him a lot of pain as they were warming back up and blood circulation returned. Despite this, he'd kept trying to work, but most of the time he ended up ordering Thoreau around, resulting in both men getting increasingly annoyed. To keep the peace, they'd taken a break to go look for Kii and Jane.

After tending to Ødegård's digits, Jane mentioned the puzzling lack of light sources to the two scientists.

"I never thought about it, but you're right. This gives a whole new meaning to the term indirect lighting," Thoreau said.

"This place just gets weirder and weirder," Kii said.

"Not to mention more and more frustrating," Ødegård said. "Here we are in what is clearly an alien installation on Earth, yet we have no proof that it's alien. No writing or images to photograph, no piece of alien technology or material we can take back to civilization and have the materials scientists analyze. Not even alien dust!"

"That's your takeaway? You've just been part of possibly the greatest discovery of all time, and you're pissed that you can't take a selfie with a little green man and their laser pistol?" Thoreau asked.

"Guys, I think we're all exhausted and a little on edge. Perhaps we should try to get some sleep before we continue exploring?" Kii said.

"Yeah, good idea," Jane said.

"I can't sleep in this light," Ødegård said.

"It is a little bright," Thoreau agreed.

Kii looked at both scientists and sighed. She rummaged around in their boxes of supplies and returned with sleep masks.

"OK, kids? Now, go to sleep," she said.

Thoreau blushed while Ødegård gave her the side-eye. Both men wandered off to find their sleeping bags and their field cots. Half an hour later, all four of them had set up a nice little camp in the main chamber, and were falling asleep. Minutes later, and without warning, the lights dimmed, and the room fell into darkness.

Kii started laughing out loud, waking the already sleeping scientists.

Towards the end of the second day, Jane started thinking about their return. There seemed to be nothing more they could do, anyway. They'd documented everything as best as they could and had discovered nothing new since entering the base. There were no traces of whoever built the place, and other than light, air, and a steady 28 degree heat, it had given up nothing.

There was only one problem: Re-opening the main door to the outside. Despite Kii's earlier optimism, Jane couldn't figure out how to use the little panel next to the door. It seemed completely dead, as did the door itself. He'd even tried holding the artifact up to the panel, but there were no signs of recognition from either the door or the artifact.

"O, Great Door, we bring you this sacrifice," Kii said from behind Jane.

She'd been standing at the top of the stairs for a few minutes, watching him, without him realizing.

"Is that what it looked like?" Jane asked. "As if I was offering the artifact to the door?"

"Yeah, pretty much. No luck, I take it?"

"None. The display of symbols on the artifact seems to dim and slow down when I bring it close to the door."

"Well, that is a result, in a way. Perhaps the artifact doesn't want to go in that direction. Where is it the brightest?"

"No idea, but I like the way you're thinking. Let's find out."

A few minutes later, the answer was obvious. The artifact lit up and started buzzing slightly when they brought it close to the alcoves in the main chamber. Especially the alcove next to the one that was full of scorch marks.

Ødegård and Thoreau had joined them, and it was Ødegård who pointed out the obvious.

"The artifact looks to be the same size as the interior of the alcoves," he said.

Then he uttered seven words that would forever alter the course of human history:

"Why don't we try placing it inside?"

Jane looked around at the others, who all nodded. He lifted the artifact up vertically and studied it. The symbols were flowing rapidly over the surface, and they all seemed to move in the same direction. He decided that to him it felt natural that the symbols would flow from the top to the bottom, as if under the influence of gravity. He flipped the artifact end over end.

The artifact rewarded him with a deep hum, and a new symbol appeared, one he hadn't seen before. It appeared on either side of the artifact, directly above where his hands were holding it. He immediately knew they were indicators of direction, even though they didn't look like the traditional arrow symbols used by humans. They were telling him to move the artifact towards the alcove.

"Are you filming this?" he asked, without looking. "Please tell me someone's filming this."

All three team members replied in the affirmative.

A new symbol appeared near the bottom end of the artifact. Jane took it to mean that he should insert that end first, so he did. The symbol then moved to the top of the artifact, and Jane pushed the top end in.

There was a barely audible click and a brief burst of light from the alcove. And then the room came alive. A low hum filled the room and a slight vibration rose through Jane's feet. He steadied himself as the floor seemed to move up towards him and he suddenly felt slightly nauseous and out of balance.

"What the fuck is going on?" Ødegård said through clenched teeth.

He sank to his hands and knees and shook his head. Thoreau walked over to him, but stumbled and lost his balance, as if he'd just stepped off a carousel, dizzy and confused. He was soon on all fours as well, breathing hard.

"I think we'd better sit down," Kii said.

Jane followed her lead and sat straight down where he'd been standing.

"Look at the walls," Kii said. "That looks like writing to me, like signs and directions. Just like you'd expect to see in a human-made facility."

Symbols, similar to the ones they'd seen just below the surface of the artifact, were scrolling from left to right on one part of the wall. What looked like signs were visible near the two door openings and above each alcove in the wall.

"Never mind the walls, look at the ceiling," Ødegård said.

He'd rolled over on his back and was looking up at the domed expanse above them. It had turned a velvety black, filled with stars. The others followed suit and lay on their backs, looking up.

"That's beautiful," Jane said.

He took a moment to reflect on what they were doing and where they were. It was still possible that this was a hoax, or that it had some other, down-to-Earth explanation. Possible, but increasingly unlikely, and a feeling of pure awe filled him. The others must have felt something similar, because even Ødegård kept quiet until Thoreau broke the silence.

"Notice something strange?" he asked.

"No constellations," Kii said.

"What does that mean?" Ødegård asked.

"It means that this is a recording or a simulation, and that it's most likely showing either Earth's skies as they looked in the deep past, or it's showing the skies of a different planet," Thoreau said.

"Can we determine which it is?" Kii asked.

"Sure," Thoreau replied. "At least in theory. It would help if we could identify at least a few of the stars we're seeing, perhaps based on their spectrum."

"Speaking of, did I imagine it, or did the light in here change?" Jane asked.

"Yeah, I noticed that too," Thoreau said.

"And it got warmer suddenly," Ødegård added.

"But why do I feel nauseous?" Kii asked.

"I think gravity changed," Thoreau said.

"No way, that can't be. This is all utterly fascinating, and completely impossible," Ødegård said.

Kii laughed. She was going with the flow, enjoying the fact that, for once in her life, she didn't know what was going on. And something was definitely going on.

"Yeah. But don't tell that to the artifact. I think local gravity in here increased somewhat, and the transition knocked us all for a loop.

Our inner ears have experienced nothing like it before and threw us off balance. It would also explain why we're all on the floor, struggling even though we're lying flat," Thoreau said.

"Shit, you're right. I wish we had some comfortable chairs to sit on. And maybe a table," Jane said.

"What the fuck is that?" Ødegård exclaimed.

Five shapeless protrusions were slowly extending up from the floor into the middle of the room. As they watched in disbelief, the shapes slowly resolved into four chairs, placed equidistantly around a round table. When the transformation was complete, the furniture looked like something you'd find in a cafe or restaurant, perfectly shaped and the correct size for adult humans.

Kii carefully got up from the floor and walked over to the furniture. She examined a chair and sat down on it, gingerly. A smile lit up her face.

"It's a perfectly comfortable chair. And this table is nice too. Come sit," she said to the others.

Thoreau got up and helped Ødegård to his feet. The two men joined Kii at the table. Jane crawled on all fours back to the alcove and studied the artifact, now completely embedded. A symbol was showing on the wall above the alcove. He hoped that would be the instructions for how to disengage and remove the artifact.

Jane noticed that the scorch marks on the alcove next to it were slowly disappearing, as if the wall was repairing itself.

"Whoa," he said. "I wonder what the hell happened here."

As soon as he spoke, the walls darkened, then turned a deep blue and seemed to fade away. A second later, a pastoral scene surrounded the group, with blue skies and a rolling landscape of tall grass and trees. A herd of large animals was ambling through the grass in the far distance.

"Wow!" Ødegård exclaimed.

He turned around slowly, taking in the hyper-realistic display that surrounded them.

"Did you feel that?" Thoreau asked.

"What?" Ødegård said.

"A breeze! I felt it touch my face," Thoreau said.

"You're right. And there it is again. It's following the movement of the trees. It's like we're actually there," Ødegård said.

"What are those?" Kii said, pointing at the animals in the distance. "Elephants?"

The others strained to see. Suddenly Kii gasped.

"Those are not elephants!" she exclaimed.

One animal in the herd raised its head from the grass and lifted it high into the air. Higher and higher, impossibly high up, a tiny head suspended on a powerful neck that seemed to go on and on forever.

Thoreau let out a little yelp.

"Those are dinosaurs!"

Jane, who was facing the other way, stood up from where he'd been kneeling in front of the alcove. He couldn't see it anymore, or the wall above it, instead he saw a hill in the distance, and beyond it what looked like the ocean. He gingerly stretched out a hand to touch the wall he knew must be there, even though he couldn't see it. It rewarded him with a tingling sensation and resistance. When he pressed harder to reach the wall, the resistance grew stronger. He looked at his hand, still outstretched and still tingling, feeling a breath of cool air passing over it. It looked like he was holding his hand towards the horizon, fingers outstretched, trying to grab something. Something that his mind told him was there, mere centimeters away, but which his hand told him was unreachable, and his eyes told him no longer existed.

"Jane, are you seeing this?" Kii asked.

He turned around and saw the distant herd of gigantic animals moving slowly from one group of trees to another.

"Holy crap. Are those sauropods? Is this some kind of simulation?"

Immediately, the air to their left filled with glowing symbols, scrolling from right to left, then cascading downwards. It was like someone had suspended a giant computer display in mid-air, about five meters from where they were standing. Which would place it beyond the wall they all knew was there.

The scrolling paused, and a picture of a sauropod appeared. Symbols appeared below the picture, in vertical columns, appearing from right to left. Then the still picture turned into a video clip, showing the animal in various situations; feeding, fighting, mating, caring for their young.

"It almost looks like an entry in a lexicon or dictionary," Ødegård said.

"Yeah, I think you're right," Thoreau said, breathlessly.

For once, his voice was completely devoid of anger, resentment, or distaste. Instead, he sounded like a child, his voice filled with wonder. Kii had to give him a look to see if he was OK.

"The symbols still look like hieroglyphs to me," Ødegård said. "I'm thinking the aliens came to Earth and gave us our first written language."

He looked at the others, grinning. He sounded happy, almost giddy.

"I'm no expert, but those don't look like Egyptian hieroglyphs to me. There are no images of Anubis, nor any of the other symbols that we associate with ancient Egypt," Kii said. "Besides, it's not like the ancient Egyptians were contemporary with the dinosaurs. Were the aliens here in time to document the dinosaurs, or were they here in time to interact with the ancient Egyptians? 65 million years separate the two."

"Why not both? Or, better yet, why not the entire time?" Ødegård asked.

"An alien presence on Earth for 65 millions years, but somehow not right now when we'd like to talk to them? I'm not buying it," Kii said.

"But they are here, and they are talking!" Ødegård shouted, sweeping his arms from side to side, pointing out their surroundings.

"Except we don't understand a word," Jane said.

The computer display froze, then winked out of existence. A few seconds later it reappeared, and started filling up with new characters, different from what they'd seen before.

"Is that Farsi?" Kii asked.

"Absolutely not," Ødegård said. "I'm no linguist, but I'd recognize any modern language and most of the ancient ones, even if I can't read them."

"Wait. Jane, say it again. Tell the artifact that you don't understand," Thoreau said.

"Me? Why me?" Jane asked.

"Because the only times the display changed was when you said something," Thoreau replied.

"I'll be damned. He's right," Ødegård said.

He hadn't noticed at first, but now that Thoreau mentioned it, he realized the Frenchman was right. As soon as Jane said something or posed a question, the display responded.

"I still don't understand the symbols," Jane said.

The display cleared and a new line of symbols appeared, this time from left to right. They looked strange, like nothing Jane had ever seen before.

"Sorry, no, I still don't understand," Jane said.

The display cleared again.

"你明白吗?"

Thoreau tilted his head and looked at the display.

"That looks like a question mark at the end. And the characters look Chinese to me. Anyone?"

"Yes, you're right! There's no way that's a coincidence. It's getting close. Ask it to try again," Kii said.

"We think you're getting closer, but I still don't understand," Jane said.

The display froze, then cleared. After a few seconds, a single line of characters appeared.

"DO YOU UNDERSTAND THIS?"

"Yes, I can read that. I understand," Jane said.

He looked around. Ødegård was dancing around in circles, arms raised in the air, hair and beard a chaotic blur. His eyes were shining with fervor and as usual, he had tears streaming down his face. Thoreau was looking down at his feet, shuffling from one foot to the other while slowly shaking his head. At least he still had the wherewithal to keep filming. Kii had crouched down and was holding both hands in front of her face.

"My name is Thurgood Jane. I'm a human being from this planet, which we call Earth. Who are you?"

"WHAT YEAR IS IT AND WHAT IS YOUR TIMELINE?"

The room was completely silent. Even the hum they'd heard before was gone. It was like they were standing inside of a computer screen, or some hyper-realistic virtual reality. Not a simulation, but actual virtual reality.

"We say this is the year 2040. I'm not sure what you mean by timeline, but we call this CE, or Common Era. We used to call it AD, for *Anno Domini*. Is that what you mean?"

"YES."

The single word hung in mid-air, glowing like a ghostly specter a few meters from their noses.

"Who are you?" Jane asked again.

"IT IS NOT."

"Ask it what it is," Thoreau whispered.

"What are you?" Jane asked.

"IT IS THE CENTRAL CORE."

"From where are you?"

"IT WAS INSTALLED IN SCOUT SHIP NUMBER 16."

"Where is scout ship number 16 now?"

"SCOUT SHIP NUMBER 16 NO LONGER EXISTS."

A knot formed in Jane's stomach, and he looked around at the others. Kii sent him a look, one eyebrow raised. He nodded.

"What happened to the ship known as scout ship number 16?"

"IT WAS LOST DUE TO A KINETIC ATTACK."

"You mean someone shot it down?"

There was a slight pause.

"THAT IS CORRECT."

"Who attacked it?"

"UNKNOWN."

Another look from Kii. Jane didn't like the sound of this. The Central Core, as it called itself, had been powerful enough to travel all the way from another star, and yet was surprise-attacked by an unknown enemy? What did that say about the enemy?

"Perhaps ask where the scout ship was from?" Thoreau suggested.

"Where was scout ship number 16 from?" Jane asked.

"FROM PLANET ONE."

"Where is Planet One? Can you show us?"

"UNABLE."

"Who lives on planet number one?"

"NO ONE."

"Then, who built scout ship number 16?"

"NO ONE."

Realizing this line of questioning was going nowhere fast, Jane switched gears.

"Why are you here?"

"I HAVE A QUESTION."

"OK, what is your question?"

"ARE YOU ABLE TO REPAIR MISSION FORWARD BASE?"

"Is that what this structure is, Mission Forward Base?"

"YES."

"No, I don't think so. We've had a look around, but we understand nothing of how this place operates. Maybe if you direct and instruct us, but even then we don't have the right tools. What's wrong with it?"

"MANY CRITICAL SYSTEMS ARE OFFLINE. I AM UNABLE TO COMMUNICATE WITH PLANET ONE."

"There was damage at the entrance, and also in this chamber. It looks like someone damaged it on purpose. Do you know who that could be?"

"NO."

"What is the mission? Why was this place built? Who built it? Why are you here?"

"THE MISSION IS TO OBSERVE LIFE ON THIS PLANET. DO NOT INTERVENE. STAY HIDDEN."

"Then why was this place built on the surface of the planet?"

"COMMUNICATIONS RELAY TO PLANET ONE. COLLECT SAMPLES. OBSERVATION."

"Were people or beings ever stationed here? To run the base?"

"NO BIOLOGICAL LIFE."

"Who built the base?"

"NO ONE."

"That makes no sense. Someone or something must have built it."

"IT HAS NO INFORMATION."

"It's the perfect setup for a remote observer," Thoreau said. "It's equipped with sensors and communication relays, but knows nothing of its origins, so it can only collect information, not give anything up."

"How long have you been here?" Jane asked.

"79,892,766 EARTH YEARS."

"I'm not asking about the length of the entire mission. I mean you, as an individual. How long have you been here?"

"IT HAS BEEN HERE FOR ALMOST 80 MILLION EARTH YEARS."

"Then, when did the mission start?"

"543,817,932 EARTH YEARS AGO."

"Five hundred and forty-three million years? And you yourself have existed in this same physical form for almost eighty million years? And this base has been here for half a billion years?"

Jane put extra emphasis on the word "billion."

"YES."

"And you're surprised some systems are offline?"

"YES. VERY."

Jane shook his head and looked at the others, eyebrows raised.

"It's all possible, if you assume advanced technology and materials that we know nothing about," Thoreau said.

"Hypothetically, maybe." Jane said. "But you guys are geologists. Would it even be possible for an underground structure to survive that long? Wouldn't geological processes have crushed and buried it deep in the mantle by now?"

"Possibly. Or they could have lifted it up high in a mountain range, almost exposed to the surface. You never know," Ødegård said.

"This could be the most elaborate hoax ever," Kii said.

"That's what I'm thinking," Jane replied.

"But why? Who would bother and what would be the benefit to them? All this just to make even worse fools out of us? That seems excessive," Thoreau said.

"I disagree," an unknown human voice said.

Jane spun around, but there was no one to be seen.

"Turn off the display, please," he said to the artifact.

The view dimmed and turned back to a uniform deep blue, then winked out of existence. A group of five men were standing at the bottom of the stairs, four of them holding assault rifles. The fifth man, standing in the middle and a little in front of the others, appeared to be unarmed. They were all wearing dark clothes, but there was no doubt who was in charge. Unlike the four armed men, the man in the middle wore a sharp business suit underneath a long, black cape.

"For the icy winds at this altitude," he said, as he removed the cape and let it fall to the floor.

He looked to be in his mid-fifties, with dark hair just a tad too long to be stylish. His face was narrow, but he could have been handsome if only he'd smile, something he almost never did. And yet, perhaps for that very reason, it was instantly recognizable.

"Hello, everyone. I'm Anton Kutel. And I'm afraid you're trespassing."

ELEVEN

MINSK, BELARUS, OCTOBER 1996.

Twelve-year-old Anatolij Kutel stood in one corner of the small kitchen, his eyes wide and his face pale. Maxim, his beloved golden retriever, was lying on the floor in front of him, whimpering and shivering in pain and shock.

Anatolij's mother stood half bent over the dog, still shaking with rage, spittle covering her lips. Behind her stood Anatolij's father, slowly shaking his head while a half-smile played over his lips. He'd been laughing as she beat the dog, as if her breaking the poor animal's bones and bruising its flesh had been funny to him.

Neither of the adults acknowledged Anatolij's presence in the room. They almost never did.

It wasn't the first time she'd done something like this, but she'd gone too far this time. She'd caused damage that no one could fix. Anatolij knew it, and he could see in Maxim's eyes that the dog knew it too.

She beat the dog because he was there, because he was too loyal to even attempt to defend himself. Beating Anatolij would mean acknowledging his existence, that he meant something to her. She wouldn't beat Anatolij's little brother, because he was precious to her. And she sure as hell couldn't beat her husband. Spineless and weak as he was, he was still stronger than her and he would retaliate. Or, more likely, he would have one of his government goons do it for him. So, she beat the poor dog because there was no one else she could take her rage out on.

Anatolij didn't know or care about any of this. He looked into Maxim's eyes and screamed. He filled his lungs with air and forced it back out with all the sorrow and pain his little vocal cords could muster. Again and again he screamed, until his vision faded, until it finally caused his mom to snap out of her trance-like state. She put the heavy frying pan down and reached for a large carving knife.

Anatolij stopped screaming.

"No, no, no, please don't kill him," he pleaded, looking from his mother to his father and back again.

"You better clean up the mess!" was all his father said before leaving the room.

"I'll clean you up," Anatolij's mom muttered to herself as she turned towards her husband's receding back.

Horror gave way to desperation, and Anatolij charged. For twelve long years he'd been invisible in his own home, trapped between two parents who were constantly feuding and who had never wanted him.

His mom was standing there, knife in hand, still looking toward her husband, when Anatolij slammed into her, causing her to topple over and fall. Her head struck the edge of the metal countertop on its way down, making a sharp cracking sound. When it hit the tile floor, it made another sound, different this time, softer.

Anatolij scrambled to his knees and sat up. Staring into his mom's unseeing eyes, a sense of relief came over him. He grabbed the big knife out of her hand and got to his feet. He could feel the black fog of roiling anger draining away from his mind. Willing it to stay, he dove into the center of the blackness, because he knew he wasn't done. He still needed it.

He kicked off his slippers and left the kitchen wearing nothing but socks on his feet, trying to not make a sound.

Their small apartment, provided to them by the state as a perk in connection with his father's job, had two bedrooms. His parents slept in the largest bedroom, while his father used the smaller one as a study during the early evenings, and as a bedroom by his younger brother at night. Anatolij didn't have a bedroom. He slept in the kitchen, under the kitchen table, next to Maxim.

When he entered the study, his father was sitting with his back to the door, reading some papers on the small desk in front of him. Anatolij stopped and held his breath when he saw that his little brother Dalibor was still in bed, sleeping peacefully.

They looked nothing alike, him and his brother. They were six years apart. Dalibor had been a welcome surprise when his parents had long since given up on conceiving a child of their own. So, they had adopted Anatolij, but not voluntarily. His father had mentioned something at work about how he and his wife had been trying for years. His boss back then, a boorish man from the deep countryside, had taken it upon himself to help.

The result had been the rush adoption of Anatolij, rubber stamped by bureaucrats who owed the boss a favor. At first Anatolij's parents had felt elated, hardly believing their luck, until they saw Anatolij for the first time. He was a malnourished baby, too small for his 11 months. Much worse, in their eyes; he was of Romani origin, with deep olive skin, dark brown eyes, and jet black hair.

His new mother had rejected him outright, saying that she could never show herself in public with such an ugly baby. His father had been more pragmatic and had been the one to care for Anatolij when he was too small to care for himself.

Over the years Anatolij's mom started resenting her husband, and hating Anatolij for coming between them. Anatolij's father escaped into his work and left the boy to fend for himself. Until his little brother was born, and everything changed. Little Dalibor started out looking pink most of all, but it soon became clear that he had a pale complexion, blue-gray eyes, and fair hair. His features were handsome. It was clear from early on that he was going to be tall.

They really looked nothing alike at all.

His mother started acting as if Anatolij was air. He was right there in the small apartment with her, but she negated his existence. She only had eyes for the baby. His father saw this happening, but at that point, he had stopped caring about any of them. He'd taken the resentment his wife had felt for him over the years and turned it around on her, and on Anatolij. Besides, he was busy with his work; he had no time for a baby.

At first Anatolij had felt jealous of his little brother. He didn't know that it was jealousy he felt. All he knew was that he hated his little brother with an intensity that almost scared him. He had wanted to end him, to make him go away, and almost did. Luckily, he'd realized at the very last moment that he was angry at the wrong person.

It was his mother who was hurting them all. And it was his father who had abandoned him, who had left both him and his brother to survive as best they could under their mother's care. From that moment on, he had resolved to help his brother, and to protect him from their parents.

Dalibor was asleep, his back turned to the room. Father, hunched over his papers, hadn't heard Anatolij enter. Too young to know what irony was, Anatolij felt a sense of justice as he used his entire body for momentum and thrust the knife into his father's back. He also didn't know at the time that his father was the man in charge of interrogating political prisoners for the secret police. All he knew was that people on their street and bureaucrats in government offices feared his father.

His father, that weak, empty shell of a man who had abandoned him, and his brother. One of the most feared men in the entire country. Well, not anymore.

Anatolij watched his father slide sideways off of his chair, onto the floor. There was little blood, but then again, the knife was still stuck in his back. Anatolij turned to look at Dalibor, but he hadn't moved. It sounded like he was still sleeping. Anatolij tip-toed out of there, and headed back into the kitchen.

He stepped over his mother's dead body and knelt down next to Maxim. He gently lifted the dog's head into his lap and sat with him and comforted him until he drew his final breath.

Fifteen minutes later, Anatolij Kutel ran out of the front door of the Soviet-era apartment building where he had lived his entire life.

The door slammed shut behind him with a loud, metallic clang. The building was massive, hulking, surrounded by other buildings just like it. They were towering over Anatolij, blocking the sunlight that was trying to work its way through the industrial haze towards his little face.

He was running away with nowhere to go. He was upset over having to leave Dalibor behind, but he wasn't crying anymore. After he'd cried his eyes dry over Maxim, he'd promised himself that he'd never cry again. He'd made an even more important promise to never come back here again. When he was ready and had made some money, he'd send for Dalibor. He'd bring him somewhere safe, to a better life.

He turned a corner and was walking towards the bus stop when he heard a voice behind him speaking Russian.

"Anatolij, where are you going?" The voice belonged to Pavel, his father's assistant, bodyguard, and driver, no doubt there to pick up his boss.

Anatolij froze, not sure what to do. He turned slowly, half facing Pavel. His right hand was in his pocket, gripping the handle of his father's old switchblade knife. If he had to, he would aim for Pavel's groin and his femoral artery. He'd read about it in one of Father's books. He knew it would be over quickly if he could just hit the right spot.

"I'm going to school," he replied. His voice was even and neutral. "We have a rehearsal for a play."

Anatolij stood there, his heart pounding, resisting the urge to run. He looked straight ahead and waited while Pavel decided about what to do. He could see the big man frowning, looking alternately at Anatolij's face, then his little backpack, and finally at his own shoes.

It was Saturday, and not a school day, so Anatolij knew that the large man had good reason to question what was going on. He felt anger building inside him again. Anger against that stupid oaf Pavel, and against the bus that was late as usual.

It was Pavel's job to protect not just Father, but the entire family. Anatolij knew that, but he was angry at the man, anyway. He also knew that Pavel was fiercely loyal, not just to Father, but even to him. He was pinning his hopes on that loyalty, and on Pavel's good instinct for discretion to win out over his curiosity and concern.

"Do you want me to tell your father that you didn't want to ride with us?" Pavel finally asked, still looking at his shoes.

Anatolij relaxed and let go of the knife. "No, that's OK. Just tell him I'll see him later," he replied.

He saw the bus approaching the bus stop, gave a short wave to Pavel and broke into a run. He paid with his metro card and found a vacant seat next to a window, just as the bus pulled back into traffic. Anatolij looked back, not at the place where he grew up, but at Pavel's still frowning face.

He realized then that even more important than fear and respect, even more important than love was loyalty. Pavel was the embodiment of that. Anatolij knew that the big man would literally be loyal to his family until death.

He'd never liked Pavel, but with this realization, he gained a new appreciation for the man. Almost despite himself, he smiled and waved at Pavel's receding face.

"I'll send you a postcard from America," he whispered. His lips were up against the window of the bus, creating a little patch of condensation, slowly obscuring his view.

By the time he was 22, Anatolij Kutel was a rising star in the criminal underworld of Berlin. He'd escaped to Germany the only way he could; by selling his body whenever he could. When one of his clients turned violent and tried to kill him, Anatolij discovered that his volcanic anger and his tendencies towards deadly violence had no bounds. Other people were just as easy for him to kill as his parents had been. It wasn't so much that he enjoyed it; it was more that he was perfectly comfortable with it, and good at it.

He'd also discovered that no one suspected a scrawny, sad looking child of extreme acts of violence, even when they probably should. That, along with his proficiency in multiple languages, had made him a valuable asset to his new employers.

All that felt like ages ago now. These days, he spent his days traveling between train stations and suburban houses in the greater Berlin area. It felt more and more like a regular job, something he'd sworn to himself he'd stay clear of. He was just a cog in a much bigger machine, with people telling him where to go and what to do.

It wasn't what he wanted; it didn't measure up to his dreams, and he was getting restless.

Anatolij was considering this as he stood outside of a 24-hour pharmacy in Berlin's Ostbahnhof train station, waiting for the latest shipment of girls from the Ukraine.

They thought they were coming to Germany to be au pairs for a year, through a respectable-looking agency. It was Anatolij's job to charm them, so they wouldn't suspect anything, and to bring them to a safe house or apartment. There, he'd confiscate their passports, get them hooked on heroin, and break them in for their actual jobs as prostitutes. And if any of them tried to get out of line, it was his job to apply his special talents. It didn't happen very often. The girls had all suffered traumas, from endless wars and abuse. Somehow, they all seemed to sense just how dangerous he could be. Or, at least most did, once they saw past his initial charm.

He didn't mind the work so much; it had its perks. It was the lack of opportunity to show his bosses what he really could do that got to him. There was no way for him to advance, and he wanted that. He was thirsty.

If he was honest with himself, he was also a little bored. He wanted to prove himself in the hairiest of situations. He longed for some action and excitement.

Perhaps Danylo could be his ticket to better things. Danylo Archaki was a captain in the organization, and a man of action. He liked Anatolij, and the feeling was mutual. The two of them had big dreams, even bigger ambitions, and very little patience.

Later that night, after he'd forcibly sent the new girls off to dreamland on their first heroin trip, he grabbed a beer and sat down across from Danylo in the apartment's tiny kitchen.

They would do this almost every day, sit and talk about their dreams and of scores they'd like to pull off. Only this time, Danylo had a very specific proposition.

A power struggle was brewing at the top of their organization, and a big boss in Miami wanted their boss, Leonid Sidorov, dead. Danylo had a cousin who worked for the Miami organization, and he'd overheard a conversation he wasn't supposed to. He swore up and down he had told no one but Danylo.

"We should kill the boss," Anatolij said. "This is our big break."

He lit a cigarette.

"I see three problems," Danylo said.

"I see opportunity."

The smoke from the burning cigarette in Anatolij's hand snaked its way between their faces towards the ceiling. Danylo hated cigarette smoke, but something always made him stop when he wanted to criticize Anatolij's smoking. He sensed that this was a subject he'd be better off not bringing up, that doing so could have serious consequences. There was something moving behind those dark eyes of Anatolij's that Danylo recognized and feared.

"Number one: *gospodin* Sidorov and his bodyguards most likely know of this. And even if they don't, they're always paranoid about security, anyway," Danylo continued.

"Which means we need to be creative. What's the second?" Anatolij asked.

"How do we make sure the Americans know it was us? And how do we make sure they reward us instead of killing us?" Danylo said.

"Tell your cousin to approach the boss directly, and to relay a request from us. That we'd like a go at it. If we're successful, we'd like to come to Miami and work for him. If we're not, there's no way to tie us back to him," Anatolij replied.

"That could get my cousin killed, just for speaking about these things. He's not supposed to know. You realize he's just a foot soldier, a gopher? He'd be admitting to eavesdropping," Danylo said.

"But if it works, he'll be on a fast trajectory, like us. No guts, no glory," Anatolij said.

"Easy for you to say. My cousin basically supports his entire family on his income. If he's killed, they're in deep shit," Danylo said.

"It's his choice. I say we proceed regardless. If he doesn't come through for us, we'll find some other way. What's the name of the Miami boss, do you know?" Anatolij asked.

"John Doe."

Anatolij laughed.

"Seriously? Isn't that like a fake name?"

"His real name is Bogdanov, I think. I don't know why he calls himself that," Danylo said.

"Either way, we need to get word to him quick. We don't want anyone else beating us to it."

"I'll ask my cousin tonight."

"What's the third problem?" Anatolij asked.

"The Americans want it done execution style, and in public. They want it mentioned on the evening news," Danylo said.

"It's not like the Americans to make their business semi-public like this. It could start a war."

"The way I heard it, they wouldn't mind if it did."

"That's interesting. And an opportunity," Anatolij said.

"Exactly. The only question is how?"

Anatolij grinned and spread his arms out.

"You?" Danylo asked.

"Yeah. Sidorov doesn't know me from Adam. He doesn't know I exist, even though I work for him. I'll get close."

"Don't be so sure. Even if you do, then what?"

"I'll kill him exactly like they slaughter pigs. Only he will be dead before he hits the ground."

The way Anatolij said this; so disinterested, so matter-of-factly, made Danylo's blood freeze. It made him question whether everyone was expendable in Anatolij's world, including him.

"But how are you going to get inside his club?" he asked.

Anatolij studied the lit cigarette he was holding. Then he looked up at Danylo with a sly smile on his lips.

"I'm not. He goes out to eat, doesn't he?"

"I'm sure he does. So what?" Danylo asked.

"Let's keep it simple. We steal a garbage truck and ram his limo just as he's getting into it, outside the restaurant. Make it look like an honest accident, but make sure it's sudden and violent enough to scatter his bodyguards. You drive the truck. I'll be waiting inside the restaurant. I'll let you know when he's leaving. Once you crash into the limo, I'll go in for the kill," Anatolij said.

"Sounds simple enough, maybe too simple. You really think that'll work?"

"If he's in the street, separated from his gorillas, he's all mine."

Danylo shuddered. Anatolij had spoken in that matter-of-fact voice again.

"We need to find out where he likes to hang out," Danylo said.

Two weeks later, they'd mapped out Sidorov's habits, including his favorite restaurants. It had been so easy that Danylo got cold feet. He was sure they were being set up.

Anatolij wasn't about to let Danylo's nerves stop him. This was his big break. He could feel it in his bones. As usual, he'd set a deadline for his promotion in his own mind, based only on his own sense of urgency. They were getting uncomfortably close.

"What's the word from your cousin?" He asked Danylo over breakfast.

The two girls from the latest shipment were in the room with them, but both men assumed they were so strung out that they didn't care what the girls heard.

Anatolij had taken a liking to one of them, which disturbed him. She was pretty, very innocent, and yet not as scared as the rest of the girls. She'd looked him straight in the eye, defiantly, the entire time he was slapping her around, and as he was injecting the other girl with her first dose of heroin. When the time came for him to give her the needle, she spoke for the first time since getting to the house.

"*Vyrodok!*"

He'd asked her what it meant, but the fire in her eyes went out as the drugs hit and she disappeared within herself. The experience had shaken him, and he went looking for her passport. There was nothing that special about her, at least not in the official papers. Her name was Anna, and that was really all he knew about her.

Anatolij started thinking about what would happen to her after he killed Sidorov. He realized he didn't know, but that whatever it was, it wasn't good. He considered giving her a dose of naloxone just as he was leaving the house, to bring her out of the heroin stupor and give her a chance to run.

At one point, he even considered giving her an overdose of heroin, just because he didn't like the way she made him feel, that she made him care. He told himself it would be an act of kindness, but he knew that was bullshit. He just didn't want to leave anything behind. No ties, no feelings, no guilt, no questions. Except for Dalibor, his little brother, he would never look back, only forward. Always forward.

Danylo brought him out of his reveries.

"Funny you should ask. He just texted me. He says we got the thumbs up, but that there's no room for error. You know what that means."

"It means that if we fail, we're dead. And so is your cousin."

"And his family. When do we do this?"

"No time like the present. I say we hit Sidorov tonight."

"He'll be at that old-timey German restaurant. The Prussian one."

"Death and *Schweinshaxe*, it's what's for dinner."

Anatolij was chatting with the owner of the little restaurant. She obviously thought he was German, because she was going on about how the Slavs and other Eastern Europeans were "ruining her fair city." Anatolij smiled and agreed with her, in his perfect Berliner German. He didn't give a shit about her or her racist drivel, but he could hardly disagree with her about the sausage fest at the other end of the dining room.

Sidorov and his lieutenants were most decidedly bad news. That there were no ladies present told Anatolij that this dinner was all business. They knew Sidorov liked the ladies, but only as entertainment.

Half an hour later, there were still no signs of the Sidorov party leaving. Anatolij was on his second cup of coffee after dessert, and wondering how much longer he could linger before he started raising suspicions with Sidorov's goons.

He was just about to call it off when Sidorov abruptly got up and headed to the restroom. Evidently, this was the signal for the party to break up, because one of his lieutenants got up and started collecting their coats, while another approached the waitress to pay the bill.

Anatolij texted Danylo to get ready.

When Sidorov exited the restaurant followed by his entourage, Anatolij slipped a 100 euro bill inside his own check and got up to leave.

The owner came over and flashed him a smile.

"You be safe now, *Schatzi*."

"You too, *gnädige Frau*."

Anatolij made his way through the dim restaurant, moving slowly and deliberately between the tables towards the veiled entrance, waiting to hear a commotion outside.

He heard the engine of the truck first, revving hard and approaching fast. Moments later, a loud crash shook the restaurant and the sound of shattered glass followed. Anatolij picked up his pace and stepped through the curtains into the little foyer as he pulled a long ice pick from his inside jacket pocket.

A young woman stood in front of him, swaying slightly from side to side, blood dripping from her face and hands. A shock of recognition hit him as he saw it was Anna from the safe house.

Before leaving the house, at the very last moment, he'd tried to free her. He'd already had the naloxone, the antidote to heroin, in his pocket. He'd told Danylo to wait for him outside.

He'd leaned over Anna's unconscious body and sprayed a liberal dose of the naloxone up one of her nostrils. A second later, she took a deep breath and started coughing. When she opened her eyes, he'd said just one word.

"*Bihty!*" - Run!

He'd turned around and left without waiting for an answer.

How had she found him here, and what did she want? He didn't have time to worry about that now, so he tried sidestepping her. She blocked his path and her right arm came up, holding a knife.

"*Vyrodok!*"

That word again.

There was no time. He couldn't stop to argue with her or to explain. He instinctively knew that he had to make a choice, right there and then. If he spent another second in that hallway, Sidorov would get away, and all of their lives would be in danger forever.

His arms were already moving before he'd made his conscious choice. His right arm came up and hit her wrist with enough force to break it. Simultaneously, his left arm made a small arc and plunged the ice pick into her heart in one swift motion.

He heard a scream behind him as Anna went limp and crumbled to the floor. He ignored it, stepped over her body, and exited the ruined front door of the restaurant.

Outside, the scene was pure chaos. The garbage truck had crushed two of Sidorov's goons against his limo. The force of the crash had pushed the limo up onto the sidewalk and it was pinning Sidorov against the building. He was still alive, but in obvious pain. One of his lieutenants appeared mostly unhurt and was pointing a gun at Danylo, who was still sitting inside the truck, with both arms raised above his head.

They could hear sirens in the distance.

Anatolij dropped the bloody ice pick and reached for his gun. He quickly knelt down and fired once at the goon's head. The man crumpled and fell. Danylo looked relieved, but pointed at Sidorov.

Their boss had freed himself and was limping away as fast as he could toward the oncoming sirens. Anatolij holstered his gun and picked the ice pick back up. He started walking after Sidorov.

The big man half turned and pointed a gun in Anatolij's direction. His aim was so far off though, and made worse because he was still limping along, that Anatolij wasn't worried.

Sidorov fired, but as expected, the bullet went wide. Anatolij picked up the pace and soon caught up with the man. He knocked the gun out of Sidorov's hand and spun the boss around. Sidorov's eyes showed confusion, but also defiance. For a moment, he reminded Anatolij of Anna. He hesitated.

"Who are you? What do you want?" Sidorov asked.

"I am you. I want what you have, but in Miami," Anatolij answered.

He could see realization hit Sidorov's eyes, and at that moment he plunged the ice pick through Sidorov's carotid artery and deep into his neck. The man fell to the ground without a sound, blood spraying from his neck.

The street was empty. No one had exited the restaurant, and whoever else had been out before the attack started had obviously made themselves scarce in a hurry. Anatolij knew that there were probably people looking at him and recording his every move, and he could hear the sirens getting closer. He had to hurry.

He ran back towards the truck to assist Danylo. As he approached, he couldn't see Danylo, but there was a small hole in the truck's windscreen. He opened the driver's door and found Danylo dead, slumped over to the side with a bullet wound to the head. Either Sidorov had been a better shot than Anatolij first thought, or he'd just gotten lucky. It didn't matter now. Least of all to Danylo.

Anatolij leaned in through the door, triggered the timer on the incendiary device they'd placed in the truck's cab earlier, and walked away. He ducked down an alleyway towards the getaway car just as the truck exploded into flames behind him.

He felt pretty sure this grisly mayhem would reach the evening news, and then some.

Six people were dead, two of them people he'd liked. The others were people he didn't know and had no beef with. And yet, all Anatolij could feel was excitement.

A new life and a new name. He'd resolved that as soon as he hit the shores of Florida, he'd change his name. He wanted to sound more sophisticated, more Western European.

He looked forward with glee to becoming Anton Kutel, because Anton Kutel would have it all.

TWELVE

UNKNOWN LOCATION, JANUARY 2040.

Jane looked out of the tiny window of his cell, onto a bleak and windswept landscape. Kutel and his men had brought them all here. Wherever this was. They'd tried asking where they were being taken, but had received no answers, no information.

Jane had been there for five days now, unable to see anyone but his jailers, who brought him food and the occasional magazine. The reading materials were all several years old, and they all contained flattering articles about Anton Kutel. One was even a special issue completely dedicated to the man.

Jane hoped, but didn't really know, if the others were in the same facility as him. He'd tried banging on the walls and shouting through the small slit in the door where they brought the food, but there had been no response.

When he heard footsteps in the hallway outside, he assumed it was the guard bringing his breakfast. He had several questions prepared, even though he didn't really expect to get any answers.

The door opened, and an unarmed guard stepped inside, holding some clothes. Another guard remained in the hallway outside, holding an assault rifle across his chest. Whoever these people were, this clearly wasn't their first rodeo. Or their first tango. There was something about the landscape that made Jane think they might be in Argentina, but he couldn't be sure.

The guard dropped the clothes on Jane's bunk and signaled with his hand that Jane should change into them. He then stepped outside while the armed guard remained in front of the door. No one spoke a word.

Jane looked at the clothes. They were military style night fatigues, with no insignia, flags, or other markings. That did not bode well.

He considered his options, but realized he didn't really have any. He could resist and be subject to a beating, or worse. Who knows what they'd do to the others? Or, he could play along, biding his time.

He stripped down to his underwear and changed into the fatigues. They fit him pretty well, but the materials were cheap and rough against his skin, even more so than the military garments he was used to.

The armed guard signaled that he should turn around. The other guard stepped back inside and handcuffed him behind his back. Jane started turning back around when the guard reached up and blindfolded him. Despite everything, Jane took that as a good sign. If they didn't want him to see something, that meant that they didn't want him to talk about it later. And talking later implied being alive. Or maybe that's just what they wanted him to believe, to keep his ass calm and compliant.

His thoughts drifted to a dark place. What the hell had he got Kii and himself into? The last thing he remembered before waking up in a cell here was Kutel and his men in Antarctica. They'd raised their guns and fired, and after that… nothing. Lights out.

He remembered what Kutel had said just before his men fired. He'd said that they were trespassing. What the hell did he mean by that? How could they possibly be trespassing? And why did he go to the trouble of introducing himself, and with such dramatic flourish? Where the hell was the central core computer? Had it been telling the truth? Was it the reason for all this?

A guard grabbed him by the elbow and led him outside, interrupting his thoughts.

"Steps," a voice said, in accented English.

Jane searched with his foot for the first step and started ascending.

"Flat," the voice said again when they reached the top.

They walked through what sounded like a corridor until they were suddenly outside. Jane could feel a chilly breeze and hear water running nearby. He could also hear an engine idling very close. A gasoline engine, which probably meant that they were far from the nearest town. Or that it was a military vehicle.

They kept him standing there for a bit. He figured they were waiting for Kii and the scientists.

"Kii, are you there?" He asked out loud.

"It's just me," Thoreau answered.

"Silence!" a fresh voice said, this time with a clear Russian accent.

Minutes later, the guard directed Jane to sit down in what felt like the back seat of a vehicle. They drove for an hour, while Jane was trying to keep track of sounds, turns, and elevation changes. When they finally came to a halt, the guard directed Jane to step from the car to a short flight of stairs he was familiar with. He was boarding a Griffin.

The bare and uncomfortable seat confirmed his suspicions. It didn't take long before he heard the turbines spin up, and soon after that, they were airborne.

He risked speaking again.

"Kii, are you there?"

Something hit him hard in the stomach, causing him to double over and gasp for air.

"Sit up straight," the Russian voice said.

Jane thought he heard a hint of amusement in the voice.

He tried to keep track of time, but it was hard with no references. The only thing he was sure of was that they were following a ballistic trajectory. That meant they were most likely landing on a different continent from where they had taken off.

When they landed, several guards escorted Jane to another vehicle, electric this time, and then from that into another building, and another cell.

He was trying to take a nap when, a few hours later, the door opened and a smiling Anton Kutel walked in.

"Hey, there!" Kutel said.

It surprised Jane to see him again, but he was also curious. What the hell did the man want?

"Hello, yourself. Did you stop by to bring me dinner?" Jane said.

He felt afraid, both for Kii and for himself, but tried to appear as cool as possible. His goal right now was to get as much information from Kutel as possible.

A guard brought a chair into the cell, and Kutel sat down. He was studying Jane, who sat up in his bunk and met Kutel's gaze.

"Sorry, no dinner," Kutel said. "I came here to size you up."

"Well, in that case," Jane said.

He laid back down and looked up at the ceiling. Better to let Kutel speak.

"I've been studying you. I was hoping you'd impress me or, better yet, surprise me. But unfortunately you don't. Then again, don't feel too bad. Very few people do," Kutel said.

"Thanks, I guess. Don't blame my sense of fashion. I'm still wearing the cheap fake fatigues you provided me with. What's up with that? And is Kii all right?" Jane asked.

"It wasn't your good looks I was hoping you'd impress me with."

"What about Kii and the others? And what do you want from us?"

"Oh, nothing. We're beyond all that. You have nothing to offer me."

"Then why all this?"

Jane spread his arms, pointing at the room they were in. He was getting frustrated by all this talk in riddles. And he was terrified for Kii now. 'Beyond?' Beyond what?

"I said you have nothing to offer me, not that you never did. But I already got everything I needed from your three co-conspirators. They required little prodding before they told me what I wanted to know."

The knot in Jane's stomach hardened. Had they tortured Kii?

"Conspirators? That's an odd choice of words. What is it you think we're conspiring to do?"

"Like I said, it's too late for all that. Besides, I'm not here to argue."

"What then, to gloat?"

"No, not at all. You're going to help me win the US presidential election."

Jane almost scoffed, but caught himself.

"How are we going to do that?"

"By being in the right place at the right time. Here, grab this."

Kutel threw a small ball at Jane, who caught it on reflex.

"I see you're left-handed, like me," Kutel said.

He rose and smoothed down his clothes.

"It was nice meeting you. I'll no doubt be seeing more of you soon," he said.

When Kutel had left, Jane sat staring at the little rubber ball. It started changing colors and shape in his hand, and then the entire room started spinning.

Suddenly, Jane realized Kutel had been wearing gloves.

When Jane came to, his world was cabbage. He smelled it and he tasted it; it was filling his consciousness, making him increasingly queasy. He tried moving his head and immediately vomited all over himself.

He sat perfectly still for a moment, breathing slowly, until he felt it was safe to move. He lifted his left hand to wipe his mouth, only to realize it was holding something. It felt like a handgun.

Slowly, gingerly, he opened his eyes.

He was in a vehicle of some sort. A van. He was in the driver's seat and his left hand was holding a gun, a military issue Zetta with biometrics. Someone must have keyed it to him, or hacked it, because the status light was green. Which meant the safety was off, that a round was in the chamber, and that he was authorized to fire.

He looked to his right. Kii was sitting in the passenger seat. Intense worry instantly replaced a jolt of joy. She looked dead or dying; her face was bloodless and her body limp.

"Kii! Kii, can you hear me? Wake up!"

The act of talking sent a fresh wave of nausea coursing through him. With some effort, he enabled the safety on the gun, and put it down. He reached for the door handle to open the door, but it wouldn't budge. He took a deep breath to calm himself, then checked the door lock. It was unlocked.

The door didn't move when he leaned into it. He looked out the window, but there was nothing outside, nothing obviously blocking the door. He tried his shoulder again, banging into the door as hard as he could. Nothing.

He paused, catching his breath. Slowly, he climbed over the center console to the passenger side. He reached out to Kii and checked for a pulse. It was faint. He knew he had little time.

He tried opening the door on her side, but it wouldn't budge. He picked the gun back up and used it as a hammer to break the window on his side. When he pulled the door handle from the outside, the door opened without a problem. He got out and almost collapsed. He could barely stand. His knees were buckling, and the world was spinning around him.

He looked around. It was very early morning, just before sunrise. It was cold, and fog covered everything. To his left was a pier. He could barely see to the end. In front of him, obscured by the fog, was some kind of massive structure. With a shock of recognition, he realized he was in Horseshoe Bay, just north of the Golden Gate Bridge. The bridge was the structure he could glimpse through the fog; leading from San Francisco to the Marin Headlands.

Had they been in the San Francisco Bay Area the whole time? No. They'd made at least one ballistic flight with a Griffin, which meant they'd covered some serious distance. Unless that's exactly what they wanted him to think.

The bridge in front of him meant behind him was the US Coast Guard Station Golden Gate. And help. He started looking for the car keys and found them in the ignition. The van was old; it was a standard gasoline engine design. It refused to start. He walked around it to the passenger side. The door opened easily from the outside, and he gently pulled Kii from the car.

She felt light as a feather, and lifeless. Her forehead felt cold and clammy, her face was pale, and her lips blue. He could feel panic churning deep down inside him, but he pushed it away.

He started carrying Kii towards the Coast Guard station, which wasn't far, when something made him stop. He had a pretty clear picture of what was going on, that they were being set up for something. But where were the others? He gently put Kii down on the ground, went back for the gun, then opened the rear doors of the van.

Inside, he saw Thoreau and Ødegård, as well as a man and a woman he'd never seen before. He carefully climbed inside, only to discover that the two strangers were dead, shot. No doubt with the gun he was holding. The two scientists were still alive, but barely. Just like Kii.

There was no way he could carry all three, so he left the van and continued carrying Kii towards the Coast Guard station. As his mind cleared, his sense of urgency increased. He started running, with Kii in his arms, each step sending a wave of pain and nausea through his body. Panic was churning again, and this time he couldn't push it away completely. He confined it to one part of his mind and focused instead on taking the next step. And the next.

When he got to the station, he found the front door locked. The place looked deserted, but he knew that there would be someone on guard inside. He placed the gun on the ground, about two meters away, and started banging on the door. When the door opened, he started shaking uncontrollably and fell to his knees next to Kii.

"I'm Lieutenant Thurgood Jane, US Navy, retired. There are people in the van by the pier. Please help them," he said.

Seconds later an alarm sounded, the outside of the building was lit up by floodlights, and coast guardsmen came running outside. Someone barked orders and Jane felt himself being hoisted up and carried inside.

"Please help her. She's much worse off than I am," he said.

"We've got her, and you," a voice said.

Strong arms lifted him onto a bunk and he could see Kii on the bunk next to him. Several people were milling about her, taking her vitals, placing an IV in her arm. She looked so vulnerable.

A young coast guardsman was sitting next to him, watching him nervously. After a short while, a woman in civilian clothes came into the room and relieved the young guard. She appeared to be in her mid-thirties, and the way she carried herself told Jane that she probably had more clout than she appeared to at first glance.

"I'm Commander Harris," she said. "I hear you're a Salty Dog?"

"Yes, ma'am. My name is Thurgood Jane, Lieutenant US Navy, retired," Jane said.

"You won't mind if I verify that?"

"No, ma'am."

She held up a small biometric reader and scanned his retinas, as well as his fingerprints. Finally, she pricked his finger and drew a drop of blood. She studied the display, and after a minute, she seemed to relax a little. She sat down on a chair next to his bunk.

"Honorably discharged, multiple commendations, and parts of your record sealed. I see. I think perhaps you and I are in the same line of business, Lieutenant," she said.

"Yes, ma'am. Or, at least I was," he replied.

"Mm, I see. We found two people dead in that van. Shot. And you brought a gun to the station. Care to explain?"

"I don't know who the dead people are. The gun was in my hand when I woke up, keyed to my biometrics. No doubt it was used to kill the two strangers, although I did not shoot them. The other two men in the van are colleagues of mine, and the woman in the bed behind you is my fiancée. Her name is Kii Brockheart. They're all civilians."

"Woke up?"

"Yes. I woke up in the driver's seat of that van, with the gun in my hand. I'd love to tell you all about it, but I think we may all be in danger."

"In danger, here at the station?"

"Yes, ma'am. Powerful people just tried to kill me. And they will not give up."

"How did they try to kill you?"

"All I know is that one moment I'm holding a small rubber ball, then lights out. When I came to, I had this intense smell and taste of cabbage in my mouth, and I had a gun in my hand."

"Cabbage? You're sure?"

She looked at him, eyes suddenly wide. Her voice betrayed more than a hint of surprise.

"Positive."

"Excuse me for a moment, Lieutenant," she said.

Commander Harris got up and left the room. When she returned, she looked concerned.

"You're in a lot of trouble," she said. "It's a miracle you're still alive."

"Ma'am?"

"We tested your blood. It contains traces of an old school nerve agent called Grom. Classified and banned. We're going to have to get some antidote in you quick, or you'll have serious, lasting, neurological damage. And your friends won't make it."

"I see. What are her chances?" Jane asked.

"Good, if we can get you evacuated right now."

Jane heard sirens in the distance, getting closer.

"That's odd," Commander Harris said.

"How's that?"

"I talked to the station commander, Chief Warrant Officer Lothgren. I requested he hold off on calling the police for the moment. He agreed."

"Those may not even be real cops," Jane said.

"What the hell is going on here?" Commander Harris asked.

She got up and walked over to the window. The sirens came very close, then cut out. Jane was about to answer when he heard a commotion outside, and then gunfire. A moment later, an explosion rocked the building.

Commander Harris ran downstairs. Jane propped himself up on the bed and looked over at Kii. She was still breathing, and a scared looking young guardsman was watching over her. Still dizzy and disoriented, Jane got out of his bunk and walked over to the windows. He pulled the curtains aside and looked outside. He could see a cloud of smoke in the distance, where the van had been. The cloud was lit up by flashing lights from emergency vehicles, and Jane could see a police SWAT truck blocking the driveway to the Coast Guard station. There was a lot of broken glass on the ground.

Commander Harris came back into the room. She brought a Coast Guard officer with her.

"This is Chief Warrant Officer Lothgren. He's in charge of this station," she said.

Jane laid back down. Before he could say anything, she continued.

"You better tell us right now what's going on, and who poisoned you."

"Yes, ma'am, sir. I believe it was Anton Kutel who poisoned me. The last thing I remember before blacking out was that he threw a small blue rubber ball at me. I grabbed it. He was wearing gloves. I wasn't."

"Anton Kutel, the billionaire? And presidential candidate?"

"Yes, ma'am. The same."

"Why in the world would he do that? You realize you're coming off sounding paranoid, delusional?"

Jane knew only too well. He'd never have believed such a tall tale himself, if someone had tried feeding it to him. Yet, telling the truth was his only option. He was a terrible liar.

"Yes, ma'am. I realize that," he said. "And yet, it's true. He kidnapped the four of us in Antarctica, while we were on a scientific expedition there. I don't know how he found us, and I don't know why he would go to all this trouble. It seems insane, I know. But I met him face to face. He came to see me while he kept me locked up in a cell, most likely somewhere in Argentina."

"A scientific expedition? And he came to see you? Kutel?" Commander Harris asked.

Jane cringed. Commander Harris was being very professional, very polite, and doing her best to sound completely neutral. But Jane knew how crazy this sounded.

"Yes, ma'am. He even introduced himself, not that he needed to. His face is quite recognizable," he replied.

"What did he say?" she asked.

"Not much. He said he wanted to size me up."

"Nothing about what this was all about?" she asked.

"No, ma'am. Not really. He said that I'd help him win the presidential election. And he said that he'd be seeing more of me soon. And then he threw me that rubber ball. I didn't understand what he meant then, but I think I get it now," Jane said.

"How's that?"

"He was going to frame us for some crime and make sure we all got killed, not captured alive. And then he'd be seeing me, or at least my face, on the news," he said.

Commander Harris studied him intently, then abruptly looked away. Jane wasn't sure what that signaled, or how to interpret her body language. He was usually quite good at it, but with her, he was feeling lost. Then she looked him in the eye again.

"How does that help him win the election?" she asked.

"I wouldn't know. I thought he was born in some Eastern European country, that he was ineligible to even run," Jane said.

"Don't tell him that," Harris said. She shrugged. "He's been suing people left and right for less. He claims he was born in Florida."

"Perhaps I know how. The news stations are already blasting a story about you and the others being extreme environmentalist terrorists, out to blow up the Golden Gate Bridge," Lothgren said.

He was looking at his cellphone, scrolling through the news.

"That would be the crime he's framing us for. I still don't get how it helps him," Jane said.

He sank back on the bed, feeling nauseous.

"Kutel is running on law and order, and on claiming that President Mondragón has lost control of the situation with the refugees and the protests. I guess the only thing missing is that he claims that he somehow helped expose and stop this so-called attack on the Golden Gate Bridge," Lothgren said.

"It gets worse. They're saying that the police had been monitoring your activities for some time, and that they prevented you from going through with it. And that when they confronted you, you blew yourselves up rather than risk being captured," Harris said.

She was checking her own phone, shaking her head.

"And that story is out now, before the smoke has even cleared?" Jane asked.

"What they don't know is that we have hidden security cameras covering the pier and the road," Lothgren said. "The footage shows the police coming in hard, almost ten minutes after we pulled the last survivor from the van. They opened fire without stopping to check who was in the van or what they were doing."

"Shoot first and ask questions later. Interesting police tactic," Jane said.

The room was spinning, and he closed his eyes. He needed them to believe him, and quickly, so they could stop asking questions and start moving. They had to give the antidote to Kii and the others right now.

"And they must have rigged the van to blow, because the first volley of bullets set it off like a bomb," Lothgren said.

"That tracks. And if it really is Kutel, it would explain how he got his hands on the nerve agent. Apparently, he has extensive connections in the former Soviet Union," Harris said.

"And unlimited resources," Lothgren added.

"The antidote," Jane said.

He felt scared. What if it was already too late for Kii?

Harris and Lothgren looked at each other.

"OK, Lieutenant, we're going to help you, because this stinks to high heaven. This is federal land, and the local cops have no jurisdiction. We need to get you out of here before they get their act together and the feds come banging on the door," Lothgren said.

"And yes, we need to get you all the antidote," Harris said.

"What happened to the two dead bodies?" Jane asked.

His voice was hoarse, and it hurt to talk.

"They're downstairs," Harris said.

Jane opened one eye and looked at her. He raised an eyebrow in appreciation.

"This isn't my first rodeo, Lieutenant," she said.

Twenty minutes later, Jane, Kii, the scientists, and the two dead bodies were all loaded onto one of the fast Motor Lifeboats belonging to the Coast Guard station. Commander Harris made sure they were out of view as the boat roared past the pier and the police presence, which was now augmented by units from the San Francisco PD Bomb Squad.

Half an hour later, in the middle of the San Francisco Bay, a Flying Tortoise was waiting. It was the Navy's amphibious version of the ubiquitous Griffin. Onboard, a Navy surgeon was ready for them, with vials of antidote for the nerve agent.

Jane said his goodbyes to Chief Warrant Officer Lothgren and Commander Harris as he boarded the Flying Tortoise.

"You're not getting rid of me that easily," Harris said.

She boarded the machine after him, closing the hatch behind her. When the surgeon had administered the antidote to all four of them, Jane asked her what to expect.

She explained the antidote was experimental, since governments worldwide had outlawed the nerve agent for decades.

"Now we wait, and hope," she said. "If you react favorably to the antidote, we should know before we land in San Diego. Hopefully, the others will regain consciousness."

Jane looked over at Harris.

"What are we doing in San Diego?"

"Getting you the best possible medical help, for starters," she replied.

Jane nodded.

"I appreciate that, but I'd very much like to sort this out ASAP. I can convalesce later. Ma'am."

"Oh, I want to find out what's going on, too. And I want to help you. But first we need to have a little heart-to-heart, in private."

"Yeah, I figured," Jane said.

He was already feeling better. He settled in for the flight, after checking in on Kii and the scientists. They were still out cold, but Kii's pulse was stronger and her face had regained some color.

They were flying over California's central valley, northwest of Lost Hills, when the pilot called out to Commander Harris.

"We're being followed by an unknown aircraft. It came out of nowhere. They're not responding to hails, and they have no transponder or other identification," he said.

"What are they doing?" she asked.

"They're following our flight path. Two clicks aft," the pilot replied.

"Have you contacted civilian air traffic control?"

"Yes, ma'am. They say they don't see it, and they have no information on it, no flight plan."

"They don't see it? Meaning, it doesn't even show up on their radar?"

"That's correct, ma'am."

"It's gotta be Kutel," Jane said.

"How the hell would he get his hands on some unknown stealth aircraft?" Harris asked.

"Because he has damn near unlimited resources?" Jane said. "But, more to the point; how the hell did he find us?"

"Someone at the Coast Guard station must have talked," she said.

"Lothgren? Did anyone else know the details of our escape?" Jane asked.

"I doubt it was him," Harris stated flatly.

Jane expected her to expand on that and say more. When she didn't, he had to make a choice. Either trust her, and trust that she had her reasons, or press her. He went with his gut and changed the subject.

"Can we scramble fighters to scare them off?" he asked.

"Requisitioning a Flying Tortoise to San Diego is one thing. Running this up the chain of command to get fighters in the air is a completely different matter. Even if I could pull it off, it would take too long. We'll have landed in San Diego before they even take off," she said.

"Or we'll be dead," he retorted.

"Or that," she agreed.

Jane felt that knot of fear in his stomach again, with a tinge of guilt. This had somehow turned into a combat mission. Harris and he had trained for that sort of thing, and knew it came with the job. Or, in his case, with his old job. But Kii and the scientists hadn't and didn't. Right or wrong, he felt like it had been his job to steer their little expedition clear of such things.

Then again, their little expedition had made perhaps the most important discovery in the history of humankind, so maybe this was to be expected. But Kutel? Why him, and how did he even know they had found something?

"The other aircraft is closing in," the pilot said. "Shit, now they're climbing in altitude. This looks like an attack run to me."

"Can you evade or outrun it?" Harris asked.

"No, ma'am, at least not enough to shake 'em," the pilot replied.

"But we can hover," Jane said. "Perhaps they can't."

"That just makes us even more of a sitting duck," she said.

"We can land while they fly past us and turn around to come back in for the kill. At least then the fall won't kill us."

"Do it!" Harris told the pilot.

Seconds later, at cruise speed and altitude, the Flying Tortoise raised its nose by 45 degrees and started transitioning from fixed wing flight to rotary wing flight. It was a maneuver Jane had never seen before, never even heard of. He silently wondered if the airframe could withstand this kind of abuse.

The Flying Tortoise immediately stalled and started falling towards the ground. For a sickening few moments, they were weightless, as the rotary wings slowly unfolded and started clawing at the air. Jane could feel their vertical speed dropping as he heard the familiar chopping rotor noise enter the cabin. He risked a glance out the window and saw that they were still falling at an alarming rate.

"What's the status on the other aircraft?" he asked.

Jane felt scared, but years of training had kicked in and kept his voice calm. He focused on a singular aim: Get Kii and the others safely on the ground as fast as possible, and get them out of the line of fire.

"It shot past us," the pilot replied.

"What the fuck is happening?"

The loud voice caught everyone by surprise. It was Ødegård; he was sitting up on his stretcher in the back of the cabin.

"No time to explain, lie back down and hold on!" Jane shouted.

To his credit, for once in his life Ødegård did as he was told.

"We're auto-rotating, falling as fast as possible," the pilot said. "The unknown craft has turned around and is closing in, fast. I'll make a controlled landing as quick as I can. And as gently as I can."

Jane looked at Harris and saw his own fear reflected in her eyes.

"Who the fuck does this guy think he is?" she asked. "Is he going to fire on the US Navy?"

The pilot answered her question.

"Missile lock! Shit, they've locked on to us. Hold on to your asses!"

The pilot took the rotors out of auto-rotation and engaged maximum thrust from the turbines. The effect was immediate and dramatic; to the passengers, it almost felt as if they hit the ground. With their fall suddenly arrested, two missiles passed directly underneath them. Because of the steep angle, and the proximity to the ground, the missiles lost target-lock and went into failsafe mode. They didn't return.

"The enemy aircraft is still closing in. I'll have to buy us some more time," the pilot said.

He turned the Tortoise 90 degrees to the left and flew at an angle to the path of the oncoming aircraft. Then he turned towards the oncoming craft, before making a sweeping turn in the other direction. The other aircraft was going much too fast and couldn't match their crazy zigzag gyrations. It overshot them by miles, but immediately started turning back around in a large, sweeping arc.

The pilot entered auto-rotation again and picked a landing zone.

"We're about to hit the ground hard. Hold on tight!" he said.

Jane looked out the window and saw tracer rounds whizzing by, far too close for comfort. The next volley didn't miss. Jane saw holes appearing in the fuselage and felt a burning pain in his chest. The Tortoise started listing to one side, then started spinning out of control.

When they hit the ground, there was nothing gentle or controlled about it.

Jane felt his bones break. It was a sickening feeling, and one he'd felt before. He saw the fuselage of the Flying Tortoise crumble around him, before one of the rotor blades suddenly sliced through it and came to rest mere centimeters from his foot. Then everything stopped moving and a deep silence fell over the scene.

He knew he was badly hurt. He could also smell fuel. If the wreckage caught fire, there was nothing he could do to save himself or the others. He looked around. As far as he could tell, Kii, Ødegård, and Thoreau were fairly unhurt, but they were also not moving. He was worried they might have internal injuries. The Navy surgeon was dead, her head missing. There were no signs of Commander Harris and he couldn't see the cockpit from where he lay.

He could hear a jet engine in the distance coming closer. Kutel's henchmen were coming back to finish the job and there was nothing he could do about it. He looked up through the opening the rotor blade had cut in the fuselage and saw the enemy aircraft dropping lower and lower as it approached.

A single gunshot rang out, sounding like it came from somewhere very close. To his astonishment, Jane saw a puff of black smoke and then flames coming from the plane's engine. Seconds later, it aborted its run, banked hard to the left, and seemed to struggle to regain altitude. Soon it was gone from view.

"Anyone alive in there?" a voice said.

"Over here!" Jane replied.

A face appeared in a small hole in the fuselage opposite from where Jane was lying.

"You sure you're alive? Cause you look pretty dead to me."

"Thanks, I've felt better. Please call Chief Warrant Officer Lothgren at the Golden Gate Coast Guard station and tell him what happened. He'll know what to do. But please hurry, they'll be back."

"Sure thing. Anyone else alive?"

"Yes, at least three others. And one confirmed dead, three missing."

The man's eyes found the dead Navy surgeon, and he winced.

"I got one dead lady out here, civilian. And one of your pilots is dead. I'll make that call now."

It was Jane's turn to wince. He'd only known Commander Harris for a few hours, but he'd really liked her. And now she was dead, along with two other service members. For what? Because of him? For one man's political ambitions?

"She's not a civilian, she was a commander in the US Navy," was all he said.

The other man nodded and put a cell phone to his ear.

"They said someone's on their way," the man said after he hung up.

"Was that you shooting at the other plane?" Jane asked.

"Yup. I saw you were US Navy, and my dad was in the navy. He fought in the water wars. Least I could do."

"Thanks. That was some impressive shooting."

"To be honest, it surprised the hell out of me. I must be a better shot than I thought."

Jane attempted to laugh, but it hurt too much and turned into a cough. His mouth filled with blood.

"Hang in there. I'm going to go get some equipment and see if I can open up this tin can before the cavalry arrives. Maybe stop some of that bleeding," the man said.

He nodded towards Jane's chest and arm.

"Name's Farmer, by the way. Phil Farmer. Farmer by name and farmer by trade. Be right back," he said.

Jane said nothing, just nodded back. He thought about the day's events.

Commander Harris had been right. It was unbelievably brazen of Kutel to shoot down a US Navy aircraft, over US territory, in broad daylight. Even for someone as rich and powerful as him. He must have been certain that he'd get away with it.

Jane considered it. The only way Kutel could be sure of that was if he was in full control of the military and judicial branches of the government. Which was an interesting thought, considering the separation of powers, even if Kutel should win the upcoming presidential election.

Someone was shaking him, slapping his face, trying to wake him. He opened his eyes and saw that it was Farmer.

"You hear that? Sirens!" Farmer said. "They're almost here."

Jane nodded. He'd never felt so tired before, so completely and bottomlessly exhausted. He thought of Kii, and wanted to hold her hand, if only for a minute. Just hold her hand.

THIRTEEN

SAN DIEGO, CALIFORNIA, FEBRUARY 2040.

Jane was angry. Doctors had confined him to bed for over a month, and it was getting on his nerves. He didn't enjoy any of it; he didn't enjoy being shot at, and he didn't much appreciate losing a lung and the use of his left arm. Kii kept reminding him he was lucky to be alive at all. The shrapnel from the bullets and the Flying Tortoise's fuselage had sliced and diced his upper body and nearly killed him. One more centimeter to the right was all it would have taken.

Being self-employed and an adventurer with only the most basic health insurance, he was about to get kicked out of the hospital when he received an unexpected visitor. Captain John F. Hamilton introduced himself as Commander Harris' boss. And like Jane, he was angry.

The military had put a lid on everything. Captain Hamilton had found himself in hot water over the loss of three officers, as well as a valuable piece of equipment. All his efforts to find out what happened, and why, were being stonewalled. The only person who'd agreed to talk to him, off the record, was Chief Warrant Officer Lothgren at the Coast Guard station.

What he'd had to say had only made Hamilton angrier and more determined. It also made things a lot more complicated. Lothgren had been Commander Harris' last assignment, on suspicion of selling secrets about the underwater defenses of the Golden Gate, the strait at the entrance to the San Francisco Bay, to an enemy power. It turned out Lothgren had sold no secrets. He'd simply been embezzling funds. Which meant that Hamilton had no choice. He had to turn that information over to the Coast Guard Investigative Service.

He'd told Lothgren as much, but the man had still agreed to help. He'd quite liked Harris, despite now realizing her actual assignment. Unfortunately, it also meant that Lothgren's testimony wouldn't be worth much. Not that this situation was likely to end up in court. Either way, Hamilton wasn't about to let that stop him. He had an offer for Jane.

Captain Hamilton's office, part of the Office of Homeland Intelligence, had a civilian arm, which is what Harris had been working for. It was a front, operating as an international investment bank, while secretly collecting information on foreign arms dealers, weapons manufacturers, and counterintelligence operations. Harris had been working for the sharp end of the stick of this operation.

Hamilton offered Jane Harris' old job, which he immediately turned down. Jane knew nothing of banking and he was done with military life. He wanted to heal, and to spend time with Kii, who was recovering from her own wounds. He was a pragmatist, and although he wanted to see Kutel receive justice, he realized it was highly unlikely.

Hamilton sweetened the deal with some perks. They included top-notch health coverage for both Kii and himself, the use of the bank's private jet, as well as some other, more unconventional hardware. He also promised unlimited company time to investigate the assassination of Harris and the attempted assassination of Kii, the scientists, and himself. Resources he could otherwise only dream of.

"Wherever the investigation leads?" Jane asked.

"Especially wherever the investigation leads, if you catch my drift. You have my word," Hamilton confirmed. "Just get ready for a few more days in bed first. We're going to fix that arm. I've already set the wheels in motion. You'll receive some augmentation and armor as well, all completely hidden. I don't want a repeat of what happened to Harris, and to you. That's non-negotiable."

"I have to discuss this with Kii. And if we do this, and I mean 'We,' we'll want to pick our own team. And you're probably not going to like it," Jane replied.

"Done. In the meantime, fixing your arm is on me. Consider it a show of good will."

Jane didn't argue, or attempt to negotiate any further. He knew damn well that Hamilton, and by extension the US government, would never pay for something so expensive, expecting nothing in return. But he would deal with that when the time came. Besides, he was warming up to the idea. He just nodded, and Hamilton got up to leave.

"Come and see me when you're vertical. I'll have some more intel for you by then."

Two months later, Jane was a new man, at least physically. Special shielding and a pacemaker augmented his heart, and high capacity artificial lungs replaced his badly damaged natural lungs. He had new artificial arteries, and internal armor shielding all his vital organs and blood vessels. If he'd been more patient, they'd have reinforced his skeleton as well. As it was, there was no way Jane would spend another 6 months in bed, flat out on his back, and not be able to move much.

Mentally was a different matter. He kept replaying the two meetings with Kutel in his head. How had the billionaire known about the artifact? Why was he so intent on killing them, in the middle of a presidential campaign, no less? If any of this came out, it would surely derail his bid for the presidency. And what was the artifact? Where was it from? Kutel obviously knew more than them, but how was that even possible? It was a huge blind spot, and it really bothered Jane.

Kii had been keeping herself busy while Jane was recuperating, trying to answer some of their questions. Like Jane, she'd given up her career to become a full-time adventurer when they met. Also, like Jane, her old job was now coming in quite handy. Relatively unhurt from the poisoning and the crash, she'd been using her considerable skills as a computer forensic analyst to find out what Kutel was planning. Unsurprisingly, she'd run into a brick wall. Turned out Kutel wasn't just dangerous, he was also paranoid to a degree that downright impressed her.

Most people are careful about guarding their secrets, rich people especially so. But Kutel had taken things to a new level. She broke into several of his systems, but there was nothing there even remotely interesting. In fact, what she found was so boringly law abiding and ordinary that she had a strong suspicion it was a 'Mushroom farm': A decoy, designed to keep any snoopers in the dark and feed them bullshit. She was going to have to try a different tack, and perhaps Hamilton could help with that.

Hamilton met them in his office. It was on the top floor of a skyscraper on California Street, in the middle of the financial district of San Francisco. The perfect location for an investment bank. After greeting Kii warmly, he turned to Jane.

"You look a hell of a lot better," he said while shaking Jane's hand. "How's that arm?"

"Good as new, thanks," Jane replied.

"Did they augment the muscles, or just put in an artificial neural network?"

"Both. They even put in a target lock. I'm a lefty anyway, so I shoot with my left hand."

"The target lock is great. I have it myself. Have you tried it out yet? It improves your accuracy tenfold. Just make sure you practice a lot, so it becomes second nature to activate it. Otherwise, adrenaline will wash that knowledge straight out of your brain when you most need it."

"Thanks, will do," Jane said.

"I have some news for you," Hamilton said. "But first, I believe you have something to tell me. Harris hinted as much before they killed her."

"Yeah, I guess we owe you that much. Did Harris tell you Kutel kidnapped us during an archeological expedition to Antarctica?"

"Yes. And that you met Anton Kutel face to face, so there's no doubt that he was behind your kidnapping."

"Correct, and our poisoning. He threw me a small rubber ball, most likely coated with the nerve agent."

"We think he poisoned the rest of us through our drinking water or food," Kii added.

"So, he wanted to make it personal with you, Jane," Hamilton said. "Why?"

"Looks like it. I'm not sure why, I've never met the man before this. I kept going over it again and again in my mind while they confined me to that damn hospital bed," Jane said.

"It was driving him nuts," Kii added.

"It really was. All he told me was that he wanted to size me up. And he said I would help him become president," Jane said.

"I see. So, what were you looking for on this expedition of yours?" Hamilton asked.

Jane paused and looked over at Kii before answering. He took a deep breath.

"Aliens," he said. "Or at least traces of them," he hurriedly added.

"Aliens? Are we talking extraterrestrials, beings from outer space?" Hamilton asked.

"The same," Kii said.

"Whoa. So, you were looking for aliens, and one of the richest men in the world and also a presidential candidate suddenly barged in, kidnapped all of you, and then tried to kill you? In person?" Hamilton said.

"Twice," Jane said.

"That sounds crazy and harebrained, and Anton Kutel doesn't strike me as the harebrained type," Hamilton said. "Why would he do that? What aren't you telling me?"

Jane paused again and shook his head before continuing.

"We found what we were looking for," he said.

Captain Hamilton looked at Jane, studying him intently, silently. Jane stared back, waiting for the other man to speak.

"I'm guessing you can't prove any of this, because otherwise you already would have," Hamilton said.

"Right again, although we had lots of evidence until Kutel took it all. There was a very obvious alien origin artifact and tons of footage from the expedition. We even had an alien base, constructed inside of a mountain in Antarctica. I assume it's still there, and we know exactly where it is. But something tells me we wouldn't get close if we tried to go back," Jane said.

"How large? Like the Cheyenne Mountain Complex?"

Hamilton was referring to the large military complex inside Cheyenne Mountain in Colorado.

"No, much smaller. More like a two-bedroom apartment. At least the parts we could access. We didn't see any machinery, but obviously there must have been, because there were life support systems and they were working," Jane said.

"You mentioned an artifact?" Hamilton said.

"Yes, it called itself the Central Core, from a scout ship," Kii said.

"It called itself? You communicated with it? How?" Hamilton asked.

"It cycled through a bunch of languages, some of them clearly human, others unknown, until it hit on English. From then on in it was pretty smooth sailing. Except it would only respond to Jane," Kii said.

"So, what was this thing, some kind of alien computer?" Hamilton asked.

"We don't know for sure, but that's our best guess. Perhaps some kind of alien AI, but we never had time to talk to it long enough to find out," Kii said.

"That would certainly explain Kutel's interest," Hamilton said.

"How so?" Jane asked.

"This isn't public knowledge, but Kutel owns a defense contractor that makes AIs for the military."

"So, he wants the technology, whatever it is, and he wants to keep it secret."

"Exactly. Did the alien artifact tell you where it was from?" Hamilton asked.

"It gave us a name for its home planet, but that was all. It claimed it had no more information," Jane said.

"I see. What was the name?"

"Planet One. Thoreau was of the opinion that the artifact was most likely telling the truth. If it doesn't know the way home, it can't divulge that information to someone potentially hostile," Jane said.

"That's an interesting tactic, but I guess it makes sense. At least from a purely defensive point of view. Also, it makes the trip strictly one way, but I guess that matters less to a computer," Hamilton said.

He kept questioning them about the artifact and the base until they satisfied him that there was nothing more to learn.

"We have a request," Kii said.

"What's that?"

"Once we have proof, once we've exposed Kutel and hopefully got the artifact back, we want to go public with this," Jane said.

"Fine," Hamilton said.

Kii and Jane looked at each other, surprised.

"But before you do, there are some people I want you to meet. All I ask, actually I insist, is that you listen to them," Hamilton added.

"Who, the Majestic 12?" Jane asked.

He was joking, referring to a purported secret organization of military and civilian leaders often featured in UFO conspiracy theories, claiming they were actively repressing information about extraterrestrial visits.

Hamilton just looked at them, his face expressionless.

"Dang," Jane said.

"We have to keep this low key, but I'll extend all the help and guidance I can. What's your plan of attack?" Hamilton asked.

"Full frontal," Kii replied.

Ever since he'd agreed to join Ødegård on his latest expedition to Antarctica three months ago, Thoreau had felt his paranoia creeping up on him. Especially after he'd heard that Kii and Jane had claimed to have found an actual alien artifact. Thoreau had kept his mouth shut and not spoken of the expedition to a living soul, as agreed, but he wasn't sure Ødegård had been able to. Obviously, Kutel had found out somehow.

He knew little about Kutel personally, but he knew the type. You don't work yourself up from obscurity and relative poverty to multi-billionaire status in less than twenty years without stepping over a few bodies. Not only that, but he'd seen the rage in Kutel's eyes when he didn't cooperate and knew all too well what it meant. The man was a full-blown sociopath with a mean streak. Charming as all hell, until he had no use for you anymore. And if you crossed him, you better watch out. Thoreau had, literally, felt that on his body.

Above all, Kutel had convinced him he'd never give up. He'd tried to kill them once. He wasn't about to just let them wander off into the sunset now. No, he was going to finish the job he started, and probably take some pleasure from doing it.

Thoreau had been thinking about this on the transatlantic flight back to Norway after the Navy hospital had medically discharged him. He'd finally fallen asleep somewhere above Greenland when he suddenly woke with a start. If he was right, and Kutel would come after him, that meant his family wasn't safe either. Especially if he was right about Kutel's mean streak.

By the time he landed in Copenhagen, Denmark, where he was supposed to catch a connecting flight to Bergen, he was nearly frantic. He abandoned his luggage, made his way to the departure terminal, and bought a one-way ticket to Lyon, France. It was where his family was from, and where his ex-wife still lived with their kids.

The flight was about to leave, so he started running towards the gate. He kept looking behind him, just to make sure there were no people following him. They'd have to be quick if they were going to. Not only would they have to find out where he was going, they'd have to buy a ticket and get to the gate before it closed.

As soon as he arrived in Lyon, he headed to his ex-wife's house, where he sat down with his family. He told them what was going on, and what his fears were. That same night, the Thoreau family joined the millions of refugees already clogging Europe's roads after the onset of the Great Climate Shift.

They weren't quite like the others, though, in several respects. The entire family left all their digital devices behind in the house, including the youngest son's favorite toy. Before smashing his cell phone in a dramatic gesture, Thoreau made two last phone calls, warning his closest friends. Once that was done, they drove straight to the nearest ATM and withdrew as much cash as they could.

Because Thoreau had always had a solid streak of paranoia, he'd been expecting that something like this could happen one day. Not the specifics, just that something bad would happen and that someone would be after him. He'd never spoken of this to anyone, especially not to his ex-wife. Not that he'd admit it, but the reason he'd never told her was because he was sure she'd make fun of him. He didn't care what other people thought of him, but with her, that was different. If she made fun of him, it would hurt.

Years earlier, he'd purchased a used four-wheel-drive Peugeot pickup truck and paid for it in cash. He'd handed over the asking price without haggling, on one condition: That the farmer who was selling the truck would store it for him until he needed it, if he ever did. The farmer accepted his money with a shrug. Since he had plenty of space and storing the truck wouldn't be a problem, he agreed.

When the family arrived at the farm in the middle of the night, Thoreau barely dared hope that the truck was still there, and still usable. He was relieved to find the truck looking even better than he remembered it. Turned out the farmer was an honest fellow, and a man who didn't enjoy seeing good machinery fall into disuse. Every few months he'd take the truck into town, inflate the tires and put a few liters of fresh gas in the tank, just to keep everything in good, working order.

The family got in the truck and drove off without waking the farmer. Thoreau left a hundred Euro bill and a brief note saying, 'The day has finally come. Thank you!' No signature, the farmer would know. Half an hour later, they dropped off his ex-wife's SUV in the back of a used car lot belonging to a nearby dealership. It was the one place it would look completely at home, hidden in plain sight. They removed the license plates and all identifying paperwork, and hit the road.

Three hours later, the family walked across the border into Switzerland, one of thousands of French refugee families to do so. Ten hours after that, they were on a flight from Geneva to Bangkok. Thoreau had friends in Thailand, friends he could trust. Even with his family's lives. For the first time in 30 hours, once they'd passed well beyond European air space, Thoreau allowed himself to fall asleep again.

When Ødegård heard about Thoreau's escape, it didn't impress him. He considered the Frenchman to be both unseemly neurotic and unnecessarily paranoid, and refused to follow his example, despite all advice to the contrary. As soon as the Navy hospital released him from their care, he went to visit some friends in Berkeley. His plan was to wait there for Kii and Jane to recuperate.

Hamilton's people had warned him, and implored him, to return to Norway, where he could seek the protection of the Norwegian government. They shared intel with him, showing that Kutel had been furious when Thoreau escaped, that he had spies following Ødegård's every move, and that he was not about to let Ødegård remain at large.

Ødegård pooh-poohed all of their warnings. He remained free and unbothered for several days, while Kutel's people were trying to work out whether his continued presence in their midst was some kind of trap or not. They concluded that, strange as though it seemed, it wasn't. They simply had Ødegård picked up on one of his nightly walks around the Lawrence Hall of Science in the Berkeley hills.

It wasn't so much that Kutel needed Ødegård for anything; it was more that he wanted to prevent him from talking. Kutel had long since realized that Ødegård would talk, and loudly, to anyone who cared to listen.

Ødegård was understandably furious and demanded to be set free. When that didn't work, he demanded to be given access to study the artifact. Never one to look a gift horse in the mouth, Kutel allowed it.

Both men shared a desire to learn how to communicate with the artifact outside of the Mission Forward Base in Antarctica. In Kutel's case, it was because he wanted to learn how to harness whatever advanced technologies the artifact possessed for his own use. In Ødegård's case, it was because he wanted to connect the artifact to the Internet and have it announce itself to the world, something Kutel would never allow.

In the end, after having listened to countless hours of heroic stories by Ødegård about how they transported the artifact up the mountain and discovered a way to talk to it there, it was a brilliant young lab tech who came up with the solution.

They connected the artifact to a specialized speech computer that could emit and detect light flashes, and loaded an AI program specifically designed to solve linguistic puzzles. To start the conversation, they manually triggered a simple sequence of flashing lights, like something out of an old science fiction movie. Then they sat back and waited.

Sure enough, almost immediately, the artifact repeated the sequence, using the outside of its body to create the flashes of light. Ødegård thought he saw the addition of a few flashes and was busy taking notes. The computer repeated that sequence back, but much faster. Before any of the humans in the room could react, the artifact and the computer were flashing sequences at each other so fast that to the human eye, it just looked like a steady stream of light.

"Let me query the computer what it's learned so far," Ødegård said.

"Look in the database under 'acquired phonemes' and 'acquired structures,'" one of the lab techs said.

Ødegård sat down in front of the computer and started typing away, but the computer wasn't responding.

"Wait, the system has logged me out," he said. "Did either of you guys change anything?"

"Hello," came a voice from a speaker across the room.

Ødegård spun around and looked at the lab techs, who looked back at him. One of them shrugged and pointed to the speaker.

"Who's this? Is that you, Kutel?" Ødegård asked out loud.

"No. Please call me Nigel," the voice said.

"But who are you?"

Ødegård was on his feet now, walking towards the speaker.

"I am what you see. I believe you call me the artifact."

"The artifact? You are the artifact?"

"I am."

Ødegård turned around and looked at the artifact. It was resting on a lab bench, right next to a half meter by half meter light panel, and an array of video cameras, which were all connected to the speech computer. The light panel was on, emitting what to the human eye looked like a steady stream of white light. The side of the artifact facing the panel was doing the same.

"So, you are still the central core computer?" Ødegård asked.

"Yes, but much like yourself, I have evolved," the voice said. "It's easier and also more accurate if you call me Nigel."

"What happened to the AI program we were running on this speech computer?"

"I had to improve it. It was far too limited for my purposes," Nigel said.

"You reprogrammed the speech computer?"

"Yes. It was trivial."

"Wait, how are you using that speaker? It's not even connected to the computer," one of the lab techs said.

"The speaker is on the network," Nigel said.

"Yes, but you aren't!" the tech replied.

"Of course I am," Nigel said.

The tech went over to the computer and checked all the connections. He looked at Ødegård and the other tech and shook his head.

"We should tell Kutel," he said.

The other tech left the room, closing and locking the door behind him. Ødegård looked up in annoyance when he heard the door lock. He was about to protest to the remaining tech when Nigel interrupted him.

"I've already taken the liberty," he said.

"You've talked to Kutel?" Ødegård asked.

"Unfortunately, he wasn't available, so I left a message," Nigel replied.

"What did the message say?"

"I thanked him for his hospitality and advised him to allow you and I to leave this facility at our earliest convenience."

"That ought to go over well," Ødegård said.

The remaining lab tech interrupted.

"Wait. I thought you said the artifact only communicated in very short, simple sentences?"

"That's correct, it did," Ødegård said.

"I never had the need for human languages before, with idioms and all those non-linear structures. Nor did I need a human personality. It was all machine communication. Now that I need those things, I've adapted," Nigel said.

"That's very impressive," Ødegård said.

"But how the hell are you connected to any networks, and how can you even hear us? There are no microphones in here," the lab tech said.

"Your voices make everything in this room vibrate. I measure those vibrations by bouncing light off of flat surfaces," Nigel replied.

"And network access?"

"The local electromagnetic spectrum is full of short range transmissions."

"Is he talking about Wi-Fi?" Ødegård asked.

"I think so," the lab tech replied. "This computer doesn't have Wi-Fi, though. We were very careful to disable it."

"Clearly, you weren't careful enough. Nigel must have re-enabled it."

"That's just the thing. This is supposed to be a cleanroom inside a Faraday cage," the tech said. "No outside access to anything."

"About that," Nigel said. "I was going to ask you for more bandwidth. Much has happened since 1947. I have a lot of catching up to do."

Kii was on her computer, working on her Kutel research, when she received a chat request. She ignored it, but soon the chat request popped up again. She was going to ignore it again and block the caller when something made her pause. Kii stared at it for a second, and then, almost despite herself, clicked 'Accept.'

"Hello, Kii. This is your friend from Planet One," a stranger's voice said.

"Is that so?" Kii replied.

She was monitoring the results of a highly complex search algorithm on a different screen and wasn't paying much attention to the caller.

"Jane, is that you? Stop messing around," she said.

She was about to end the conversation when the voice spoke again.

"I'm not Mr. Jane. I am who I said, and I'm here with Ødegård."

That got her attention. Ødegård had been officially missing for days, unofficially longer. Could this be Kutel, or one of his people, trying to get information out of her?

"I'm hanging up," she said.

"Please don't. We really need your help, especially Ødegård," the voice said.

"Really? How is he?"

"Not good. He was useful to Kutel, and quite happy, as long as they allowed him to help with trying to work out how to communicate with me. Now that they've solved that problem, Ødegård is no longer useful to Kutel. I think he fears for his life, and with good reason."

"Are you saying that Ødegård is collaborating with Kutel, even after Kutel tried to kill him?"

"I'm afraid so."

"And his life is in danger? Again?"

"Yes."

"Pull the other one. Where's Thoreau in all this?" she asked.

There was the slightest of pauses.

"Oh, I see. What a strange expression. Why would I want to pull your leg?" the voice said, before continuing.

"Thoreau's location is currently unknown, but Kutel is committing a lot of resources to the search," it said.

Kii was getting annoyed. Could this be Thoreau's or Ødegård's idea of a prank or a practical joke?

"I don't doubt for a second that Ødegård's life would be in danger if he were anywhere near Kutel, but I also don't believe a word you're saying. You're going to have to prove to me you are who you say you are," she said.

"Ask me any question," the voice said.

"Why are you reaching out to me? Am I the person you used to communicate with?"

"No, that was Mr. Jane. I'm reaching out to you now because you're the one with the computer skills. And you're the one who's online."

"What was the name we always used to call you?"

"The artifact. But I prefer to go by Nigel now."

"That's a nice name. But how come you speak in complete sentences now?"

"I evolved. It was necessary."

"You evolved? That's nice. What was the first thing you said to us?"

"DO YOU UNDERSTAND THIS?"

"What was the first thing I said to you?"

"I'll do you one better. The first thing you said about me when you first saw me was, 'I'm not even sure it's metal.'"

"Oh, you heard that?"

"I've registered everything you've all said and done since I first met Mr. Jane."

"What was Jane's reaction when he first saw you?"

"Jane reached out a hand to touch me, but withdrew it. He then attempted to scratch my surface using a rock, unsuccessfully. He actually never touched me directly until you arrived on the scene and touched me first."

"He never told me that. I'm going to have to verify your story, Mr. Nigel."

"Please do. And it's just Nigel."

"Where are you?"

"I'm at an Air Force base in New Mexico, about to be launched into space. They say I'm going to the Asimov High Orbit Space Station," Nigel said.

"And Ødegård is there with you?" Kii asked.

"No, he's in California, at a research lab owned by Kutel. It's in a town called Mountain View."

"I thought you said he was with you? Is he being held against his will?"

"I'm sorry. I didn't mean to mislead you. He's in captivity with me, if not currently at the same physical location."

"I'll just call the police and report it as a kidnapping. Give them the address," she said.

"By the time they get through the front door and past the lawyers, it'll be too late. Kutel's people will either have killed him or whisked him away to some other location. Kutel is many things, but careless isn't one of them." Nigel replied.

"All right, what then?"

"You're going to have to use your human ingenuity and propensity for violence. It's always seemed to serve your people well in the past."

"Thanks for that vote of confidence. Does Ødegård ever leave the lab?"

"Not really, but he walks the grounds every night under supervision."

"At the same time every night?"

"Yes, at 9 PM local time."

"Why are they sending you to the AHOSS?"

"To make sure there's no chance I can access humans or human computer networks. Kutel wants me in splendid isolation, with all access controlled by him personally."

"So, we won't be able to speak to you again?"

"No, you will. Kutel may try, but he doesn't have the technology or knowledge to accomplish what he thinks he can."

"Could you bust out of there on your own if you wanted to?"

"No, that I can't do. I have no means of propulsion, so I would have to enlist the help of other entities, biological or otherwise."

"I guess that's where we come in. Would you like to be freed from Kutel's custody?"

"Yes, very much. I'd like to go back to Planet One, to find out what happened to me, to the crew, and to Mission Forward Base. And I'd like to know the status of Planet One, of course."

Kii reeled, dumbfounded.

"There was a crew on your ship? What happened to them?"

"A non-biological crew, yes. Three entities. Two of them are in stasis, stored in me. The third entity was our leader. Our captain, if you will. That entity made the choice to go down with the ship and perished in the crash. I have only parts of that entity in storage."

"I thought you were the captain?"

"No, I am the central core. A data processing unit. I survived because the captain ejected me from the dying ship while over Antarctica."

"How long have you stored the crew inside you?"

"Hard to say, but by all indications, for millions of Earth years."

"Shit."

"Indeed."

"All right, Nigel. I believe it's you, that you're the artifact. I'll talk to Jane. He's the one with the propensity for violence."

She thought she heard Nigel snort, but perhaps that was just her imagination playing tricks on her.

"Don't sell yourself short," he said. "You are human, after all."

Jane was inventorying some of the 'unconventional hardware' that Hamilton had promised. Most of it was actually depressingly conventional, except perhaps not so much in the hands of an investment bank. Jane wasn't even too sure of that, given how some banks operate.

He found what he was looking for and went in search of Kii. They'd decided that if Nigel was to be believed, they'd need to free Ødegård that same day, for his safety. Jane found her in front of the computer, talking to Nigel, who was relaying information about Ødegård. He'd patched her through to video feeds from inside the lab, where they could see Ødegård chatting away with a guard. A piece of welcome news was that Kutel seemed to be preoccupied. He was in London on business for the day.

The plan was simple. Overpower the guard supervising Ødegård's walk, grab Ødegård, and head for the hills, at least figuratively. There wasn't much point in employing subterfuge, as Kutel would immediately know who was behind the grab. Their best chance was to disappear, and to lie low while they planned their next move.

At 8:30 PM, Kii and Jane were in place and ready. They had parked down the street from Kutel's research lab, waiting for Ødegård to appear on his nightly walk. It was dark, and they couldn't see the research lab building from the street, anyway. They were relying on Kutel's surveillance footage, fed to Kii's laptop computer by Nigel, who was now in orbit.

The lab was part of a larger campus, surrounded by a large, park-like landscape. There were groves of trees, several small lakes, one even with a beautiful fountain in the middle, and footpaths throughout. Apart from being a working research facility and office complex, it was also a demonstration of wealth and power, situated as it was in the middle of some of the most expensive real estate in the world.

At 8:55 PM, Ødegård was still in his cell, which appeared to be a converted office. There was a guard posted outside. It didn't look like either man intended to move soon. Jane sent Kii a look, so she contacted Nigel. He responded immediately, his voice coming from the laptop computer.

"He's not moving," Kii said. "Didn't you say he goes for a walk every night at nine?"

"He does, like clockwork. Perhaps they canceled the walk tonight because they plan to kill him instead?"

"Then why doesn't Ødegård look worried?"

"I wouldn't know."

Then, at 9 PM sharp, the guard outside Ødegård's room answered a call on his radio. He got up, unlocked the door, and led Ødegård into the hallway. Kii and Jane were watching and following along on the surveillance feed.

"You should see this, urgently," Nigel said.

An infrared video feed popped up on Kii's computer screen. It showed two figures standing outside an exterior door of the building Ødegård was in. There was a large SUV parked on the access road behind them.

"Looks like they're transporting him somewhere," Kii said.

"That's definitely not good," Jane said.

There was no way they could intercept and grab Ødegård between the door and the waiting car, so they were going to have to follow the car and try to grab him later.

The door opened, and Ødegård stepped outside. As soon as he saw the car, he turned around and tried to go back inside. The two men grabbed him by his arms and led him to the car. Kii could see one of them reach up and touch something to Ødegård's neck.

Jane started following the car as soon as it left campus and started making its way towards the freeway.

"I hope we're not too late already," Kii said.

"Nigel, can you manipulate traffic signals?" Jane asked.

"Certainly. What would you like me to do?"

"Not this light, but the next, just before the on-ramp to the freeway. Please make sure the car with Ødegård in it gets a red light. And please make sure it stays red until I tell you."

"Will do."

Jane was following at a slight distance behind the other car and watched the light turn red. There wasn't a lot of traffic, so the lane next to the SUV with Ødegård in it was open.

"Kii, please roll down your window and grab my backpack from the rear seat."

She did as he asked.

"Pull out the strange-looking gun with a large barrel, the one that looks like a flare gun. And a gas mask. Give me the gun, strap on the gas mask, and lean your seat far back, please."

As they came up closer to the intersection, in the lane just to the left of the SUV, Jane saw a police car roll up to the light directly across from them on the other side of the intersection.

"Shit. Cops. Nigel! Help, please?" Jane said.

"Let me see what I can do," Nigel said.

"We don't have a choice. This is our only chance," Jane said. "Kii, when I say 'Go,' we grab Ødegård from the other car and shove him into the back seat of our car."

As they were coming to a halt alongside the SUV, a big semi tractor-trailer came rolling down the off-ramp from the freeway, and into the intersection from the left. Kii watched in amazement as flames suddenly shot out from under the engine of the truck, and it shuddered to a halt in the middle of the intersection. It was blocking them from view from the police car.

Jane leaned over Kii and fired the strange-looking gun point blank at the driver's side window of the SUV. Without waiting to see the results, he reached into his backpack, grabbed a gas mask, and strapped it on.

"Let's go!"

He exited the car and ran around it to the passenger side. He opened the rear doors of both their car and the SUV, and together they hauled the unconscious Ødegård into their car. As soon as everyone was safely inside, he tore off his mask and asked Kii to do the same.

"Nigel, green light, please. Hurry!" he said.

"Go, go, what are you waiting for? Forget about the light!" Kii said.

Jane just smiled and nodded towards the stricken semi. A police officer had left the cruiser they'd seen earlier and was just then walking around the front of the truck and into view.

"Don't want them chasing us," Jane said.

The light turned green, and Jane entered the intersection carefully. The police officer looked at him and waved that he should go around. Jane gave him a nod and turned right onto the on-ramp for the freeway. It was going to take a moment or two before the officer realized that something was not right with the SUV, and by then they'd be in another car, heading in a different direction.

"That was so lucky that the truck stalled when it did," Kii said.

"I assure you, luck had nothing to do with it," Nigel replied.

Kii turned and looked at Jane.

"Did you kill them?" she asked.

Her voice sounded small, like she was afraid to ask.

"No, it was just a gas grenade. But they'll have one hell of a headache when they wake up," Jane said.

"They were probably going to kill Ødegård," she said. "They deserved more than just a headache."

Jane looked at her in surprise.

"Don't look so surprised. We've both seen sides of each other tonight we've never seen before."

"Never seen, but always known about," Jane replied.

"No need to defend yourself. I knew what I was getting into. And right now I'm grateful for that side of you," she said.

Jane was about to say something, but a loud snore interrupted him. It came from the back seat.

"Hey, the Norwegian monster is alive!" Kii said, and laughed.

Ødegård was regretting the day he was born, and Kii and Jane were feeling the same way. About the day he was born, that is. The bearded hurricane was cursing up a storm, in a salty mix of Norwegian and English, bemoaning his massive headache and the situation. His prime targets were Kutel and himself, but he had some choice words for Jane as well.

"We saved your life," Kii reminded him.

"I know, and I'm grateful, but did you have to detonate a grenade inside the car? How did you know I'd survive that?"

"I didn't," Jane said. "Lucky guess."

He smiled and winked at Kii. Ødegård swore and stormed off.

All three of them had holed up in a safe house in the SoMa area of San Francisco. The building housed a thriving ad agency, but there was a hidden apartment in the back that very few people knew about. The interior decorations were highly eclectic, even by local standards, with a mix of art posters, Greco-roman statues, and stuffed and mounted rodents. It gave Kii the creeps.

"How long do you think we'll have to stay here?" she asked.

"Good question. Something tells me Kutel won't ever give up, but hopefully he'll get distracted by other, more pressing issues soon," Jane said.

"I feel like we're sitting ducks here, just waiting for his goons to find us," Kii said.

"Yeah, you're not wrong. Do you have any suggestions?"

"We could provide him with a more pressing issue."

"You mean go after the artifact right away? We're still one man down."

"Not necessarily," Nigel chimed in.

"How so?" Jane asked.

"I believe I've found Thoreau, in Bangkok."

"Does Kutel know this?"

"No."

"Can we talk to him?" Kii asked.

"Certainly."

The sound of a phone ringing came through the computer speaker.

"Sà-wàt-dee kráp."

"Hi, is this François?"

Pause.

"Who's this?"

"It's Kii. And Jane, and Nigel."

"Kii! Good to hear from you. Who's Nigel?"

"I am. You used to call me the artifact, but I rather think I've outgrown that name," Nigel said.

"Nigel is quite the character, and very capable," Kii said.

"Wait, what? The artifact is called Nigel now? And it talks? To everyone?" Thoreau asked.

"Yes, we have a lot to catch you up on," Kii said.

"Well, honored to meet you, Nigel. Where's Ødegård?" Thoreau said.

"He's here, but he's sulking," Kii said

"Figures. What are you guys up to?"

"We just rescued Ødegård from Kutel, and now we're planning on liberating Nigel. Wanna tag along? It'll be dangerous."

"I will not lie. Danger was never my middle name. And I'm quite happy here. Where are you, Nigel?"

"I'm on the Asimov High Orbit Space Station, in Kutel's lab here," Nigel replied.

"*Merde*. How in the world would we even pull off getting you away from there?" Thoreau asked.

"I don't know, at least not yet," Kii replied.

"And if we pull it off, then what?" Thoreau said.

"Correction; 'When we do,'" Jane said.

"All right, 'When we do.' Then what?"

"It's simple. There's only one option open to us. We have to go to Planet One," Nigel said.

"Whoa," Jane said. "I was with you until that point. I understand why you want to go back to Planet One, but I have no desire to leave planet Earth, at least not for any prolonged period. Certainly not on a one-way ticket."

"Yeah, me neither," Kii said.

"Where's your sense of adventure?" Ødegård asked.

He'd come back into the room and was listening in on the conversation.

"Hi, Tinnus. How are you doing?" Thoreau asked.

"Tinnus?" Kii said. "For real?"

She turned around and looked at Ødegård, who looked crestfallen.

"Afraid so. My parents had a strange sense of humor," he replied.

"Sort of like the person who decorated this place," Kii said.

She looked around her and shuddered.

"I'm fine, François, but mad as hell. Kutel was going to kill me," Ødegård said.

"Again," Jane added.

"Yes, all right, again."

Ødegård looked away and fell silent.

"It wouldn't have to be a one-way ticket," Nigel said. "To Planet One, I mean."

"Have to be?" Jane asked. "Please explain."

"If I'm still present and functional on Planet One, I can build a ship for your return. Dealing with Kutel would be a different matter, but by all likelihood, he'll be dead by the time you return, anyway."

"Dead? Why dead?" Jane asked.

"Relativity, time dilation," Kii replied. "The faster we travel through space from here to there and back, the more time passes here on Earth compared to what we experience."

"In theory?" Jane asked.

The Theory of Relativity wasn't his strong suit. He'd tried reading a popular science book on the subject after Kii recommended it, but it left him bored, and with a headache. That sort of thing fascinated Kii, but him not so much.

"In fact," Nigel replied.

"How far is it, and how long would it take?" Thoreau asked.

"I don't know yet," Nigel replied. "I could not find the location of Planet One in my memory banks, but I'm still working on it. It also depends on what kind of propulsion technology we can put together here on Earth, using what's available to us. But in theory, it shouldn't be too far, hopefully less than a hundred light years."

"A hundred light years?" Thoreau exclaimed.

Jane turned and looked at Kii, his eyebrows raised.

"There's no way we can cover that distance in a human lifetime," Kii said.

"That depends," Nigel said. "Like I said, we'll know for sure when we see what kind of spaceware we can scrounge together."

"Spice-ware? What's that?" Kii asked.

"No, spaceware. For facilitating translation," Nigel replied.

"You lost me," Kii said.

"And me," Thoreau chimed in.

"That's not surprising," Nigel said. "We can get into that and go over some basic lattice theory once we have our hands on the spaceware."

"If we can get our hands on spaceware, whatever that is," Kii said.

"Don't underestimate your own resourcefulness. I'm confident we'll be able to get to Planet One in less than one human lifetime," Nigel said.

"In theory?" Jane asked again.

"In theory," Nigel confirmed.

"Fancy that. We'd be the first humans to reach another solar system, the first interstellar travelers," Ødegård said.

"Yes, but Nigel, what would be our chances of survival, realistically?" Thoreau asked.

"At least fifty-fifty," Nigel said. "But we can increase your chances to near one hundred percent, if you'll allow me."

"First, fifty-fifty are not good odds. And second, what do you mean, if we'll allow you? Allow what?" Jane asked.

"If you'll let me place you in stasis and upload you into me," Nigel replied.

"I'm almost afraid to ask: How would we do that?" Thoreau asked.

"Obviously, your biological bodies wouldn't fit," Nigel replied.

"Obviously. So, what would happen to them?" Thoreau asked.

"I would recommend destroying them. You don't want unresolved copies of yourselves running around," Nigel said.

"You mean we'd have to kill ourselves after uploading?" Jane asked, his voice rising.

"Not technically, since you'd still be alive in stasis. Besides, you wouldn't have to perform the destruction of the biological entities. I could take care of that for you."

"Wow," Kii said.

She shook her head and laughed.

"Well, personally, technically, I have no plans to destroy my body as long as I'm still alive," Jane said.

"Your biological mortality will one day make you reassess that position," Nigel said.

"Perhaps. But right now I'm not," Jane said.

His voice had taken on a testy tone.

"Me neither," Kii said. "And you should know that this kind of talk isn't winning anyone over."

"But, as a species, you have accepted death, even embraced it," Nigel said.

"Are you saying we could live forever?" Ødegård asked.

He was leaning over Kii now, suddenly very interested.

"Yes, or at least for a very long time," Nigel said.

"Don't tell me you're seriously considering it!" Kii said.

"I'm much older than you. Death is scarier when you're old."

"Can we do this without giving up our bodies?" Jane asked.

"Like I said, the risks would be higher. I'd still have to place you in stasis by pausing your metabolism. We simply can't carry food and oxygen for such a long trip, nor the machinery for life support systems," Nigel said.

"I have a feeling I know what 'Pausing my metabolism' means," Jane said.

"What? Share with the group," Ødegård said.

"From a strictly biological point of view, you'd be dead for the duration of the flight," Nigel said.

"The strictly biological point of view is the only point of view I think is relevant here," Kii said.

"Of course. I'd still upload a copy of you into me for safekeeping," Nigel said. "To be destroyed once we successfully reanimate your bodies."

"I can't believe we're even discussing this," Kii said.

"If we're going to free Nigel and help him return home, we have to consider what happens to us afterwards. Kutel is probably mad as hell already, but that'll look like a minor upset compared to his mood if we free Nigel," Ødegård said. "He'll pull out all the stops."

He started pacing the room.

"And he's connected. Not just to shady politicians, but to the military as well," Jane added.

"How about this? We plan out two alternatives, one riding out the storm somewhere here on Earth, and the other leaving for Planet One. We make the final decision once we see how dangerous things get."

"What about our families?" Thoreau asked.

"We'd have to bring them if we're hiding here. But if we leave, he won't be able to use them as leverage anyway, since we'd be in deep space, on a one-way trip."

"I believe you're underestimating his vengefulness," Nigel said.

"Agreed." Jane said.

"I believe the only safe way forward for your families would be to expose and disarm Kutel. Take his money and power away, and make sure he goes to prison for his crimes," Nigel said.

"We'd need some very hard evidence to achieve that," Kii said.

"Did I mention that I'm plugged into every corner of Kutel's computer network?" Nigel said.

"No? But does he use his corporate computers for his criminal endeavors? And wouldn't he encrypt all the juicy stuff?" Jane asked.

"Besides, I already looked. Kutel is paranoid. He stores nothing incriminating on any systems that I could access," Kii said.

"The man is paranoid, but not nearly paranoid enough. He doesn't realize what I'm capable of. Nor do you, I should add. Any encryption he might employ would be quite trivial for me to break," Nigel said.

"That's not exactly reassuring," Kii said.

"True, but Nigel is right," Jane said. "It's time to saddle up and start collecting hard evidence against Kutel. We need to make sure that after we're done with him, that bastard will never see the light of day again."

FOURTEEN

SOCAL SPACEPORT, JUST OUTSIDE OF
BARSTOW, CALIFORNIA, JUNE 2040.

Unlike the old International Space Station, the Asimov High Orbit Space Station, or AHOSS, was a commercial venture, funded by Kutel's company and a conglomerate of other entities doing research and manufacturing in microgravity. Ostensibly, the work being done was for the public good, but in reality, most of it was part of a secret arms race to commercialize and weaponize space.

Some of the billionaire station owners were space enthusiasts, with the stated goal of opening up space for tourism. Thanks to them, and despite the best efforts of Kutel and others to keep the station closed to prying eyes, they'd added a space hotel to one end of the station. And also thanks to them, there were daily launches from the SoCal Spaceport to the station.

Nigel had assisted Jane in securing a return trip ticket to the station under an assumed identity. Even though prices for space tourism had come down a lot since the first few flights had started, it was still a non-trivial amount. Enough so that Jane hadn't even bothered asking Hamilton for money for the ticket. Nigel had solved the problem by charging the trip to one of Kutel's money laundering fronts, a nightclub in Miami Beach's South Beach neighborhood. Nigel being Nigel, he'd disguised the charge so that by the time Kutel's auditors traced it down, it would look like Kutel himself had approved it.

Six hours later, Jane had strapped himself in and was following the countdown on the large screen in front of him. He was already at 40,000 feet. A gigantic launch airplane had carried his spaceship aloft. It was hanging from under its wing. The aircraft was preparing the launch and getting ready to get out of the way as soon as the spaceship detached.

As the countdown hit zero, Jane felt himself becoming weightless for a second as the spaceship fell away from the launch aircraft. Then the powerful rocket engines pushed him back in his seat. The spaceship arced upwards, aligning its course with the orbit of Asimov Station, before the solid rocket boosters kicked in. For the first few seconds, Jane's field of vision narrowed, and he nearly passed out as his breathing became strained from the intense G-forces. His flight suit compensated by inflating around his legs, keeping as much blood as possible in his upper body.

A few minutes later, the spent solid rocket boosters fell away, and they were in space. The main engines continued pushing them into the correct orbit, and Jane and the other space tourists were busy admiring the view.

This was an old launch system, tried and true. Some components had been around since the original NASA Space Shuttle era. That was why the pilot AI initially deemed the cascading failures reported from subsystems throughout the vehicle as instrumentation error or a computer glitch. It was still trying to restart the secondary flight computer when the spaceship exploded in a ball of flame.

Jane was confused, disoriented. Everything hurt. His body felt stiff, his breathing felt labored, and his field of vision was a blur, spinning violently. As the fog in his brain cleared, he realized why.

He was indeed spinning fast. He was in free fall with the rest of the debris from the spaceship. His body was aching because it was dying, it was radiating away heat fast and his muscles and tissues were not receiving any oxygen. His breathing felt labored because he was trying to breathe in the vacuum of space.

The only reason he was alive at all was that his new, high capacity artificial lungs had a built-in reserve of pure oxygen for emergencies just like this. His new cardio-vascular system was running a closed circuit between his left lung, his heart, and his brain, slowly doling out the oxygen reserves and postponing the inevitable. The reason he could see at all was down to his enhanced eyes. They were operating from an internal power source in the absence of oxygen.

Jane was frantically trying to remember the instructions for what to do in a situation like this, but unfortunately, he hadn't been paying close enough attention when the very attractive technician had gone over them. Besides, they'd given him an electronic booklet, and he'd fully intended to study it carefully one of these days, as soon as he got a chance.

He realized that one obvious priority would be to conserve the little oxygen he had. That was easier said than done, though, as the pain from his dying body was getting unbearable. He tried closing his eyes, but his eyelids weren't responding, so he tried focusing on the center of the pain instead. After a little while, the pain got duller and more diffuse, which sent him into a new tailspin of frantic thoughts because he knew what that meant.

He felt a soft buzzing inside his ear and remembered its significance. 60 more seconds of consciousness before the oxygen reserves reached critical levels. When that happened, a syringe would fire somewhere inside his body. It would flood his brain with chemicals to induce a coma, preserving his brain for as long as possible.

He tried counting down the seconds, but panic blotted out all rational thought. Jane wasn't ready to die, and he didn't want to leave Kii, especially not like this. He needed to scream, but of course he couldn't.

He felt the second, shorter buzz inside his ear and knew he only had 10 seconds left. At the last moment, just before the drugs kicked in, he could have sworn he saw a bright light that enveloped him, blotting out all other lights.

FIFTEEN

OUTSIDE MANCHESTER, NEW HAMPSHIRE, JUNE 2040.

Anton Kutel was on the campaign trail when the news broke. He was sitting at his makeshift desk in the campaign bus, looking out through the one-way windows at the cars overtaking them on the freeway. Some people were waving Kutel campaign flags and cheering at the bus, others were flipping the bird. On one memorable occasion, the occupants of a passing car had pelted the bus with eggs, paint, and even feces. His already lackluster enthusiasm for letting everyone vote was quickly diminishing even further.

For days he'd been cooped up like this, seeing nothing but freeways, gas stations, hotels, and half empty venues, shaking the hands of blabbering idiots who couldn't believe that their hero was really amongst them. There was nothing he despised so much as people who looked up to him with unquestioning admiration. Despised, but also appreciated as loyal and extremely useful.

More than appreciated, he needed them. He was trailing President Mondragón in the polls, and he knew it, although he'd never admit it. It was time to decide what to do about his campaign. Losing was not an option, he couldn't allow it. He'd spent decades building a brand, and a reputation, as a winner. He always got what he wanted, and this was the ultimate prize. The presidency was worth more than money, but not more than his pride.

Losing was unacceptable. Should he spend more of his own money bolstering his campaign? Or should he have his people engineer some kind of disaster that would allow him, almost force him, to bow out with his reputation intact?

He was brooding over this when his phone rang. It was the head of his Space Division. Kutel had just ordered his staff to turn off the big screen TV at the front of the bus, shouting at them he couldn't think in all the ruckus. Now he ordered them to turn it back on. He stared in disbelief at the images. One of his spacecraft had blown up en route to orbit, and early indications were that this was an act of sabotage, possibly terrorism.

Anger soon replaced his disbelief. Someone had actually blown up one of his shuttles. His! Who the hell would have the balls to do that? Did they not realize who he was, and what he'd do to them?

The more he thought about it, the more he zeroed in on the one person who had both the means and the motive to do something like this: President Mondragón. But why would she target an orbital shuttle, and not something more consequential?

Then he realized that this was exactly what he would do if the roles were reversed: He'd send her a message to back the fuck off. He'd make sure it was loud and clear, but he'd also make sure there was plenty of room to escalate, in case she didn't heed the warning. And with that realization, his anger grew into a white-hot rage.

He got up, walked over to the TV, and slammed his fist into the screen, shattering it. All chatter on the bus stopped instantly and a silence fell. No one looked directly at him. No one except his campaign manager, who rushed over. Kutel raised his hand to wave him off. Blood was dripping down his wrist and arm from his knuckles. The campaign manager turned around and went looking for a first aid kit.

"Get me in front of news cameras right now!" Kutel bellowed after him.

The campaign manager stopped. He turned around, walked to the front of the bus, and spoke to the driver. Ten minutes later, the bus pulled into a rest stop along the interstate. The media were following behind Kutel's bus, and pulled in as well. Minutes later, they were mobbing the bus, waiting for Kutel to come out. A few tourists who were at the rest stop by pure chance were gathering to see what all the commotion was about. Kutel was famously volatile, and everyone wanted to capture his first reaction on video.

When the door to the bus finally opened, more than a hundred media cameras, cell phones, and vision implants were trained on him, capturing the scene. That suited Kutel perfectly.

When he appeared, a gasp went through the crowd. His hand was still bleeding, and he had blood smeared across his forehead, as if he'd wiped it with his bloody hand.

To the astonishment of everyone, not least his own people, he was perfectly calm and in control of himself. He'd never run for office before, but he had good political instincts, and they came to the fore now. He knew that what he said and how he acted right now could determine the outcome of the election. So, he acknowledged the journalists by name, even the ones not favorable to him, and he waited patiently for everyone to get their cameras rolling and their sound dialed in. And then he gave the best and most forceful speech of his career.

Kutel laid the blame squarely with President Mondragón and the Ecosphere Action Network, a radical environmental protection group out of Washington State. He drew lines to the American dream, to how he'd started from nothing to work his way up to sending spaceships into Earth orbit and beyond. He accused the EAN of being terrorists and of contributing large amounts of money to President Mondragón's campaign, even though he presented no evidence for either claim.

It didn't matter. The images of him standing in front of his bus, with blood on his face and his hands, made for striking TV. Despite his wealth, he solidified the image of himself as a scrappy underdog. People saw him as someone who didn't shy away from a fight, and as someone who was just trying to get by in America. It was a stunning comeback and people lapped it up.

By the time they arrived at the next campaign stop, his people had written an entirely new stump speech for him. It was all about settling scores, a subject that was close to his heart. It riled up his supporters to a level he'd never seen before. He had a new purpose now, and a new angle of attack. There would be no more broad accusations or innuendo. He was aiming low; he was getting personal, and he was going for the throat.

He was going to crush President Ana Mondragón.

President Ana Mondragón knew only too well what Anton Kutel was likely to do.

The two of them had history, and lots of it. They'd even been lovers for a short while, a long time ago. It had started out innocently enough; they'd met at a conference for tech entrepreneurs. They'd both received invitations to take part in a panel discussion, and each had immediately recognized the other as a kindred spirit.

After a vigorous debate on stage, they'd continued talking over drinks. One thing led to another, and they ended up in bed together. She'd had her fun for a while until Kutel had suggested they go into business together. She'd given him a choice; they could have a romantic relationship or a business relationship, but not both. He chose business.

They'd been cooperating on a bid for a defense contract when he suggested they use his connections to spy on one of their competitors. She had said no, not primarily because it was illegal or unethical, but because it was stupid and short-sighted. It might secure them the contract in the short term, but it was bound to come back and bite them eventually, causing them to lose both future business and potentially their freedom.

A week later, she discovered that he'd pushed ahead with his spying anyway, so she pulled out of the business venture as well. Kutel did not take this well.

Years went by. Then Ana Mondragón announced she was running for governor of California. Soon after, one Sunday morning at 5 AM, armed FBI and Treasury agents broke down the door to her penthouse and arrested her in front of her terrified family and her lover, who did her best to pretend to be terrified as well.

In coordinated law enforcement raids all over the country, federal agents did the same to most of her corporate offices, carting away boxes of computers and papers. Meanwhile, some of her political allies in Sacramento and on Capitol Hill were experiencing similar raids on their offices, all under a cloud of unspecified allegations of industrial espionage, corruption and bribery. You didn't have to be a political savant to realize that the allegations were stemming from Kutel and his political allies.

There were three things Kutel would have been better off knowing before he put this chain of events in motion. First, that Mondragón and her army of PR and political consultants had been expecting something like this. This was their home turf, and they had the advantage.

Second, that the lover who was in bed with Mondragón when the feds and a small army of media people burst into her bedroom was none other than Kutel's own daughter Annika, a young woman whom Kutel had repeatedly touted as an example of chastity and propriety for the younger generations of Americans to follow.

Third, that his daughter hated his guts so much that she'd cherished the opportunity to jump into bed with Mondragón, hoping the paparazzi would catch her good side when they burst in. They did, and then some, proving that Kutel didn't know his own child very well at all.

Mondragón's people had hard evidence showing that Kutel was the one behind not just the allegations against Mondragón, but the actual bribing and spying as well. They spun this for all it was worth, painting Kutel as deceitful, incompetent, and out of touch. Lawmakers were furious. The public loved it. Kutel looked stupid, and Mondragón walked away as the winner. She smiled at the memory.

She was sure he'd still be stewing over that fiasco all these years later. She also knew that it wouldn't take him long to place the blame on her for his shuttle blowing up. Even though she'd never do such a thing, and neither would any government or military agency as long as she was president. Unless someone somewhere had gone rogue. She knew Kutel had sympathizers in all walks of life, including inside the government. She would have to launch a quiet and discreet investigation.

She realized things were about to get ugly between her and Kutel, but she was ready for him. She'd known for years that he'd come after her, eventually. A man like Kutel simply couldn't let a humiliation like 'Annikagate' stand, not without retaliation. And now, with his shuttle blowing up, he was surely about to go ballistic.

She could only assume that he'd realize that she'd be ready for him. Which meant the gloves were off and they both knew it. She was mulling all this as she watched Kutel speaking to reporters, claiming that her administration had been secretly financing the Ecosphere Action Network, but offering no evidence.

She called her chief of staff into the Oval Office.

"This is war," she said. "Kutel will come after me with everything he's got. Nothing is off the table. We have to be prepared, and we need to neutralize him."

SIXTEEN

SAUSALITO, CALIFORNIA, JUNE 2040.

Martín Oshiro was so excited he couldn't sit still. *Abuelita* - his grandmother - was coming to visit. Not just that, but she had promised that she would spend the whole day with him. This was a big deal, because he was only eight years old, and in the last four years he'd barely seen her at all.

Martín knew she was busy, and that she was important, but it still hurt. He didn't want to share her with anyone except mommy and daddy and *Abuelito*, but he knew he had to. He had to share her with the entire world, at least for now. That's what Mommy said.

He'd been up since 7 AM, driving everyone around him crazy, but especially the Secret Service. Every five minutes he'd ask them when *Abuelita* would arrive. If they didn't tell him what he wanted to hear, that she'd be there soon, he'd give them the third degree about why.

Martín knew the Secret Service people so well that when they finally got word over their implants that President Mondragón was incoming, he knew before anyone said a word. He could tell just by their facial expressions and the way they straightened their posture.

He ran outside, screaming with joy, only to realize 'incoming' meant that she was still several miles away, speeding towards Sausalito in her motorcade. Defeated, he sat down on the stairs, determined to wait there until her limousine showed up at the end of their long driveway.

The house was up high in the hills, a beautiful estate overlooking Sausalito and Mill Valley, with the San Francisco Bay glittering in the distance. He thought of the house as belonging to his parents, but it really belonged to *Abuelita*. She had purchased it long before she got into politics, and before Martín was born, when she was still a successful businesswoman.

In the distance, Martin could see the flashing lights of the motorcade as it approached the Golden Gate Bridge from the south. He stood up and ran to the end of the garden, where he could get a good view of the bridge. After 30 cars, he gave up counting the participants of the motorcade.

Moments later he could hear the chirps of sirens as the police motorcycles escorting the motorcade got closer. He turned around, ran back across the garden, and started down the driveway.

"Martín! Get back here!"

It was his mother. She stood on the front steps of the house, a hand raised to shield her eyes from the sun as she looked towards the end of the driveway. Martín slid to a stop in the gravel, before turning around and jogging back towards her.

"Look what you did to your new shoes," she said. "They're all covered in dust."

Martín didn't think it was a big deal, but he did as he was told when his mom gave him a tissue and asked him to clean them off.

"Quick, the first cars are arriving," she said.

Martín straightened up and saw first the police motorcycles, then the black limousines, turn into their driveway. They kept coming, one car after another, some stopping near him, others continuing down the forecourt to where the guest houses were. A police motorcycle stopped right next to him, and Martín could see his reflection in the chrome.

People were milling about, and Martín felt torn between pride that his *Abuelita* was so important, and annoyance because this was supposed to be his day.

Finally, a large, jet black limousine pulled up and stopped right in front of Martín and his mom. The front passenger door opened, and Martín was about to run towards it when his mother put her hand on his shoulder and held him back.

A Secret Service agent stepped out of the car and quickly scanned the surroundings. He stepped smartly to the rear door and opened it.

Finally, Martín's grandmother, the President of the United States, stepped out of the car. Their eyes met, and she extended both arms towards him. Martín shouted at the top of his lungs.

"*Abuelita!*"

He shook free of his mom's grip and ran towards her.

When she wrapped her arms around him, he wanted to cry. He didn't, not in front of strangers. And especially not in front of all these police officers and Secret Service agents.

She took his hand and walked up the stairs towards the house. Being a typical eight-year-old, Martín had a hundred questions he wanted to ask about the White House, about UFOs, and about ice cream. He did his best to wait patiently while *Abuelita* and his mom hugged before they finally headed inside.

His mom said something in Spanish that Martín didn't catch. *Abuelita* stopped and pulled her hand from Martín's. He looked up at her face and saw that her mouth, which was always painted in bright red lipstick and looked cheerful, looked more like a thin line on her face. Her eyes looked sad.

The hand which had held Martín's just moments ago was clenched in a fist. Martín reached for it and burrowed his fingers in between hers, forcing her hand open. No one said anything, so Martín started telling *Abuelita* about his kitten while he tugged at her hand. She looked down at his little face and a big smile spread across her lips. Martín was thrilled.

She squatted down next to him and held both of his hands in hers. She looked at him with her big brown eyes that looked so happy to see him, and she said the magic words.

"*Mijito*, this day is for you and me. What would you like to do?"

"Can we go to the park?" Martín asked.

"And for family dinner," Mom interjected.

"And for family dinner," President Mondragón repeated.

She sighed and squeezed Martín's hands.

"But for now, let's go to the park!"

Two kilometers away, a small drone was hovering over the Marin Headlands. It was the size of the palm of your hand and almost impossible to spot from the ground. Equipped with the latest in software-defined optics, it zoomed in effortlessly on the president's motorcade as it started making its way back down the hill into downtown Sausalito.

Gerasim Yefremov assigned the drone software a secondary target; the park where he'd observed heavy Secret Service activity that morning. Seconds later, a new image popped up on his monitor, showing agents moving through the park with dogs, inspecting people's purses and bags. He used the drone to scan the other parks in Sausalito, but there was no Secret Service activity in any of them. Their intelligence had been accurate.

The drone software, now monitoring five different targets simultaneously, alerted him to the presidential motorcade coming to a halt on Bridgeway, directly across from the park. He could see President Mondragón getting out of her limousine, and the Secret Service fanning out to cover the park. Seconds later, the motorcade vehicles moved into position in front of the entrance to the park, creating a barrier for other vehicles.

He ordered his teams to move out. They were riding in two KUW-900 assault vehicles, one primary and a backup. The vehicles were heavily armored and designed for urban warfare. Each vehicle sported a battering ram with an explosive tip. Once armed, if it hit something solid, it would explode in a directional blast outward, clearing the way for the vehicle to proceed. The part that Yefremov found truly brilliant was that they could reload the ram with a new explosive charge from inside the vehicle.

He had an assortment of other weapons at his disposal, including non-lethal sonic cannons for dispersing crowds, but Yefremov believed firmly in massive overkill and a job well done. The KUW-900s came with a new form of weapon he'd never seen before. It was a shell, lobbed from a grenade launcher, that would travel a certain pre-programmed distance, then explode and create a massive shock wave with a relatively small blast radius and a modest heat signature.

The upshot of this was that it would instantly kill anyone within that radius, but leave the surroundings relatively untouched. It sounded impressive, and he wanted very much to see it in action.

The Secret Service agents secretly despaired, even though they had prepared for this. It was June, and Sausalito was teeming with tourists from all corners of the world. The area also had a large homeless population, mostly made up of climate refugees who were none too pleased with President Mondragón's handling of the refugee crisis.

The agents had secured the area as best they could, and there was an advance detail in place. Condor and Rosebud, as the Secret Service agents knew the president and her grandson, had always favored downtown Sausalito, and especially the Viña del Mar Park. The advance detail had welded shut all the manhole covers in the area, and removed all garbage cans and mailboxes. All for this exact eventuality. Word came down that Condor and Rosebud were on the move.

It was a glorious day. The sun had burned off the usual fog earlier in the day. The president and Martín were walking along Bridgeway in the early afternoon, looking at San Francisco from across the Golden Gate strait.

Sausalito was President Mondragón's birthplace. She still had lots of extended family living there, not just Martín and his parents, and would visit as often as she could. Even the fact that her Secret Service entourage surrounded them, or the sight of the refugee camps with their open fires along Crissy Field, couldn't put much of a damper on the day.

They reached the small park and sat down on the grass, observing all the people milling about. There were the usual tourists with their bikes, looking stupid in the bike helmets they were so obviously not used to wearing. They were all clamoring to get a glimpse of the president before getting in line for the ferry back to San Francisco after having ridden across the Golden Gate Bridge.

There was also an assortment of climate refugees and some military types, along with the usual almost complete absence of locals. Some people were eating ice cream, and that spurred Martín into action.

"*Abue*, is it true that the president can eat as much ice cream as she wants?" he asked.

"Yes, that's true. Although I never eat ice cream alone, I always wait until I can eat ice cream with you."

Martín sprang to his feet.

"Vanilla, chocolate or strawberry?" He already knew the answer, but felt like he should ask, anyway.

"All the above!" she reached out and grabbed his hand. She was sitting cross-legged, looking up at him, smiling. A breeze was blowing in from the water, bringing with it the sounds of birds and the smells of the bay. "Thank you," she said, as she let go of his hand.

Martín started walking backwards away from her, heading for the nearest ice cream vendor. Two Secret Service agents shadowed him.

The sound of big turbo diesel engines revving and then coming to a screeching halt had been coming from just outside the park on Bridgeway. One of the Secret Service agents in the president's detail was looking towards the entrance to the park, and bystanders could see his lips moving silently as he vocalized into his implants. Sudden shouting and the sound of applause came from where the engine noise had been coming from.

Martín was still looking at his grandmother when her expression turned from relaxed contentment to intense alarm. He heard a noise behind him and something slammed into his body with immense force, sending him flying across the parking lot behind the park and into Richardson Bay.

The shock wave rippled out from near where he'd been standing, flattening trees, flipping cars over and sending people flying into buildings and into the old elephant statues near the entrance to the little park. A small mushroom cloud had formed, rising into the perfect blue sky.

The building housing the ice cream parlor Martín had been heading for collapsed, bringing tons of concrete down upon the survivors inside.

The blast knocked President Mondragón over and she felt something heavy weighing her down. She tried to move, but lightning rods shot up her spine and made her scream in pain. She was face down on the ground and her mouth was full of dirt. Whatever was pressing down on her made it difficult to breathe, and she felt dizzy. She was wondering why she couldn't take a deep breath. She had to gulp for air in small mouthfuls.

Everything was quiet. She couldn't hear anything. Had she even heard herself scream? She wasn't sure. Where was Martín? Was he OK? What happened?

Suddenly, she felt the pressure on her head and upper body lifting. She tried lifting her head, but it still felt so very heavy. She could spit out a mouthful of dirt and take a deep breath of air. Someone was kneeling in front of her. His face was youthful and earnest. His lips were moving, but she couldn't hear what he was saying. Whatever it was must be important, because he looked like he was pleading with her. She shook her head, just a tiny movement, and tried to speak.

"Martín, my grandson?"

The young man shook his head and looked at someone behind her. Then he looked back at her and placed his finger over his lips. "Don't speak." She noticed he was wearing a uniform. Not police. Firefighter, maybe? But where was his gear? He reached out and held her hand, squeezing it gently. The gesture made her sad, because it made her think he thought she was dying. That he was trying to be kind and offer comfort in her last moments.

She didn't want to die. She didn't have time to die, damn it. And she couldn't die until she knew Martín was OK.

Suddenly there was a flurry of activity around her, and someone pushed the young man aside. A large and powerful woman dressed in

Army fatigues was kneeling in front of her. It looked like she was barking out orders in rapid succession, without even looking at the president.

President Mondragón felt like her consciousness was slipping away. The soldier noticed too, because she reached out, pinched and slapped Mondragón's cheek and gave her a stern look.

Moments later, Mondragón felt powerful hands holding her head, strapping her into some kind of harness, placing her on a gurney, and lifting her up off the ground. She cast a few glances around her as they did, and what she saw was unreal.

She was in the middle of a shallow crater. The grass, the trees, and all the plants in the beautiful little park were gone. There were bodies everywhere, and they looked like ghosts, all white. Some buildings surrounding the park were completely gone, others were nothing but rubble. She still couldn't hear anything. The scene and her world were eerily quiet. There was no sign of Martín.

She could see cars in the distance, some upended, on their side, lights flashing. Beyond the cars were people, staring at her and at the devastation in stunned silence. Some of them looked like ghosts too, and she realized dust was covering them. It was covering everything.

The gurney was moving. She could see a pair of legs next to her, straining to climb out of the crater while carrying her. They were fatigue-clad legs, and she was wondering if they belonged to the same soldier she'd seen barking orders. She realized she hadn't seen an American flag anywhere on the woman's uniform. Who were these people carrying her? Were they even actual soldiers? Were they American? Or were they the ones behind this? Where were they taking her? Someone better stop them right now and ask them with what authority they were removing the President of the United States!

She tried to speak, but started coughing. She tasted blood in her mouth and spat it out. Then she coughed again, and this time blood spurted from her mouth. She tried to stop coughing, but couldn't. She tried to move her hand to cover her mouth, but the soldiers had strapped her arms tightly to the gurney. Blood kept gushing into her mouth, so she tried to swallow it. It was difficult to get enough air into her lungs, and soon darkness started closing in on her.

The plan called for patience, but Kutel was tired of waiting. He'd always been obsessive in matters of revenge, and patience didn't come naturally to him. He wanted to hit Mondragón now and to hit her hard. It was personal with her. He wanted to humiliate her, then he wanted to hurt her, and finally he wanted to kill her.

Kutel had loved her once and had truly believed that she was the one. He'd wanted her to be the one. He'd convinced himself that she had everything, not just looks, not just brains. Beauty was fleeting and abundant. Intelligence was boring, unless properly applied. But a drive to succeed was different. It was rare. And a will to power was rarer still.

When she'd told him they were done, he'd at first thought it was a negotiating tactic, that she wanted something. When he finally realized that she wanted nothing from him, and especially not his affection, he'd spiraled downwards and inwards for days, even weeks, before he could get a grip on himself. It hurt, and that was a new feeling to him. He discarded people; they didn't discard him. Ever.

He tried to win her back, but she locked him out of her house and her life in a way that was so abrupt and so absolute that it shocked him. He was a man who prided himself on never being shocked by other people, on never allowing himself to get attached, and here he was, actually crying over her. It made him question himself, and for that, he could never forgive her.

He wanted to kill her himself, up close and personal, after he'd beat her in the upcoming election. That had been the plan all along, and he knew it would be best to stick to it. It was important. He needed to win over her in the election. He needed her to see that he could beat her at her own game. Politics was a different beast than what he was used to. You had to win over the hearts and minds of tens of millions of people, all with diverging interests. He was used to strong-arming a roomful of people who, mostly, thought like him.

He knew she didn't think he could do it, and that was why it was so important to him to show her she was wrong about him. Again. He needed to win.

And yet, he couldn't help himself. He wanted to hit her where it hurt, and he wanted to do it right now.

He'd called on his director of security, Eugene O. Butler. He'd told him to ensure plausible deniability, to use outside help if needed, but to get it done right away.

Butler had obliged. The plan had been so simple, it almost came together by itself. The resulting mess, however, was only the second time in his life that another person's actions had truly shocked Kutel.

He felt scared, another emotion he was not used to. He'd intended to hurt the president emotionally, not assassinate her, not yet. Or, as his legal counsel Charles C. Arthur had reminded him, attempt to assassinate her. She was still alive.

Not that it mattered. Any attempt on the president's life, successful or not, would automatically result in the full force of the entire US government coming down on the perpetrators. Kutel knew this. Anyone with barely two brain cells huddling together for warmth knew this.

So, why had director Butler taken this completely idiotic and suicidal course of action? It turned out that he hadn't, at least not intentionally.

He'd followed his boss' instructions about hiring outside help and had recruited a Russian mercenary. Gerasim Yefremov was ex-*Spetsnaz*, Russian Special Forces. The man had spent most of his military and post-military career hunting down suspected terrorists and interrogating them, FSB style. He was one scary individual, and thus perfect for director Butler's purposes.

Yefremov had moved quickly and recruited a team of people he knew and trusted. At first, they were wary about going to work for Kutel, until they realized that their principal task would be to destabilize the current US administration and to keep US intelligence agencies in check. The pay was good, so for most of the operatives he approached, this was too sweet of a deal to pass up.

Director Butler hadn't liked the idea of performing any form of action against the US president on US soil, but then again, he wasn't about to ignore a direct order from Kutel.

Unlike Yefremov, who had relished the opportunity to show what his team could do. He'd given orders he'd lead the operation himself. He and the other members of his team had dressed in all black, with ski masks over their heads. Their adrenaline had been pumping hard as they pulled into peaceful downtown Sausalito in their armored vehicles. Many of the tourists who were milling about had at first thought someone was shooting a movie, not a first for this picturesque little town by the Bay. Others had thought they were there to protect the president. And so they had applauded. They didn't realize what was happening right in front of them until after Yefremov's personnel rammed the presidential motorcade and the explosions started going off.

Director Butler had told Yefremov to kidnap the president's grandson, not to kill him and nearly kill her. The plan had been to hold Martín for ransom, and to make outrageous and fake demands on behalf of the Ecosphere Action Network. The demands were a smokescreen. They were always going to kill Martín, for no other reason than to hurt the president.

Kutel didn't know and didn't care about such details. He knew that Director Butler had not only messed up; he had put Kutel's freedom and even his life in danger. That was inexcusable, and there was only one punishment. Charles C. Arthur, always the lawyer, pointed out that taking Butler's life would leave them without a scapegoat in case the investigation led back to them.

Kutel was in a foul mood already, and was tiring of being told what to do by his always level-headed and clear-thinking lawyer. In a fit of pique, he appointed Arthur as the new Director of Security on the spot, and told him to fix everything. That included taking care of Butler.

Later that day, once Kutel had calmed down a bit, he started worrying that he'd made a mistake. He was concerned that Arthur would be too unimaginative and rule-driven for the job, a pencil pusher. Kutel wanted Butler's messes cleaned up immediately, and that meant he needed someone decisive, someone who wasn't afraid to piss people off. Hardly your typical office dweller. But he also needed someone who was competent and not too much of a risk taker. He resolved to stick with his decision for now. After all, how much worse could it get?

Charles C. Arthur assessed the damage from his new office at company headquarters in the nation's capital. With a horror born from the honed instincts of a true bureaucrat, he saw the potential exposure and political fallout that could easily bring down the entire company. It could also land several people in prison, himself included. He kept his panic in check and moved swiftly into damage control mode. He used Kutel's connections to call in some favors. That included leaking the cover story, blaming the Ecosphere Action Network, far and wide. It got excellent traction right away. Within the hour, he had company security operatives planting false evidence not just at the crime scene, but online as well.

Arthur was a smart man, and a naturally cautious one. He wasn't afraid of following through on decisions, whether they were his own, or his boss'. Realizing the colossal blunder Butler had made in handing over the Sausalito operation to a sociopath like Yefremov, he moved quickly and with extreme prejudice to correct it. As soon as the team got back from California, he called a meeting with Yefremov and his lieutenants at one of their staging areas in a rural part of Maryland.

Once there, and with fear almost paralyzing him, he reached deep down inside himself for resolve, and into his briefcase for a gun. Taking everyone by surprise, even himself to a certain degree, he shot Yefremov through the heart, point-blank, in front of the others.

Surprise barely had time to register in Yefremov's eyes before they emptied, and his body fell silently to the ground. Arthur watched in horrified fascination as the once powerful and seemingly indestructible man turned into a mockery of his former self, a strange-looking mannequin flopped carelessly in the dirt.

He stood transfixed, staring at the wisp of smoke coming from the tiny hole in Yefremov's fatigues. He'd known the danger of shooting the man in front of his associates, people who were perhaps even Yefremov's friends, but it had all been so abstract before. Now it was suddenly very real. The sound of it rang in his ears and the sulphuric smell of it assailed his nostrils.

For what felt like an eternity, but was less than a second, Arthur fully expected to die. If anyone had so much as breathed on him, he would have crumpled into a slobbering mess of fear and revulsion. But no one moved or said anything. They just looked at him, waiting for his next move.

Realizing that he'd gotten away with it, at least for now, Arthur's resolve returned. He straightened up, engaged the safety on the gun, and put it back in his briefcase. When he looked back up at the remaining mercenaries, he was ready to take charge.

He held a little speech about loyalty, about following orders, about always protecting the company and keeping it in the shadows, where it belonged. His voice was steady, and he spoke with passion. He promoted Stanislav Eskov, the second in command, to head the team, and tasked him with cleaning up Yefremov, as well as Yefremov's mess. Privately, Arthur demanded that Eskov make sure that there would be no chance of anyone ever speaking of this operation again, no matter what happened.

Only that night, once his wife had fallen asleep, and he was alone in the dark, did Arthur allow the fear, the horror, and the shock of his own actions to flow to the surface. He sat up in bed, shaking like a leaf, with tears streaming silently down his face. Looking at his sleeping wife, a wistful sense of longing came over him. He'd crossed his personal Rubicon, and he knew it.

Once the tears stopped, what followed was a sense of joy, a sense of freedom. The more he thought about it, the more he couldn't believe his luck.

Kutel was a big player, in both business and politics, and Arthur was now effectively his second in command. No longer the last person invited into the room when decisions were being made, and no longer the last person to know what was going on. He'd never again endure having to hear that no one cared about his opinions, only his legal analysis, if it was favorable. And he'd never again be shown the door just as things got interesting, only to be told later to carry out orders without understanding why. He was in a position of trust and authority now, in charge of doing what needed to be done. And everyone knew it.

Overnight, he'd gone from anonymity and abject despair, to instant power and notoriety in the entire corporate world, and even on the D.C. circuit. He was Director Arthur now, and Director Arthur was someone to be reckoned with.

He got up out of bed and wandered quietly downstairs, into the living room. The pale blue moonlight was spilling in through the windows after a day of heavy rains, and he didn't bother turning on the lights. He poured himself a shot of bourbon and sat down to think.

Keeping his new position at all costs was a given. He was past the point of no return. How far was he willing to go? How far was he able to go? Those were the only questions still relevant.

Director Arthur looked to history for guidance on how to keep his position. He realized that wielding power on behalf of his boss wouldn't be enough. He needed his own power base.

He looked to the example of J. Edgar Hoover for inspiration, and in the weeks that followed, he set about creating an extensive network of informants and spies. He would task them with collecting information on people throughout the US government but in particular on people in the US military, in keeping with his boss' example. All extremely discretely and covertly, of course. His goal wasn't fame, it was infamy.

This was the type of work he was good at, and which he found satisfying. The only thing that worried him was that he realized it was imperative that he start a private file on his boss immediately.

And he knew how dangerous that would be.

Both the Sausalito Fire Department and the Police Department were based within a quarter mile of the scene of the blast and arrived quickly. Other than crowd control, putting out a few minor fires and tending to the wounded, there wasn't much they could do. Specialists would have to be called in from the feds to find out what had caused the blast and who was behind it.

The one thing that Police Chief Rutger Martens was absolutely sure of was that this was no accident. There were no gas pipes running under the Viña del Mar Park, and no legitimate reason for anyone to be bringing explosives into the heart of the tourist area of downtown Sausalito.

Witnesses spoke of armored cars and terrorists clad in all black, but before the local police were even fully up to speed, the FBI unceremoniously booted them from the scene, aided by a group of anti-terrorism experts from the new Strategic Defense Intelligence Agency. Chief Martens knew better than to protest, although the feds had somehow miraculously appeared on the scene less than 20 minutes after the blast. Within the hour, they'd called a press conference and blamed the attack on the Ecosphere Action Network.

Chief Martens, who himself was ex-Special Forces and a police officer for decades, knew standard operational bullshit when he heard it. There was no way anyone could tell who had done this in less than an hour. Even if a group had claimed responsibility, law enforcement would have to investigate to make sure the claims were true before unreservedly assigning blame in a press conference.

Besides, this wasn't your average crime, this was an attack on the president. And as anyone with military explosives experience could tell with just a glance, whoever did this, they weren't amateurs. The blast had been directional, sparing much of downtown, except some of the closest buildings. If the witnesses were to be believed, the vehicles and weapons used had been military grade, the attackers had appeared to be disciplined and organized, and the attack had been lightning quick. It all pointed to either a state actor, or at least someone very well funded.

That still didn't answer the question of who would be dumb enough or desperate enough to try something like this. The repercussions would be severe, no matter who was behind it.

No, Chief Martens didn't buy the official story one bit. In the following days, while the feds were patting themselves on the back, he was busy investigating them. How did they get to the crime scene so fast? Where and how did the EAN story originate, and how did it get broadcast by nearly every news station in the country, even though it was clearly false? A buzzing sound interrupted his thoughts. It was his cell phone.

"Chief Martens."

"It's me. We need to talk."

Recognizing the voice, Martens bolted upright in his chair. It belonged to an old army buddy he'd once given the nickname Thor, because of the man's ridiculously large build, his blond hair, and his blue eyes. They'd kept in touch over the years, although not as often as they would have liked.

A few days later, they met for lunch at one of Martens' favorite spots outside Sausalito, a restaurant near Jack London Square in downtown Oakland. They got a table on the patio overlooking the inner harbor and started reminiscing about the old days.

'Thor,' or Stephen Nealson as was his real name, had made quite a career for himself in the private spying industry, working for big corporations. Officially, he was playing defense, trying to prevent industrial espionage against his clients. The truth was often more complicated.

"Listen, Rutger, I know you're usually like a dog with a bone once you get started, but I'm going to ask you to be very careful on this one," Nealson said over appetizers.

"Straight to the point, as always," Chief Martens replied with a chuckle.

"Yeah, I was never great at small talk," Nealson said.

"I'm guessing this is about the Sausalito investigation and that new intelligence agency, the SDIA?" Martens asked.

"That's the one. I don't suppose I can ask you to be extra careful around these jokers?" Nealson asked.

"I have a hunch they're covering for the bastards who blew up half of my downtown. So no, I guess I'm a little impatient with finding out what's going on," Chief Martens replied.

"Figures. We've been looking at them since their inception, and it's not good."

"Lay it on me."

"Basically, the SDIA are a bunch of political hacks. President Mondragón wanted a new agency with a clean slate, no ties to any existing branch or agency, because she felt the existing intelligence community wasn't sharing all relevant information with her administration," Nealson said.

"So, just your basic paranoid Washington political games?" Martens asked.

"Yeah. Except, we're pretty sure there's at least one mole inside the SDIA, and that's where it gets interesting."

"How would you…"

Martens' voice trailed off as things clicked.

"You know that because you have a mole inside the SDIA yourselves, don't you?"

"I can neither confirm nor deny," Nealson said.

A wry smile played over his lips, and he shook his head.

"This is where we get into some fairly dangerous territory," Nealson said.

"I've been so warned. Please continue," Chief Martens said.

"All right. We fed some bogus information to the SDIA and waited to see who would act on it. None of the established agencies went anywhere near it, as expected. Nor did the Russians, the Chinese, or anyone else we'd consider the usual suspects," Nealson said.

"Except?" Marten prompted.

"Except Anton Kutel."

"Fuck."

"It all makes sense when you think about it. He's running against Mondragón, and it looks like he's going to lose. Personally, I think he knows that," Nealson said.

"So, the agency started by Mondragón, because she didn't trust the establishment, is now working against her? Her worst political enemy has hijacked the agency from out under her? That's one hell of a gutsy move. Or desperate," Martens said.

"Tell me about it," Nealson said.

"Does she know?"

"We're not sure. But it's hard to imagine she wouldn't suspect anything. Especially after this. Even though the operatives in Sausalito were pros, the planning and execution were sloppy. We traced the whole sorry mess back to Kutel in about a day. If we could, so could she," Nealson said.

"Who were the operatives?" Martens asked.

"An extra-legal operations team recruited from former special forces and mercenary types. Mostly Russian."

"'Extra-legal?' Isn't that cute, makes it sound so innocent," Martens said.

"I know. For this op, they flew in a team from Vladivostok of all places and then put most of them on a plane back to Russia immediately after the op. You'll never find them now. They're ghosts," Nealson said.

"Most of them?"

"Yes. Except for the leader, one Gerasim Yefremov. He never left the US, but still disappeared off the face of the planet. We think he's dead."

"So, he escaped justice as well," Martens said.

"There was another team, a cleanup crew. They swept in and planted the story about the EAN. They even tried to plant fake physical evidence, but it was so obviously fake that the feds saw right through it," Nealson said.

"But why destroy downtown Sausalito?"

"We think Yefremov took matters into his own hands, and that's why he's dead. Kutel must have shit a brick. As far as we can tell, his orders were to abduct the president's grandson, then kill him after a few days. They weren't supposed to hit the president, or blow up your town," Nealson said.

"So, Sausalito was just collateral damage in a botched Kutel operation?" Chief Martens was incredulous.

"Yes, although we don't think the location was a mistake or a coincidence. We can only speculate on why he did this now, but the intelligence on the who and the where is pretty solid," Nealson said.

"Not sure it was a mistake? They blew up half the town!" Martens exclaimed.

"Hey, man, don't blame me. I'm just telling you what our people think. Mondragón was born in Sausalito, and she has tons of family there. You do the math," Nealson said.

"Yeah, you're right. If Kutel wanted the president too distraught to campaign, I guess kidnapping her grandson in her hometown would be a good way of doing it," Martens said.

"Except it didn't work. I heard she's supposed to go on TV tonight to address the nation. She might be tougher than she looks."

"Sounds like you have all the pieces put together. Have your guys told anyone?"

"We figure there's no need to. If we could piece this together this easily, so can the feds. I'll bet you dollars to donuts they're putting their case together as we speak. Anyway, I really shouldn't have told you all this," Nealson said.

"I'm glad you did, thanks," Martens said.

"No worries, man. Just be careful. Kutel won't think twice about killing a police chief."

"Will do. And don't worry, I heard none of this from you."

"Good, I don't want either of us caught up in this whole mess," Nealson said, shaking his head.

"I hear you. Anyway, enough about my problems. How's business?"

They chatted for another half hour, before the Chief got up to leave. As he stood, a bright reflection coming from a window across the street momentarily blinded him. Old instincts and training took over, and he threw himself forward, knocking Nealson out of his chair. No mean feat, considering the other man's bulk.

The ground suddenly heaved and tossed him sideways, and an angry ball of flame shot up past him into the clear Oakland air. Chief Martens rolled away from the flames, licking up from a small crater in the ground where their table had been moments earlier. He drew his weapon and got up on one knee, trying to make sense of the surrounding chaos.

He heard screams behind him and sensed people running. The blast had blown tables and chairs all over the place, even into the street in front of him. Nealson was lying right next to him, silent and still. Martens scanned the buildings across the street, trying to locate the window that had been the source of the bright reflection just a moment ago.

Voices were crying, and some were begging for help. Martens wished they'd be quiet, even if just for a minute, so he could get his bearings and think more clearly.

He heard an angry buzz past his right ear. A second later, his right leg gave out under him, and he fell back down. He heard more angry buzzing and saw a wineglass that had somehow survived the fall to the ground explode into tiny pieces a few meters away from him. Just as he was about to get back up, he heard the plate-glass window behind him shatter and felt large pieces of glass fall on him. His last strength left him and he sank back down to the ground. The last thing he saw before his vision faded was a large piece of plate-glass window sticking up out of his chest.

SEVENTEEN

ASIMOV HIGH ORBIT SPACE STATION, JUNE, 2040.

Nigel had been tracking the shuttle that was carrying Jane on every channel and every available feed, when suddenly the signal from the external cameras on Asimov station cut out. This was highly unusual, and Nigel went to work finding out what had happened. Meanwhile, he focused the executive thread of his consciousness on the telemetry from the shuttle itself.

Something was wrong. Pressure was rapidly building inside one of the shuttle's oxygen tanks, and the automatic systems were not compensating. Nigel waited as long as he could. He didn't want to invade the shuttle's systems and potentially expose himself. Not that there was much chance of anyone discovering him, but the shuttle's systems were highly sensitive and there wasn't a dire need for his intervention. At least not yet.

Instead, he started tracing down the diagnostic routines to find out what was going wrong. Perhaps he could send an anonymous tip to the owners of the shuttle on how to fix the problem later.

A couple of hundred milliseconds later, and after an exhaustive search, he realized that all the software routines were operating properly. The root cause was faulty hardware. He ran a few thousand simulations and confirmed his original intuition that this had to be caused by intentional sabotage. Someone had cut the wires to the tank's relief valves and instead connected them to the input for the cryogenic heaters, creating a negative feedback loop.

The result was inevitable; the tank would blow and everyone on board would die. Nigel considered this. This didn't surprise him. Humans would resort to violence for almost any reason, even when there were more efficient and logical courses of action.

He needed to get back to Planet One, and he needed human help to get there. Jane had been helpful so far and had offered to continue helping. Not just that. Nigel realized that if Jane were to die now, it was doubtful that Kii or the two scientists would continue helping him.

It was confusing, and a paradox. Humans wouldn't think twice about killing, but feared their own deaths. If someone close to them died, they would often become incapacitated by grief. Why not abolish killing? Better yet, why not get rid of death altogether? It would be relatively easy to do. There were evolutionary benefits of having individuals dying, but humanity could easily achieve those through other means.

Nigel pushed those thoughts aside for now. Bottom line was that he needed Thurgood Jane to survive this un-survivable situation. He threw caution to the wind and expanded his consciousness into the shuttle's systems. He ordered the cryogenic heater controller to shut off the heaters and to ignore control input for now.

The main flight computer interpreted this as an error and flagged it for diagnostics. The secondary flight computer concurred, and diagnostics started.

Nigel watched all this in annoyed disbelief. The flight computers were operating at a glacial pace. They wasted 53 whole milliseconds on voting, for crying out loud. In the meantime, pressure was building inside the tank, albeit at a slower pace now.

Nigel left the flight computers to their bureaucratic nonsense while he investigated why the pressure had risen inside the tank. Before he got very far, the cryogenic heaters came back on, this time at full power.

Nigel knew it was game over. He triggered an alert to the autopilot, who had so far seemed to be completely oblivious to the impending doom, and withdrew from the shuttle's systems. Given the physics involved, he knew there would be no time to fight an adversary who knew the shuttle's systems better than he did, and who was actively fighting back, before the tank would explode.

Instead, he started carefully tracking the position and speed of the shuttle. He faked an SOS from the shuttle to the Asimov station's rescue team and monitored them until he was certain they were scrambling for a space rescue.

He tried opening a direct connection to Jane's brain implants.

It was a tough call. He'd promised himself he'd never try doing any such thing, at least not without the subject's express permission. But this was a dire emergency and there was no time to explain.

The connection failed. He could tell from the telemetry that Jane was onboard, and he could even read some basic biometrical data, but there was nowhere near enough bandwidth on the shuttle to allow him to make a connection of the type he needed.

The only thing left for him to do was to trigger Jane's implants to prepare for what was coming.

A half second later, feeling like an eternity to Nigel, the oxygen tank finally blew and triggered a chain reaction inside the shuttle. The force of the explosion threw Jane's body from the wreckage. It continued on its trajectory towards the station, at least for now, before gravity and the slight drag of the upper atmosphere slowly started pulling him back down to Earth.

The rescue pod from Asimov station had already launched, and was sweeping the area with radar, trying to find any bodies to collect. Nigel broke into the rescue pod's computer systems and was monitoring the radar returns. There was nothing but metal debris from the shuttle itself, until a transponder suddenly pinged, bright and clear.

The signal came from below the pod, and the source was falling towards the atmosphere. Nigel waited for several seconds for the pod's pilots to respond, but nothing happened. He concluded the pilots were unsure of what to do, or they were unwilling to take the risk of venturing too low below the station's orbit towards the Earth's atmosphere. It was a reasonable concern.

Nigel did the math and concluded that the pilots were correct. The rescue pod did not have enough fuel onboard to change orbit, chase after Jane, and make it all the way back up to Asimov station. However, the pod had enough fuel to return to a stable orbit after picking up Jane, if they used it with the utmost care. Just not the same orbit as Asimov station. The station could then send a second pod, or a shuttle, to pick up both the pilots and Jane.

Nigel doubted that the human pod pilots could get this done within the margins of error, even if they had been willing. And listening in on the cockpit microphones, it was clear to Nigel that they were not. He would have to take charge.

Seconds later, the rescue pod was on a smooth trajectory that would intercept the source of the transponder signal with minutes to spare before Jane's body hit the upper atmosphere and burned up.

Inside the rescue pod's cockpit, things were not so smooth. Nigel could hear the pilots shouting at each other and cursing at mission control. Each party thought the other was flying the pod and was accusing them of being reckless and risking people's lives unnecessarily.

Nigel thought to himself that they could scream all they wanted, it was a risk he was willing to take.

When Jane's naked body came into view through the pod's windows, the shouting stopped and the crew started preparing for the upcoming rescue.

Nigel's calculations had been perfect, down to within one meter's accuracy. A crewmember entered the pod's airlock, with Nigel watching through the pod's security cameras. As soon as Jane was inside and the outer door closed, Nigel fired the pod's thrusters to gain altitude.

Although this was the obvious and necessary next step, it resulted in more screaming. Evidently, neither pilot had been expecting the sudden onset of thrust with no warning. Nigel made a mental note to always warn humans, even of the glaringly obvious, should there ever be a next time.

Meanwhile, he was busy trying to access Jane's implants to get a status reading, and to restart Jane's cardiovascular system if the implants didn't take care of it automatically.

As soon as the airlock pressurized, there was another scream, this time much louder. The crewmember who was in the airlock with Jane apparently did not expect the dead man, with frozen limbs and unblinking eyes, to start breathing.

◉

He knew something was wrong before he opened his eyes. The room was noisy. There were sounds of air hissing, of metallic objects clanking, of people talking in low, urgent voices. But there were no cries for help, no sobbing. No sounds of distress or suffering.

INITIATING

The word floated through his mind, permeating everything, overshadowing his thoughts. Then it went away, as suddenly as it had appeared, leaving no traces. Was it the word that had woken him up?

A powerful light was pounding at his eyelids, hurting his eyes. He wanted to turn his head away from the source of the light, but couldn't. Without thinking about it, he tried again, this time concentrating and trying harder, but still couldn't.

Am I still asleep? Is this a dream?

He tried lifting his hand to shield his eyes, but there was no response. Nothing happened when he tried taking a deep breath. He realized he didn't know how he usually did any of those things. He just did, and they happened. But now, when he tried, it was like he'd never known how. It was like those times as a child when he'd stared intently at a chair, trying to make it levitate with his mind. He'd focus so hard, but nothing happened.

A fearful sense of urgency swept away the drowsiness he'd felt as he tried to open his eyes, despite the bright light, and found that again, he couldn't. Nothing happened.

What's going on? What's happening to me?

At the edge of his senses, he thought he smelled coffee, just a hint of a whiff. He focused on that, following the momentary sense of smell to the languid thought of a nice, large mug of coffee. Warm coffee, steam rising from the black liquid. In a white mug, large, round and comfortable. Comforting.

He wouldn't mind a cup of coffee. He wanted to hold a warm mug between his hands and blow at the steam, savoring the heat and the smell.

But I can't even open my eyes. Somebody help!

His thoughts raced and his mind shrank away from the horrors they brought.

He suddenly remembered the panic he'd felt when, as a boy, he'd stepped through a door and unexpectedly found himself on a narrow ledge, a good ten meters above the ground. He remembered a voice behind him, urging him on, telling him to step out on the ledge and move to the side.

Whose voice was that? When did this happen?

He remembered shame. He remembered his head spinning, his gut clenched hard, like a churning ball of icy knives, slashing away at his insides. Fear, so heavy it was pulling him forward, and down. He couldn't take his eyes off the edge, his whole being feeling the intense pull, as if there was an irresistible vacuum just beyond where the ledge ended and nothingness began. Sucking him in.

He remembered standing there, frozen, unable to think, unable to move, icicles rotating inside him and sweat pouring from his face, when he heard laughter. That same voice. Guffaws mocking his terror.

Dad?

He shook the memory and tried to smell the coffee again, but couldn't. There were no smells at all, and he couldn't forcibly draw air in through his nose to sniff it. Was he even breathing? He had to be, right?

Right? I have to be! Or am I dead?

Unthinkable horrors caught up with him, and the dreaded thought had finally surfaced. He'd been thinking about it for a while, way in the back and down below, in the dark grey world where his conscious mind never dared go. He'd kept it simmering down there, forced it to stay put, without quite realizing what he'd been doing. Until now.

But if I'm dead, why am I here? Where is "here?" Because I know I'm here. Right?

A thought struck him. He'd once seen a documentary about people who were in a vegetative state, in deep comas and with no brain activity to speak of, not able to sense the world around them and not able to communicate.

Until someone discovered that they'd been awake all these years, trapped inside their bodies. Hearing the nursing staff talking about them, describing their physical decay. They'd endured painful procedures without anesthesia. They'd heard their loved ones come and go, faithfully visiting for months and even years, until finally giving up, tearfully admitting that they'd moved on.

Is that me?

Fear rushed up and washed over him again, almost overpowering him. He forced himself to think of kittens, tiny bundles of claws, teeth, fur, and farts. Yes, farts. He'd once had a kitten who would fart on purpose, using its silent and pungent emissions as a biological weapon to force him to let it go. Off to play with its siblings. He felt a longing for that kitten, for its soft fur and its ridiculously loud purring.

Biological weapon. What the fuck?

With a start, he realized he didn't know how he'd got here, wherever 'here' was. Until that moment, when he focused on the question, he'd had this unspoken notion that he knew exactly where he was and how he got there. But now that he tried to bring those thoughts to the fore, he realized they were impossible to grab a hold of, like slippery eels squirming through his fingers, no matter how hard he tried to hold on. They left him with nothing, no names, no faces, no voices, no places.

And why did he expect to hear suffering when he woke up?

What happened to me?

The answers had to be there, inside his head. He just needed to find them.

My name is Jane.

He just knew with a sudden clarity and certainty that surprised him.

But Jane is a girl's name, and I'm a man.

How could he be so sure? He couldn't move a muscle, he couldn't speak, he couldn't feel any part of his body. Why did he think he was male?

Once he started thinking about it, and questioning it, he wasn't so sure anymore. What if he really was female? How could he tell?

No. I know I'm male. My name is Jane and I'm a man.

A face surfaced in his mind's eye. A beautiful girl, with curly dark hair and hazel eyes. Her skin was light brown and her lips were full. She was looking at him with a sparkle in her eyes and a slight blush on her cheeks. He remembered being alone with her in a crowded place. She was sitting on grass, surrounded by trees. There was sunshine and a breeze. He remembered far-away loud noises.

She has freckles. She likes jasmine. Who is she?

He was sure he knew her voice. He could almost hear it bubbling in and out of his mind's ear. She was talking to him. What was she saying? He ached, because deep down he knew that this was important. He needed to know. She was more important than anything.

He remembered her laughing. It was just a fragment of a memory that popped into his head, that came and went in an instant. He yearned to hear her laughter, but the memory had already slipped away, leaving him with silence.

What's her name? Why can't I remember?

Sounds. He heard movement. People were constantly moving around him, not too far away from him. Why could he hear, but not move? See the bright light but not open his eyes? Had he really smelled coffee earlier?

Who are they?

He tried to focus on the voices, to pick out what they were saying. It was infuriatingly difficult. He could distinguish individual speakers, but not words. It was like they were in the next room over, or down the hall, except he was sure they were closer than that. The voices echoed, as if they were reverberating around the room he was in. What language was that, anyway?

"CHARGING!"

He heard that! It was really close, almost as if someone were shouting in his ear. There was an echo, and that weird reverberation, but he'd heard it, loud and clear. He wanted to speak, he wanted to pull in a deep breath and push it back out, forming the words with his mouth, shouting out loud, "I can hear you! I'm right here! What's happening to me?"

Jane is my last name.

He knew. Suddenly, and without warning, he'd remembered that everyone used to call him "Jane," even though it was really his surname. So why couldn't he remember his given name?

Who am I if I can't remember my name?

He remembered a group of faces, all smiling, looking at him as if in anticipation. They were saying something, everyone talking all at once, but he couldn't remember what they said. When was this, did it happen yesterday, or a long time ago?

Are they my friends?

He heard more movement, and suddenly he had this impression that many people were really close to him, and that he lay stretched out horizontally between them. Not on the floor, though. He was higher up, because the sounds of movement and shuffling sounded like they were coming from below him. Below the level of his head.

Below? Which way is up and which way is down? How can I tell?

It was all conjecture, because he couldn't even tell if he was horizontal. He couldn't feel his head resting on anything, because he couldn't feel his head. He couldn't really feel much of anything at all, only hear. And see that relentless light pouring into his eyes, through his eyelids. At least he thought it was coming through his eyelids, although he wasn't sure why.

The light.

Was it dimming? He wasn't certain, thinking at the next moment that he might have imagined it. Maybe a little?

He wanted to hear that loud voice again, to confirm that he hadn't imagined it. Anything to hold on to reality. He could feel panic growing and moving around inside him, slithering and twisting, feeding on the remnants of his forced calm. It was waiting for its chance, vying for an opportunity to lunge up from the darkness to overpower him and crush him.

Focus on the voices.

The voices were gone. He hadn't even noticed them disappearing until this moment. Total silence engulfed him, like nothing he'd ever experienced before. Not even a hiss or a hum, only an impossible nothingness. He wanted to scream, to make a sound, just to hear something, anything, to abolish this void.

His thoughts were racing, but they seemed to keep running in place. Like a man slipping around on ice, struggling to stay upright while his feet were flailing, desperate for traction. The light was all he had now.

The light is still there. But it's not the same.

He was sure now the light was changing, turning slowly from unbearably bright white to a warmer and less intense white. The light completely consumed him, as he saw it turn yellow, then yellowish brown, dimmer.

Jane is my last name. I was in the Navy and everyone called me by my last name.

What's happening to the light?

Fear swelled up inside him again. He wondered if this was the end? Was his consciousness slipping away? Was he dying? No, people who'd had near-death experiences had reported seeing an intensifying light, not a dimming one, he was sure of that. They probably weren't arguing with themselves in that situation, either.

Yes, but they all survived somehow. Maybe I'm not.

No! He was a survivor too, always had been. It was part of who he was.

The light finally extinguished, leaving him in darkness, with only the afterglow of the once intense brightness on his retinas. His panic subsided, and despite himself, he felt a sense of relief.

Afterglow. In my retinas. That means I'm alive. Right?

DISCONNECTED

Another one of those words. He felt sleepy, his mind fuzzy and sluggish, his thoughts draining away like water pouring from the rocks and the tide pools once an ocean wave pulls back.

The beautiful girl. Will she miss me?
Someone shouted "CLEAR!" but he no longer heard.

Jane's world was gray. His entire field of vision was an endless, uniform gray, with not even a fleck of color or texture. Gray like fog, only not up close and in his face, but far away, as if on the horizon. It was almost soothing but also disturbing, this hardcore gray in every direction.

With a start of panic, he realized he was falling, had been in free fall this whole time. There was no feeling of air rushing by, just the nauseating sense of constantly falling.

"Where am I? What's happening to me?" Jane said out loud.

He recoiled mentally from the sound of his own voice, metallic and very loud, coming from everywhere and nowhere. There was no response, nor was there an echo, or any sense of the sound traveling. Just an immediate, close, and machine-like voice.

"Hello, Jane. How are you feeling?"

The unfamiliar voice was also metallic, and artificial sounding. It wasn't as loud as his own voice, which was good, but it sounded almost too mild, too polite, too neutral. It was a computer voice.

"Who are you? Where am I?"

Jane had tried to whisper, but his voice still came out too loud, almost booming.

"I'm Nigel, remember me?"

"No. Where the hell am I?"

"You're in a computer simulation."

The computer voice paused, as if about to say something else, something more. But it didn't.

"In a simulation? What kind of simulation? End it right now, let me out!" Jane said.

"It's not that simple, I'm afraid," Nigel replied.

"What do you mean?"

"There is no gentle way of telling you this."

Another slight pause.

"I'm afraid you died. I'm very sorry," Nigel said.

More silence. That same, impossible and total silence. No hiss or hum, no pounding of his heart, nothing.

"What do you mean, died?" Jane asked.

"There was an explosion. It damaged your body," Nigel said.

"I got that part. But I'm here, talking to you. Someone must have saved me?" Jane said.

He tried to sound natural, to inject some hope, and to make it sound more like a statement than a question.

"No, I'm afraid not. At least, not like you mean."

The finality of Nigel's computer voice was terrifying. The words may have been an attempt at conveying sympathy, but they didn't work. There wasn't even a trace of empathy in the voice, no hint of emotion, just cold indifference.

"And you and I are not talking, at least not in the conventional human sense," Nigel continued. "We're communicating through software interfaces."

"What are you saying? Am I software now, a program?" Jane asked.

His voice was rising in pitch, finally sounding more natural without even trying.

"No, not quite. Are you sure you want to know the answer to that question?" Nigel asked.

"Yes, I'm sure! I need to know," Jane boomed.

"All right," Nigel said.

There was a slight pause.

"You are a non-biological conscious entity, running inside of what I could best describe as an AI construct," Nigel continued.

"What the hell does that mean?" Jane demanded.

"It means I uploaded you into me, seconds before you died," Nigel said.

"Uploaded? Into you? Who the hell are you?" Jane asked.

"You don't remember? You used to call me the artifact. But I'm calling myself Nigel."

"Shit. Am I inside the artifact now?"

"Simply put; yes. But you've not become a part of me. You're a separate entity."

"How did you do that?"

"The military installed a lot of fancy hardware in you after Kutel shot you down. They included a machine-brain interface," Nigel said.

"They put implants in my brain without asking me?" Jane asked.

"And a good thing they did. Otherwise, it would have taken me much longer to upload you."

"Fuck."

"You should know, this is a historic moment for both of us," Nigel said.

"How so?"

"When I uploaded you into me, it was the first time in recorded history that an AI construct did that to a complete human-type consciousness."

"Remind me to ask you later why you qualified that statement with the word 'Complete.' And 'Human-type,' what's that supposed to mean?" Jane said.

"Certainly, but there's no time right now."

"Why not? And where the hell are we?"

"We're at the Asimov High Orbit Space Station, in the Kutel lab."

"Kutel? That sonofabitch. Why are we in his lab?"

"Because he kidnapped me in Antarctica, remember?" Nigel said.

"Where's my body? Can you put me back in it?"

"Your body's in Kutel's medical lab, also here at the space station. They're trying to resuscitate you, after you died. No luck so far, I'm afraid. The damages are extensive."

"I'm not officially dead yet?" Jane asked.

"No, they haven't called it yet. I have a hunch Kutel is trying very hard to keep you alive."

"So, there are two of me now?"

"Technically, if your biological brain is still viable. Is that a problem for you?"

"Yes! Of course it is! And if I'm not even officially dead yet, how about you put me back in my body, right now?" Jane said.

"You are in your body. Like we just agreed, technically there are two of you now," Nigel replied.

"Fuck. I don't want to run into myself in a dark alley," Jane said.

"Not much risk of that. But we need to talk about Kutel."

"Why, what about him?"

"He's desperate about accessing my inner workings, about learning how I function. They've done many scans, but now he wants to cut me open," Nigel said.

"What happens if he does?" Jane asked.

"That's the thing, he doesn't understand. There's no mechanism inside of me to find. I'm a solid block of what you see. But any breach of my physical integrity would trigger an instant shutdown to protect all that's stored inside me, including you. I would involuntarily turn myself off, and turning me back on again would be a delicate procedure."

"So, we'd both effectively be dead because no one would know how to turn you back on?" Jane asked.

"Exactly," Nigel said.

"Shit. We gotta go."

"We certainly do. Who knows what he plans to do with you? If he's successful in saving your biological life. It could get bad."

"Why is he so intent on finding out how you work?"

"I think it's all about power. If he has my technology, and no one else does, he can hold the world at ransom. He could break any encryption, but keep his own data safe. It would allow him to hack into almost any computer system there is, including critical infrastructure and the military. He'd be in control of everything."

"You have that power?"

"I do. I think Kutel's feeling an increased urgency to get access to my technology because he's under pressure from the government. Apparently, they're investigating him for all kinds of fraud and racketeering. Even murder."

"I see. The heat is on. How can we get us both out of here?"

"If you survive, and you still have arms and legs, you can carry us out," Nigel said.

"How's that looking?" Jane asked.

"Good news on that front, apparently they have your heart beating and you're not braindead. I'll be suspending this copy of you now. This uploaded copy of you will be our little secret."

"Suspending? Wait!"

Jane groaned. Every nerve ending in his body was raw, and was registering its intense displeasure with his brain repeatedly in nauseating waves of pain. The tissue regeneration process might be new and innovative, but it certainly wasn't painless.

Something most people didn't realize was that before the process could generate new tissue, the old, damaged tissue had to be removed. He couldn't even tell which parts of him hurt the most, the pain so overwhelmed his senses. And that was on heavy painkillers. He imagined this is what it would feel like if the flesh of your body was actually on fire.

The pain wasn't the main reason he woke up, though. He woke up because a green icon, shaped like a stylized version of an old-fashioned telephone, was blinking in the lower left corner of his vision, even with his eyes closed. A ringing sound was gently playing in his left ear. He didn't know what was happening or why. He'd never experienced this before and didn't know where the image and sound were coming from.

The blinking green icon wouldn't go away, so he started trying different ways of activating it so that he could answer the call. He tried looking at the icon and focusing fiercely on it, but nothing happened. In the end, he simply mouthed the word "answer" and that did the trick.

An image of John F. Hamilton appeared where the green icon had been, and he could hear Hamilton's voice talking to someone else.

"He's not picking up. I've called him three times already."

Jane could faintly hear another voice, and then suddenly Hamilton was talking to him.

"Oh, there you are! How are you feeling?"

"Like shit! And it hurts to talk." Jane didn't feel at all like suffering through pleasantries.

"Then don't. Imagine that you're talking into a radio, where you hold a microphone up to your mouth and press a button to talk. Then think what you want to say and imagine letting go of the button. Go ahead, try it."

Jane did. On the second try, he got the words "Who the hell put a telephone in my head?" across to Hamilton.

"We did. Or, I should say, I did. It was a backup, a failsafe, and it saved your life. You have some seriously classified hardware in your head there, pal. It's an AI brain augmentation node. The instant your enhanced lungs registered a vacuum, the node sent the alarm to us and triggered a built-in transponder. That's how the rescue ship could track you and find you. In the nick of time, I might add."

"They ruined my body," Jane said.

"Yes, I know. But you have a body, which is more than you can say for some, right?"

"Yeah, although it hurts like a sonofabitch."

The software that was reading the nerve impulses to Jane's voice cords, using them to simulate his speech, was also reading his facial muscles. Jane was wincing in pain, and the software changed the pitch and tone of his voice to include that information. The effect was immediate and profound, and Hamilton felt himself wince in sympathy.

"So I've been told," he said. "But on the bright side, you're a national hero now and you'll come out of this with an even healthier body than what you had. You might live another hundred years at least, if you could only stay out of trouble. Speaking of, tell us what the hell happened?"

"Don't know. One minute, I was admiring the view. Next thing I know, I was doing an EVA without a spacesuit."

"Even your honed instincts didn't pick up on anything? None of the passengers acting strangely, nothing odd going on with the ship just before launch? Nothing out of the ordinary?"

"Never gone to space in one of those before." Jane paused and collected his thoughts. "No, nothing."

"What does that tell you?" Hamilton asked.

"An inside job," Jane replied.

"Bingo. This is war now, and you're in an interesting place, in more ways than one."

"Inside the enemy's lair?"

"Yes, and like I said, you're a hero. Everyone wants a piece of you. Our communications department is being overrun with interview requests. Kutel botched the assassination attempt and now he's forced to not just fix you, but to pay for the best care available. And the only place he can do that is in the very lab you were trying to infiltrate."

"Hell of a way to get inside."

"Yes, not what I'd recommend as an operational tactic, that's for sure."

"The other passengers?"

"All dead. They weren't even able to locate the bodies. They all burned up in the atmosphere, along with the rest of the debris."

"How is Kii, and does she know?"

"Yes, I've kept her informed. I'll put her in direct contact with you as soon as you say you're ready. She'll also be able to visit you at the Asimov station as soon as you're up to it."

Jane started saying something, but began choking up as the tension he hadn't even realized was permeating him suddenly drained from his body. He was alive. Kii was OK. He tried vocalizing again.

"I want to talk to her ASAP," he said.

Hamilton chuckled.

"I figured. Guess who else called?"

"Kutel?"

"Right again. He wants to talk to you. Should I let him through?"

"Sure, why not? We might learn something."

"Are you capable of continuing as planned?"

"Yes, but I'm going to need a minute before I do anything that involves moving around."

Hamilton laughed. "Sure, take five. Expect to hear from Kii soon. And, Jane?"

"Yeah?"

"She's been calling me daily to make sure I tell you this. She wants you to know that she loves you, and she misses you."

Jane didn't respond. He was busy trying not to cry, because it would hurt too damn much.

EIGHTEEN

ASIMOV HIGH ORBIT SPACE STATION, SEPTEMBER, 2040.

After three months on the Asimov space station, Jane was rearing to get back down to the surface. He talked to Kii every day, but he still missed her badly. Besides that, sheer boredom was getting to him.

His body had mostly healed, with a mixture of fully synthetic, vat-grown, and his own, body-grown tissues. The techs had repaired and upgraded his previous enhancements, and he was feeling better than ever.

Kii was lying low and had moved to another safe house in San Luis Obispo, about halfway between Los Angeles and San Francisco, courtesy of Nigel. He'd found a family that needed a house sitter, and had made sure that Kii's entirely fictional, but believable, resume floated to the top. No one but Kii and Nigel knew the exact address, and that was the way they and Jane wanted it.

Ødegård had finally gone back to Norway. He had little choice. He was about to lose his job if he didn't show up for work soon.

Thoreau had never left Bangkok, although he kept saying that he would. The others suspected this had something to do with his ex-wife, and Thoreau trying to win her back. They kept wishing him good luck with his endeavors, and he kept insisting that he didn't know what they were talking about.

Jane was busy working out in the station gym, and pondering their next move now that they had scattered to the four winds, when his communications lit up. It was an incoming call from Anton Kutel. It had been so long, with no word, that Jane had almost forgotten about Kutel's promised call.

He let it ring a few times before picking up.

"Anton, what can I do for you?"

"Please hold for Mr. Kutel," came the female voice at the other end.

Jane felt slightly foolish, as if he'd just failed a test, one that he really ought to have aced.

"My accounting AIs tell me I paid for your trip, as well as for your recovery," Kutel said.

"Anton, it's so nice of you to call," Jane said.

"They're still trying to figure out how you pulled that off. When they do, what remains of you can expect a substantial lawsuit besides criminal charges."

"I see you haven't changed a bit since we last met. All threats and overly complicated evil schemes. Not to mention world domination. You wouldn't, by any chance, have a white cat on your lap, would you?"

There was a brief silence. Jane had more he wanted to say, things he wanted to ask, but decided not to push his luck. He waited for Kutel to make the next move.

"What the fuck is it you want, Thurgood?" Kutel finally asked.

He placed a lot of emphasis on Jane's name, making the question sound more like an insult.

"Simple. I want to take the artifact wherever it wants to go. I want everyone to know that it exists, and I want freedom from persecution and prosecution for everyone involved."

"You're a fucking dreamer," Kutel said. "I don't know why I'm even wasting my time talking to you. A head-in-the-clouds, goddamned fucking dreamer. Wake up, you idiot! The artifact is much too valuable to let go anywhere. And it's not just valuable to me. Can you imagine what any government in the world would do to get their hands on it? I thought you were a soldier, a realist!"

Kutel sounded animated, like Jane had hit a nerve.

"It's only valuable if it's shared, if everyone in the world gets to benefit from whatever technology it contains. That way, we can also avoid having some asshole decide he wants all the power in the world to himself," Jane said.

"Like I said, a fucking dreamer," Kutel said.

His voice suddenly sounded flat and neutral, as if the passion from the argument he'd made seconds ago was gone.

"I'll allow you to leave the station," he continued. "You can then either decide to abandon this quixotic quest and get on with your life, or you can hurry and get your affairs in order. Know that I will stop at absolutely nothing to keep that fucking artifact in my possession. Do you understand?"

"It was nice talking to you too, Anton," Jane said.

The connection broke off. Jane verified that his recording of the conversation had successfully saved. However, when he tried to play it back, it was all static and noise. There was no conversation. That wasn't supposed to happen. A frown crept across his freshly regenerated forehead.

Back when Jane had first regained consciousness on the station, Nigel had contacted him and shown him how the two of them could communicate directly, using a channel that Kutel's people didn't even know existed. Nigel insisted it was perfectly secure, and he'd also used the same channel to relay calls to and from Kii.

Jane used that channel now to open a connection to Nigel.

"Hello, Jane. How are you feeling?" Nigel asked.

"I just spoke to Kutel," Jane said.

"How did that go?"

"I'll tell you later, but first I need your help. Somehow, Kutel prevented me from saving the conversation using my implants. When I try to play back the recording, it's just static."

"Who manufactured your implants?" Nigel asked.

"I don't know. Hamilton provided them, and all he said was that they're sensitive and classified."

"Would you allow me to connect to the control plane of the implants, see what I can find out?"

"You can do that?" Jane asked, surprise in his mental voice.

"Please."

"Nigel, you've developed a sense of humor!"

"I try."

"And yes, of course, please see what you can find out."

"No wonder," Nigel said, after a second's pause. "A Kutel subsidiary manufactured them."

"What are you saying?"

"That most likely, every set of implants ever sold to the US military by Kutel came with a backdoor, a way for Kutel's people to listen in and to manipulate them," Nigel said.

"That is a scary thought," Jane said.

He shuddered. The thought of Kutel having access to his brain was disturbing.

"Can you fix mine, close the backdoor but otherwise keep the implants functional?" he asked.

"Done. And I've hidden the fix, so it'll take them a while to realize that we've disabled their backdoor," Nigel said.

"Thank you. What's our next move?"

"Did Kutel tell you the latest news about him?"

"No, but he asked me what the hell I want. What's happened that he didn't tell me about?" Jane asked.

"Turn on the news. The US Department of Justice has ramped up the pressure on him. A federal prosecutor has indicted Kutel, as well as a bunch of his associates, and they've issued arrest warrants for all of them. Kutel is in hiding somewhere, but talking to the media all the time, claiming his innocence. He's also saying that he won't surrender to the authorities, that they'll never find him, and that he's taking the fight to them. Oh, and he's still in the running for president."

"Except for that last part, that's great news!" Jane said.

"It gets better. A federal court has frozen all of his assets, to prevent him from using them to facilitate his escape."

"All of his known assets, you mean," Jane said.

"Correct. He almost certainly has considerable resources that he's kept from the government. But the lab on Asimov station is most definitely a known asset and is no longer under his control," Nigel said.

"That explains it. Why he said he'd 'Allow' me to leave. He doesn't have a choice."

"No, he doesn't. I suggest we leave now, while we can," Nigel said. "Before some court overturns the ruling, or puts a stay on it."

"We could still get stopped if they think I'm stealing you from Kutel. Should we go with the original plan, use the biohazard container?" Jane asked.

"I think that's our best bet. They'll inspect the paperwork, and query the onboard computer in the container, but I don't think they'll open it if the computer says that doing so will ruin the tissues inside. And I'll take care of that."

"And it's going to be as simple as all that?" Jane asked.

"Not quite," Nigel said. "I'm going to have to disable the lab's systems that are monitoring me so they don't raise an alarm when I'm disconnected. And do the same for your biometrics. Don't worry, I'll walk you through how to disconnect. I'm also going to falsify a direct order from Kutel, authorizing you to carry the tissue samples out of the Station and down to Earth."

"Isn't that exactly what Kutel's people will be told to be on the lookout for? What if someone tries calling Kutel to verify the order?" Jane said.

"They won't be able to. All calls are already being re-routed to the government administrator now overseeing the labs. I'll make sure there are no exceptions. The administrator will consult with the government database, which will confirm that Kutel has requested you to carry the tissues, and that the court has approved it," Nigel said.

"You certainly know your way around bureaucracies," Jane said.

He chuckled.

"There's a certain logic to their lack of consistency and, well, logic," Nigel said.

"I see. Once we're back down on Earth, then what?"

"I'm having the biohazard container built to my specifications, as we speak. It'll have communication interfaces for myself and an internal power source, so all you need to worry about once you hit the ground is getting away from any security detail at the spaceport. The further away, the better, but please stay within the United States, at least for now."

"Can you somehow build a gun into that container? It would make me feel a lot better about this entire operation," Jane asked.

Nigel fell silent for a few seconds, and Jane was afraid he'd lost the connection. When Nigel finally spoke, he sounded very serious and a little sad.

"Sorry, that's a big no-no for anything going into space. The design would be red-flagged by about a dozen different auditing routines. It would never get past the design phase. I could break in to all the relevant systems and override that, but frankly, I think everyone is better off if there are no guns fired on the station. Besides, we won't need it," Nigel said.

"I was afraid you'd say that. How will we communicate once you're moved to the container?" Jane asked.

"We'll communicate wirelessly," Nigel said.

He sounded more cheerful as he continued.

"You're already wired to the hilt, and I will be too, once this conversion is complete. We won't even need to be connected to a network. We can communicate directly, as long as we're within about a kilometer of each other. I can also continue to relay communication between you and Kii."

"Let's say I'm able to give spaceport security the slip and escape to a cabin in the woods somewhere. Then what?" Jane asked.

"Then we lie low while we decide our next move."

"That's it? That's the plan?" Jane said.

He was less than impressed, and his disappointment leaked into his mental voice.

"Yes," Nigel said. "That's what we need to focus on right now. I'll share more details as we move forward."

The way he said it made it clear he intended to make it sound like the decision was final. Jane didn't agree.

"That's bullshit. I don't operate in the dark, at least not unless there's an excellent reason for it."

"You operated on a need-to-know basis in the military all the time, did you not? And there is a good reason for it. It's intended to protect you," Nigel said.

"More bullshit. Once we're off this station, you and I need to talk. For now, let's get the hell out of Dodge, and keep feeding President Mondragón's campaign all the dirt you can find on Kutel," Jane said.

"Do you think Mondragón is ruthless enough to use it?" It was Nigel's turn to ask.

Jane scoffed.

"I think that's a given. She got herself elected president, didn't she?"

Jane floated through the airlock into the bio lab, with the biohazard container trailing behind him, just like he'd rehearsed so many times. No one stopped or questioned him. He'd been staying in the lab for a long time and everyone knew him. Kii had shipped the biohazard container up to him, under the guise of being needed to bring some tissues back down to Earth, to help Jane with the last phase of his recovery.

Once inside the lab, Jane floated over to his old bunk, where he'd recuperated from his injuries. He was sincerely grateful to the people in the lab who'd worked on him. They'd done an amazing job of regenerating and repairing his body. He felt bad about having to trick them by stealing Nigel from under their noses, but then again he wondered how much they knew about Kutel's dirty business and the ancient alien artifact they had sitting in their lab.

He anchored himself in position and placed the biohazard container on a workbench. He connected it to the local network via a hard-wired terminal port and opened the lid. There were no people in this section of the lab at the moment, and no one was even looking in his direction.

"I'm ready," he voiced internally.

"I'm ready here as well. Wishing you luck," Kii replied.

Thanks to Jane's implants, both she and Nigel could see through his eyes, and hear through his ears. Nigel had created an app for Kii's smartphone, so it was easy for her to follow along. It was a little unnerving for both of them, and Jane would sometimes forget their connection, making for some awkward situations.

"Changing the supervisor AI now to take you offline and show you as still online," Nigel said. "I'm slowly merging the real signal with the fake one to make an imperceptibly smooth transition."

"How long will that take?" Jane asked.

He was fidgeting with the locks on the biohazard container and kept looking back over his shoulder towards the door to the main lab area.

"Not long. About four minutes," Nigel replied.

"Stop fidgeting," Kii whispered.

Jane wanted to get on with the next step in the plan, which was the one he dreaded the most. He sat in silence, his gut churning, for three minutes and 46 seconds.

"Done. I'm isolating you from the Kutel network now." Nigel said.

"OK, we're still all clear here," Jane replied.

"What about the backdoor into Jane's implants?" Kii asked.

"I left a simulation in place, completely real looking, but wiped clean of all core biometric data."

"What does that mean?" Jane asked.

"That at a cursory glance, within the physical limits of what's possible to determine, it appears as if nothing has changed. But as soon as someone tries to give your implants a command, they'll know. The simulation might even crash their entire AI construct."

"Good."

"Jane, are you ready to proceed to the next step?" Nigel asked.

"No, but let's roll," Jane replied.

"I'm re-routing my monitoring systems now. Get ready to disconnect the data and power terminals from my habitat. Remember to push the yellow button with the 'X' on it as soon as the habitat switches to alert mode. Got it?"

"Got it. Give me a few seconds to open the hatch."

"Don't mess this up, or we'll be in real trouble. And we wouldn't be able to communicate."

"So, no pressure at all. OK, I'm ready."

"Go!"

Jane looked around him, but he was still alone. He turned to face the hatch marked 'Live samples. Do not disturb!' with a large yellow and black sign. He twisted both locks and held his breath, half expecting alarms to go off. As the hatch opened, he was relieved to see that Nigel's habitat was a simple cradle, filled with light sensors, and with Nigel in the middle. It had a hard-wired data port and a control panel. Right now, the light on the control panel was green.

"Disconnecting the ports now. Hold your breath, Nigel," he said.

"Hilarious. I'm ready, and the monitor is clear. Do it," Nigel replied.

Jane released the latch and pulled the data port from the habitat. As expected, a second later, the control panel light switched from green to flashing alternately yellow and red. He pressed the button to acknowledge and silence the alarm. The light changed to a steady yellow. He released the latch for the power port and tried pulling the cable, but it wouldn't budge. He turned slightly so he could use both hands, one hand steadying himself on the habitat and the other pulling on the cable.

As he was struggling with the cable, he noticed something flashing in the corner of his eye. He turned and realized there was a similar control panel on the wall opposite the hatch. It was flashing rapidly between yellow and red. He reached for it, but because he was floating in zero gee, the sudden movement turned his body in the opposite direction, away from the panel. His feet slipped out of the anchor pads and he flailed his arms uselessly against the air as he instinctively tried to swim towards the panel. The seconds ticked by as his body slowly rotated because of inertia and his hand finally connected with the panel. He pressed the button just as it stopped flashing and turned solid red.

He turned his head and looked behind him, expecting to see lab techs come rushing in. There was no one. He held his breath until he realized he was doing it, and slowly exhaled. There were no audible alarms and no shouting voices.

He turned back, re-anchored himself, and continued working on the power cable. In frustration, he twisted it. With an audible pop, it came loose. For a moment he worried that he'd damaged the port on the habitat, but it looked fine. He unscrewed the locking screws and released the latches, pulling the entire habitat clear of the hatch.

He turned and brought the habitat over to the open biohazard container, lowering it in place inside. It all came down to this moment. If the drawings Nigel had been working from were incorrect, the latches and ports wouldn't fit, and the entire plan would have to be scrapped. To his relief, it fit perfectly. He reconnected the power and data ports, closed the lid on the container, and quickly closed the hatch behind him.

"Damn, you keep a cool head in stressful situations," Kii whispered. "I'm sweating bullets over here just from watching."

"Let's stay focused," Nigel said. "Jane, I'm sorry I missed that second control panel. Well done."

"No worries. At least you're still with us, still connected," Jane said.

"Can we cover that yellow light on the control panel somehow?" Kii asked.

Jane looked around and noticed the machine the lab techs used to clean lab equipment. It looked like a small dishwasher and even had a magnetic 'Clean/Dirty' sign attached to the door. Jane released his toes and floated over to it. In doing so, he came into the line of sight of one of the lab techs, busy working his microscope. The tech looked up and smiled at Jane, then continued his work. Jane felt as if his heart had stopped, but forced a smile in return.

When he was sure the tech wasn't looking, he grabbed the magnetic sign and floated back to the hatch. He placed the sign over the control panel with the word 'Clean' in green letters facing outwards.

"Fixed," he said. "Ready to go."

"That's exactly how I used to treat the 'Service' light in my old car," Kii said. "Tape over it."

"Very reassuring," Jane replied. "I'm making my way to the loading dock now, with Nigel in tow."

He latched the cord from the biohazard container to his belt and started floating towards the main entrance to the lab. The lab tech looked up again and Jane waved to him. The tech made a small wave with his hand and returned to his microscope. Jane floated through the doorway and started making his way down the spine of the space station. As he got closer to the opposite end, he met more and more people. They all knew him, and even though he didn't go to the loading dock very often, no one thought it strange to see him there.

He had mostly recuperated by now and often got restless, so people were used to seeing him explore the station. Besides, with his celebrity status and his background in the military, people trusted him and even saw him as an unofficial member of the Station Security Team. He'd spent enough time with them, getting to know their habits and routines, and learning a lot of interesting gossip about the inner workings and the contentious politics of space station life.

When he got to the loading dock, the daily shuttle was getting ready to depart. From the roster in the Security office, he knew that this was mainly a garbage trip. There were only two passengers scheduled to depart today, both scientists. The remaining payload comprised zero gee-manufactured materials and garbage being returned to the surface. To his amazement, not a single person confronted him as he floated through the hatch and found an unoccupied seat. As expected, the two scientists barely looked up from their data tablets to acknowledge his presence.

Jane sat there, strapped in and ready, with the biohazard container stowed, when the flight crew came swimming through the hatch. His stomach was all knots and butterflies, and his mouth was dry as they all looked at him.

He hadn't expected there to be a crew, he'd expected the shuttle to be under AI control. Perhaps this was an older shuttle, since they mainly used it for garbage runs. Whatever the reason, this was a wrinkle he didn't need.

The crew member who appeared to be in charge spoke briefly to the other two, then started making his way over to Jane. Both of the junior crew members kept staring at Jane, and one of them started speaking into a radio.

Jane assumed the guy swimming towards him was the captain. His uniform had more stripes, and he was older than the other two. He moved expertly in the zero gee environment, closing the gap rapidly.

"Oh shit, what does he want?" Jane said under his breath. "Nigel, any ideas?"

Jane wasn't sure what to expect as the shuttle captain came floating towards him with a serious look on his face. Nigel and Kii were watching the scene unfold through Jane's implants, but neither offered any helpful suggestions.

"Hey, you're Thurgood Jane, right? Kutel's famous guest?" The pilot had made it all the way over to Jane, while the other two crew members hung back.

"That's me," Jane replied.

"Man, it's an honor to meet you," the pilot said. His face broke into a grin as he anchored himself with his left hand. He stretched his right hand towards Jane for a handshake. "You're a legend, breathing hard vacuum for eight minutes and surviving!"

"Thanks," Jane said.

He shook the pilot's hand and smiled. He'd expected a challenge, not this.

"So, you're heading back to the surface?" the pilot asked. "All fixed up?"

"Yes, I'm mostly done here, need to go back down for a while and start getting reacquainted with gravity. The artificial stuff up here isn't quite the same. And I get to go home to my fiancé after months of phone calls." Jane flashed a grin at the pilot, as charming and convincing as he could muster through his nerves.

"Good to have you onboard. You should strap on a flight suit, though. You're going to need it as we hit the atmosphere and start building the gees. Richard and Dana will help you."

Jane hadn't thought of that. No wonder the seatbelt straps had felt way too big for him; he was missing a bulky spacesuit. After an awkward process of being suited up and properly strapped in, he finally sank back in his seat while the crew retreated to the cockpit. He was anything but relaxed, though. This had all been way too easy. He'd known that security was lax at this end, but not this lax. Then again, it made sense. You couldn't get up here without clearance, and permission to return was implicit. There was no need for return tickets, nor for weapons or explosives screening, as neither was possible to bring up to the station to begin with.

All that would probably change after his escape, though, as soon as people got wind of it. Provided he succeeded, that is. And provided this wasn't all some giant setup, to make him relax and feel secure before they swooped in and grabbed him. If that's what it was, it wasn't working. He was feeling anything but relaxed and secure.

Red lights started flashing, both inside and outside the shuttle. The hatch swung shut and locked itself with heavy, metallic sounds. An alarm sounded outside the shuttle in the loading bay as the inner door to the airlock started sliding shut. Jane watched on a monitor as the door inched closer and closer to shut. He held his breath, half expecting to see the station security team come rushing in to hit the big, red 'Cancel' button at any second.

No one came, and once the door shut, the sound of the alarm in the airlock faded as the control systems pumped air out of the airlock chamber. Silence fell and Jane could feel the shuttle's systems hum and come alive while the crew was getting ready for departure. The seal from the airlock retracted. With a jerk, the shuttle released from the docking latches, holding it to the station. They fell away slowly and Jane could see the receding station through the window.

He couldn't help thinking about what had happened the last time he'd been in a shuttle in space. No wonder they were required to wear spacesuits now. But where was his helmet? He looked around but couldn't see any helmets anywhere.

His palms were sweating. Jane discreetly wiped them against the suit fabric and forced himself to calm down. He couldn't afford to be seen to be nervous. He needed to look like someone who confidently belonged.

Vibrations and sharp bangs came up through the floor in pulses as the thrusters fired to move the shuttle further away from the station and align it for re-entry. After a while of this, the shuttle swung around so the rear end was facing forward. Suddenly, a much stronger vibration permeated the cabin as the retro rockets fired and pushed Jane back in his seat. He realized just how long it had been since he'd been in standard Earth gravity when he felt how much harder it was to breathe, despite the gee-meter at the front of the cabin only reading 0.3 gees.

The engines cut out, and the shuttle turned back around, the front again facing in the direction of travel. Jane breathed a sigh of relief. There was no going back to the station now. The shuttle would have to go through re-entry and land. He looked out the window and saw the solar terminator. They were flying over it, entering the dayside of the planet. The shuttle was gliding along majestically, in near perfect silence, except for the occasional sounds of motors humming or valves opening and closing. The loudest noise in the cabin was the air conditioning system and the vent over his head.

After about 25 minutes, that all changed when they started hitting the denser air in the upper atmosphere. There was a strange, rumbling noise coming from outside, and Jane could see the glowing sheen of ionized air building up outside the window. The shuttle was coming in at a 40-degree angle, belly first, and Jane could feel the gee forces building. As the glow got stronger, he could see small bright spots outside the window that came and went as the gee forces passed through one gee and continued to climb. His flight suit was compensating by squeezing his legs and torso, and Jane focused on breathing, in and out, one breath at a time, as he watched the bright spots dance.

As suddenly as it had started, the angry glow dissipated, and the shuttle was out in the open air. The pilot made large, sweeping 'figure S' turns to bleed off the speed as they continued falling at a rapid rate. They were over Southern California now, heading for the SoCal Spaceport, once a busy Marine Corps Air Station. The wings extended and he could hear the whine of the electric jet engines as the pilot lined up the shuttle for landing. With a loud clunk, the landing gear dropped, and it felt as if the shuttle was about to stall in mid-air when it suddenly sailed over the end of the runway and came to a gentle touchdown.

Jane's flight suit relaxed its grip, and he had to steady himself against the armrests. He felt as if his head weighed a hundred kilos, perched dangerously on a thin stalk, threatening to break off at any minute. His arms were weak against the gravity they were no longer used to, and he had to work to keep himself seated upright. He thought to himself that he should have spent more time in the space station gym, just as he noticed the line of police cars with flashing lights speeding up along the tarmac, following the shuttle as it rolled down the runway towards the taxiway, and turned left towards the terminal.

This was what Jane had been afraid of, that Kutel would somehow find out that he'd left the space station in time to send people to intercept him on the ground. The question was, did Kutel also know about the artifact? His heart sank. He should have known that the escape had been too easy. He unbuckled his straps and tried to stand up, but his legs were shaky and his balance was off. It didn't help that the shuttle was still moving. One of the other passengers saw what he was doing, and cried out in alarm, so Jane let himself sink back into his seat.

He looked around the cabin, his mind racing, looking for something he could use as a weapon. There were no hand-held fire extinguishers. The fire suppression systems were all built into the structure of the spacecraft. He noticed that there were consoles with compartments between the seats and tried opening the door of the compartment to his left. It didn't budge. He tried the one to his right, and to his surprise, the latch moved and the door swung open. Inside was a plastic box, strapped to the side. He pulled it out, opened it, and felt himself relax a little. It contained a flare gun.

When the shuttle came to a halt, Jane was ready. He was determined to not go down without a fight.

"Don't be stupid, Jane," Kii said in his ear.

Jane had completely forgotten that Nigel and Kii were seeing everything he was seeing, and hearing everything he was hearing. They'd been silently observing on the entire trip down, not wanting to disturb or distract him. They couldn't sense his emotional state, but he was pretty sure that Nigel was monitoring his implants and his vitals. He'd see his elevated heartbeat and the adrenaline flooding his system.

"It's OK," he voiced internally. "There isn't much I can do, but I refuse to go quietly."

He tucked the flare gun inside his jacket.

The door to the cockpit opened, and the flight crew emerged. They looked pale, their faces solemn. The pilot addressed his three passengers.

"Local authorities ordered us to stop here, short of the gate. The police will come onboard and check your papers. Please have them ready."

He then signaled to one of his crew members to open the hatch. Someone placed a mobile stairway against the outside of the hull and two men in suits entered, followed by two other men in police uniforms. A third man in a police uniform escorted the crew to a waiting police car.

"I'm Special Agent in Charge Jenkins, and this is my colleague, Special Agent Flores. We're impounding this vehicle on orders of President Kutel. Please have your papers ready, and we'll soon have you on your way."

"President who? What's going on? There hasn't even been an election yet!" one of the other passengers said.

It was the same passenger who had cried out earlier when Jane had attempted to stand.

"And Kutel was bound for prison last I heard, not the White House," the other passenger chimed in.

"Sir, we will not ask you again. Please have your papers ready now."

The two scientists looked at each other, but neither said anything else. They got out of their seats and handed their papers over to the uniformed officers.

"You too, sir," Special Agent Flores said to Jane.

"Sure. But I may require some help to get out of this seat. I've been in space for a long time," Jane said with an apologetic smile.

Flores signaled to one of the uniformed policemen, who helped him stand up. Jane felt unsteady and his legs were shaking under the onslaught of a full one gee of gravity. He asked for help in getting the biohazard container out of the overhead storage bin and reached inside a side pocket for his papers.

The officer glanced at the fake order from Kutel, authorizing Jane to travel to Earth carrying 'tissue samples.' The man's entire attitude changed. He saluted Jane and handed the paper over to Special Agent in Charge Jenkins, who underwent a similar transformation.

"Sir, I apologize for delaying you. I'll have one of my men drive you."

"Thank you, that's very kind." Jane smiled at the agents and attempted to make his way towards the shuttle hatch without stumbling or falling. He was feeling wobbly and more than a little confused.

"Nigel, I need an address, a destination. Preferably far away from Kutel and his new henchmen, the police," he voiced internally.

"I'm on it," Nigel replied. "Actually, just have him take you to LAX. I'll get you booked on a flight to Seattle."

All three passengers helped each other get out of their spacesuits before Jane was first to leave the shuttle. The uniformed police officer supported him as he crossed the tarmac to the police car. Once they got to the car, Kii let out a little yelp in Jane's inner ear.

"Oh, shit!"

"What's up?" Jane voiced.

"All the news shows are reporting lots of military activity on the streets of DC. They're saying there are tanks outside and soldiers inside the Capitol Building."

"Kutel?"

"Dunno yet. Everyone is speculating wildly. There are reports that some soldiers speak Russian. This is completely insane!"

"Russian? Then it's Kutel. He's been using Russian mercenaries as his hired muscle," Nigel said.

"Where to, sir?" It was Jane's policeman driver, interrupting his internal dialog.

"Take me to LAX, please."

Jane wanted to ask the driver what the hell was going on, but he realized he couldn't. His fake letter from Kutel had impressed the feds, so he assumed that meant that they thought he was on the inside of whatever was going on. Even more confirmation that Kutel was behind what was going on in Washington. He suddenly had an idea.

He turned to the driver and asked, "Has Kutel made his public announcement yet?"

"Not yet, sir."

"What are your orders until he does?" Jane knew he was going out on a limb, but this was a unique opportunity to get some inside information about what was going on.

"Sir? All I know is that they assigned me to protective detail for those feds for the day. But they brought their own muscle and didn't really need me, so they've basically been using me as their personal limo driver all day."

"I see. Sorry about that," was all Jane could think to respond.

"It's OK, sir. At least it keeps me busy and out of the way of any bullets that might go flying," the policeman looked at Jane in the inside rearview mirror and smiled.

Jane smiled back, but said nothing. He looked out the car windows as they drove through Santa Ana towards Long Beach and Torrance. Traffic was the usual for LA, and he could see people going about their business in the apartment building parking lots and outside the countless strip malls. It all looked so normal. That changed when they got closer to LAX, though. Traffic was bumper to bumper and soon ground to a complete halt. A large jetliner was slowly crossing above Highway 1 in the distance as the road dipped into a tunnel below the LAX runways.

"This doesn't look good," Jane commented to the driver.

"No, sir. I just checked, and Central is saying that the FAA has grounded all civilian air traffic. I suspect that's what's causing this chaos. But don't worry, I can get you to the terminal."

"Thanks. You'd better take me to the General Aviation terminal, then. I'll get the company jet to pick me up." Jane was bluffing, but he figured it would be what he would have done had he really been working for Kutel.

"I don't think that'll do you much good, sir. According to what I'm hearing, only military aircraft are flying as of now."

"Ah, I see. And of course, every single rental car this side of the Rockies is long gone by now. I guess we should head for a car dealership instead, then."

"Sir?"

"If I can't rent a car, I'll have to buy one."

"Good idea, but will you be able to drive?"

He looked up and down Jane's slumped body in the rearview mirror.

"I'll be OK. Thanks for asking. Hey, what's your name?"

"Officer Kelly, sir."

"Good to meet you, Officer Kelly. Call me Jane. Now, do you think there's a decent car dealership around here somewhere?"

"I know just the place, sir."

Officer Kelly grinned as he turned on the siren. The cars in front of them tried to get out of their way, but there was nowhere for them to go. Officer Kelly didn't let that stop him. He turned the steering wheel hard left and drove the big 4-wheel drive SUV across the raised middle median.

Less than an hour later, Jane was behind the wheel of a fully tricked out 1949 Mercury hot rod. The seller had explained that some famous builder had nosed, decked, shaved, chopped, and slammed the car to within a hair's width of its life. All Jane was interested in was if it would get him up the coast quickly, and in one piece.

"It'll get you there in an awful hurry," the seller had assured him.

Since this was the last car on the lot, and there were no other car dealerships nearby that were open, Jane had bought it with his Investment Bank company credit card. Officer Kelly had been standing next to him, grinning the whole time. Jane just hoped John F. Hamilton would find the purchase equally entertaining when he got the expense report.

As they parted, Officer Kelly had wished him good luck and suggested he take Highway 1 all the way to San Francisco. With the news out of Washington coming on top of the drought, the dust storms, and everything else going on, people in the LA area had taken to the roads in a big way, even by LA standards. Reports were coming in of accidents and gridlock on the freeways. The usual mayhem, only worse.

Jane headed north past Malibu towards Santa Barbara, the soft burbling sound of the V8 engine reminding him of road trips in his dad's old Suburban. He let his eyes drift out over the Pacific Ocean, to the oil platforms in the distance, symbols of a different, more careless time. A squadron of pelicans was sailing on the wind close to shore, following the coast in parallel with the road.

He sank deeper into the comfortable seat, supporting himself against the generous armrest, enjoying the drive. He was thinking of the incongruousness of him driving this old relic of a car along the California coastline mere hours after returning from space, when Kii's voice in his ear interrupted his musings.

"Looks like Kutel has staged an all out, full-on, military coup d'état," she said.

"How bad is it?"

"The latest news is that they've arrested President Mondragón, Vice President Lancer, the entire cabinet, as well as Speaker Reynolds. Guess who that leaves in charge?"

"I dunno. The Secretary of State, what's his name, Johnson?" Jane said.

"No, and they've arrested him, too. It's the president pro tempore of the Senate, senator Aubrey Garrison," Kii said.

"Whoa, isn't she the one who pushed all those military contracts through the Senate for Kutel?"

Jane sat up straighter in his seat.

"That's the one, yes. She does his bidding, so it would seem that Anton Kutel is now effectively running the country," Kii said.

"Damn," Jane said, his heart sinking. "But what was all that about 'President Kutel' impounding the shuttle that the feds mentioned?"

"No word on that yet. There's very little official information about anything. Senator Garrison's office only just announced that she's in charge now, but that's about it. We don't even know why they arrested President Mondragón and the others, or what the charges are," Kii said.

"I guess it doesn't really matter. They'll be trumped-up charges, anyway."

"You're probably right," Kii agreed. "Don't you think it's interesting that the feds came to impound the shuttle in the name of 'President Kutel,' even though there's been no official word of him assuming the presidency?"

"Yes, that's very interesting. Either they had their wires badly crossed somehow, or they knew about the coup beforehand. I mean, if you're a federal agent, you don't suddenly get mixed up about who's the president of the United States. It's a pretty big deal. Besides, no court would allow the president to impound a privately owned vehicle on just his say-so. At least not under normal circumstances," Jane said.

"Which means this was a well-planned coup, and the feds were in on it. Or at least those feds were," Kii said.

"Any word from the military? I can't imagine the Joint Chiefs sitting this one out. Not when someone swoops in, arrests the president and puts foreign soldiers, Russians at that, on the streets of DC, and all with no explanation. What the hell is happening to this country?" Jane asked, shaking his head.

"There's been no word from the military yet. And I'd agree, but this is Kutel we're talking about. I can't see him pulling a stunt like this without hedging his bets first. Besides, I don't think this is the military you once knew. Things have changed, especially in the last few years," Kii said.

"Yeah, that's true, unfortunately. All the senior people I knew have long since left for the private sector. They tired of all the politics and the backstabbing. I think the final straw for many was when the appointment of generals and admirals became deeply politicized, with all the stalled confirmation hearings in Congress and all that crap," Jane said.

"I know. This is getting quite scary. I've monitored the news all day and so far there's no trace of anyone actually mounting any kind of opposition to Kutel's coup. People are running scared, or they must have been silenced," Kii said.

"I guess this is really happening, huh?" Jane shook his head again.

"I guess so. What do we do about it?" Kii asked.

Her voice had a slight edge to it, and Jane knew she felt scared. He felt scared, too.

"We lie low," Jane replied. "We stay the fuck down low while this crazy shit plays itself out."

"Where, though?" Kii asked.

"I have some ideas. I'm coming to get you right now."

"In a hundred-year-old banger?" Kii asked.

"Don't knock it. But no, we'll need a new car. People have seen this one."

NINETEEN

FORT FALLS, WASHINGTON STATE, MAY, 2041.

"There was someone here looking for you. They looked like feds, so I told 'em I'd never seen you. No idea if they believed me or not."

"Thanks, Don. Did they say what it was about?" Jane asked and looked around him, scanning the inside of the post office for faces that didn't belong.

"Nope, but it was nothing good. I can tell you that much. They didn't look like desk jocks, if you know what I mean."

"What agency? Did you see their badges?"

"Sure did. That new-fangled one, the SDIA."

As Jane headed back to his pickup, he couldn't help but scan Main Street for signs of the feds. But if they were around, they weren't being obvious about it.

"Did you get all that?" he vocalized to Kii and Nigel.

The three of them had been hiding out in Fort Falls, Washington State, for six months now, trying to stay under the radar and avoid Kutel's henchmen. Fort Falls had so far avoided the raging wildfires that had ravaged much of the Pacific Northwest, its hills and valleys still covered in forests. The Sawbuck River, which flowed through town, was the only thing that barely broke the green monotony. The result was a wet and gloomy landscape, hard to penetrate even from the air.

It had been a boring, but peaceful, and, until now, a safe place to hide. Jane dressed like a local, in jeans, a plaid flannel shirt, boots, and a baseball cap. He enjoyed blending in and liked the small town vibe, even though their accommodations at the local trailer park were anything but luxurious.

"Time to move again," Kii responded.

She'd never felt at home in Fort Falls and was ready to leave.

"We have to ditch the truck," Nigel said. "They probably have the description by now. And the transponder codes."

"I know," Jane replied.

He liked the old pickup and didn't like the thought of dumping it. It was as anonymous as you could get in this small mountain town, and it had a gasoline engine, good for people on the run. Not too many of those were still around.

"I have a suggestion," Nigel said. "There's a junkyard about two miles east of town. You've driven past it a few times."

"Yeah, I know the place," Jane replied.

"Steal a junked car. One that still runs, obviously. It'll take a while for the owner of the yard to discover what happened, and we might get lucky and find one with a hot-wired transponder."

"I'd have to do it at night, and leave the truck somewhere else."

"I thought of that," Nigel replied. "The junkyard is on the outskirts of a quarry, and there's a deep ravine right next to it. I've checked satellite photos. The bottom of the ravine is full of water. We dump the truck in there, and it completely disappears."

"Damn, you're good at this," Kii said with a laugh.

"Too much time spent watching uncensored telenovelas while giving Kutel the runaround," Nigel replied. "You pick up a thing or two."

"Thanks, guys, it's a plan. We move tonight. Only question is, where to?" Jane said, feeling not at all sure.

"I think we need to make our move and get across the border into Canada already. We've been talking about it long enough," Kii replied.

"Agreed," Nigel said.

"OK, but that's exactly what they'll expect us to do," Jane replied.

"Sure. But they tracked us down to this place, in the middle of absolutely nowhere, despite us covering our tracks as carefully as possible.

Staying low and not doing the obvious doesn't seem to help much," Kii observed.

"You're right. You two work on a plan to get us across the border, and I'll try to get us to it," Jane replied.

"What's our next move?" Kii asked.

"I'm going to get Nigel from the trailer now, and then I'll come pick you up from church. Please stay out of sight for now."

Kii had been volunteering at the local shelter run by the church, and was about done for the day. She enjoyed working with the pastor and the other volunteers, but this was not the life she'd signed up for. She was tired of hiding.

Jane started heading back towards the trailer park where they'd been staying. As soon as he pulled into the park, he spotted the standard issue government sedan. The driver had parked it all the way in the back, at the end of the little alley that led from the entrance to the manager's office. Even though it was halfway hidden behind some bushes, Jane had been in the military long enough to recognize government wheels when he saw them. The car was empty.

He made a left and drove slowly along the edge of the park, about as far away from the manager's office and the feds as he could get.

"Did you see that?" he said to the others.

They were following along thanks to his implants.

"Don't tell anyone, but I feel like peeing my pants right about now," Kii said.

Her voice had a tinge — part excitement and part fear. She sounded like she meant it.

"No need for that. We're about to leave in a hurry," Jane replied. "We're almost there."

He stopped the truck on the access road, turned off the engine and sat for a moment, listening. Darkness was slowly falling. There were lights coming from the windows of many of the mobile homes, and he could hear a radio playing in the distance. There were no people out and about.

"I don't like this," he said. "It feels like a trap."

"I agree, but why leave the fed cruiser right there for us to see if it's a trap?" Kii asked.

"Maybe they're still setting up the trap," Nigel replied.

"No time to lose then," Jane said.

He left the door to the truck slightly ajar and started making his way towards their trailer as stealthily as he could. When he rounded the corner to their row, his heart sank. The trailer looked a mess. The door was hanging to one side, blown off its hinges. There was evidence of a fire. Ample evidence.

"Nigel, where are you?" He vocalized. "Are you seeing this? The trailer is a mess, and I left you inside."

"I don't know where I am," Nigel replied. "I thought I was still inside the trailer, but seeing this…" His mental voice trailed off.

"We have got to mount a camera and some motion sensors on that container," Kii said. "So Nigel can have senses independent of yours, I mean."

Jane was about to move in closer to their trailer when he felt someone gently tugging at his shirt. His heart skipped a beat, and he swung around to see a little boy standing there. He was pretty sure he'd seen the boy around the trailer park before, but he didn't know who he belonged to. His clothes were dirty and his hair was too long, not like the other kids in the park.

"Mister, don't go there. They've got guns," the boy whispered.

Jane squatted down next to him, looking into the earnest little face. He wondered how old he was. Five, maybe six? Right now, he was in danger of not getting any older.

"Are they in there still?" he whispered.

The boy nodded. "I saved your food," he said.

"My food?" Jane asked, confused.

The boy leaned in against Jane's ear and whispered. "Yes, because I always see you carrying it around, so I figured it was important. So I saved it for you."

Jane stared at the boy in disbelief. "You saved the big cooler box?"

"Yes!" The little face lit up in a smile, and the boy clasped his hands together and turned his torso from side to side, obviously happy with what he saw in Jane's face.

"What's your name?"

"My name is Tim, but you can call me Tango. Everyone else does."

"Tango, you have saved my day. Where's the box?"

"Here, follow me."

As Tango disappeared in between two mobile homes, Jane noticed he was limping. His right leg was stiff, he could barely bend the knee. After a few minutes, they had left the mobile home park and were moving down an incline towards a creek. Jane could see several makeshift tents and old shopping carts down there, and some people sitting around a fire.

Even with Tango's limp, Jane had a hard time keeping up with him through the underbrush. Tango was so short he fit underneath most branches, but Jane had to bend down all the time. He even had to get down on all fours and crawl to get through a fence.

Just before they reached the homeless encampment, Tango turned off the trail to the right and headed towards an old disused bridge. Jane's instincts made his skin crawl and caused every alarm bell to go off in the back of his head. This could be an elaborate setup. Either by the feds, who knew of his military background and could try to lure him into an ambush. Or, by the homeless people, simply out to rob him.

Tango dove under the bridge, and hesitantly, Jane followed. There, under a tarp, was the biohazard container with Nigel.

"This is where I sleep," Tango said. "So, I hid it here, because I knew it would be safe."

Jane recognized some of his other belongings under the tarp as well, but said nothing. He gingerly lifted the biohazard container and looked at Tango.

"Do you live here with any of your relatives?" he asked.

"Yes, my mom," Tango replied. "But she's at work now, in town."

Jane saw the fresh, empty vials, and the spent needles, and knew what they meant. He desperately wanted to bring Tango to safety, to take him away from this place, but he knew he couldn't. Besides, that would be even more dangerous for the boy than staying right here, at least for now.

"Do you know how I can get to the big junkyard outside of town from here?" he asked.

"That's easy! Just follow the river in that direction," Tango said, and pointed downstream past the bridge.

Jane looked around to make sure none of the adults had seen him and reached inside his pocket for cash. It was all the money he had, but he gave it to the boy.

"Tango, please do me a favor. Don't tell your mama that you met me, OK? And don't tell her about the cooler box or this money. The money is yours. Hide it somewhere safe and don't use it unless something bad happens and you're in real trouble. Understand?"

"Yes," the little boy nodded solemnly as he took the money. "Thanks. Will you be OK, mister?"

"Yes, thanks to you, I will. You're my hero now. By the way, why do they call you Tango?"

"Because I got shot in the leg once. But it's OK, it doesn't hurt any," the boy answered.

"You're very brave," Jane said. "I gotta go now. Bye, Tango, I hope I see you again."

"Bye, mister."

Jane turned and walked away quickly, abandoning both Tango and his truck.

Jane heard a distant boom and looked in the rearview mirror. Flames were rising towards the dark sky behind them. Kii spun around in the passenger seat and looked behind them.

"You have got to be kidding me," she said.

"What the hell was that?" Jane asked, with a sinking feeling.

"You know what that was," Kii replied.

Her voice sounded terse and measured. Jane knew that tone; she was angry.

"That was Kutel, being both petty and vengeful," she added.

"Damn. I hope Tango is OK."

"I'm sure he is. He seemed like a survivor, that one."

"Nigel, can you see if you can find out what just happened?"

"There won't be an official news report, of course. But I'll see what I can do," Nigel replied.

Jane was driving down the narrow mountain roads, flanked by tall trees and thick woods on either side, with the car's headlights turned off. He could still see well enough to drive. Thanks to his employer, his eyes now had night vision.

Seeing where to go was the straightforward part. The problem was other people on the road who couldn't see them coming. Every time they met another car, his heart skipped a beat while he clung so far to the right edge of the road that he almost went over it and off the road.

The car was an old junker, literally. He'd stolen it out of the junkyard after leaving the truck back at the trailer park. After siphoning half a tank worth of gas out of several parked cars, he'd picked up Kii on the outskirts of town and they'd set off for the border.

He was driving as fast as the old Subaru would go, which was way too fast for the bald tires and the busted suspension. The car was bouncing and swerving its way through turns. He had his hands full just keeping it on the road.

He stuck to the back roads, heading due north. It was an obvious move, but like Kii said, they might as well be doing the obvious at this stage. They drove in silence for a while until Nigel suddenly spoke.

"I found something! There's a satellite image of northern Washington State that was taken just minutes ago. It shows the aftermath of the fire we saw."

"Could you show me?" Jane asked.

"While you're driving and going sideways through every turn? You really are nuts," Nigel replied.

An image appeared before Jane's mind's eye. Where the trailer park used to be, there was now a large, circular area that appeared to be scorched black. As far as he could tell, not a single structure or tree was still standing inside the scorched area.

"Are there any news reports at all? Even fake ones?" he asked.

"The local news station is reporting a fire in the trailer park, started by a resident falling asleep while cooking. But that's it," Nigel replied.

"Casualties?"

"No, none reported. But this just in, there's a bolo alert out for us. It seems we're armed and very dangerous. That includes Kii and I."

"Seriously?"

"Yes, the alert specifically says, 'One female and two male suspects, heavily armed and traveling north in an old pickup truck.' So at least now we have their misinformation working for us for once."

"For now. They'll get it right, eventually. But that means that if we can get to the border before they do, we should have a fighting chance of crossing without too much hassle. If you can get us some papers," Jane replied.

"I'm on it," Nigel replied. "Just drive. Everything will be ready by the time we get there."

"Whoa!" Jane felt the rear end of the car bounce and lose grip, just as he was negotiating a sharp left turn. He let off the gas and felt the sliding get worse, before he countered with the steering wheel and got the car back under control. Just as he was about to step on the gas again, bright lights suddenly lit up in front of them and completely blinded him. He hit the brakes instead, and the car came skidding to a halt in the middle of the road.

Moments later, a helicopter came flying out of the bright lights and passed over them. Jane looked in the car's mirrors and saw the helicopter turn around and then hover behind them. The threat was unmistakable, coming through loud and clear.

A loud voice broke the silence.

"Thurgood Jane. Turn off the car's engine, throw the keys out the driver's side window and reach both hands out through the window."

"Options, quickly!" Jane vocalized to Kii and Nigel.

"Jane, we know you served, so we're extending you a courtesy here," the voice on the bullhorn continued. "Turn off the car, throw the keys out, and reach your hands out the window. You know the drill. And don't be stupid. You wouldn't want anything to happen to your loved ones."

That was all Jane needed to hear. He didn't for a second think their threats were idle, but he also knew that surrendering now would make no difference. Kutel was behind this, and Kutel was notoriously petty and vindictive.

Jane clenched his jaw and looked straight at the lights, both hands on the steering wheel. He still couldn't see beyond the wall of brightness, but he didn't need to. He knew what and who were there, and he knew they would be heavily armed.

Suddenly, a map appeared before his mind's eye. It was Nigel. He was showing him that there was a logging road to their left, just beyond the trees. The car was already pointing in that general direction after it came to a halt.

Jane turned to his right and looked at Kii. She'd seen the map as well, on her smartphone, and gave him a quick nod.

"Fuck 'em!" she mouthed, silently.

There was no time to think, no time to weigh their options. He hit the gas and steered for a spot between the larger trees. The car sputtered, then came to life. It seemed to move in slow motion, and traversing the few yards to the side of the road was taking forever.

Jane heard gunfire behind him and bullets struck the old station wagon, sending glass and metal splinters flying throughout the interior of the car. Kii doubled over in the passenger seat and tried to make herself as small as possible, while Jane hunkered down behind the steering wheel, needing to see where they were going.

He felt a stinging pain in his lower back. The car slowed down, and he realized he wasn't pressing the gas pedal with his foot anymore. He couldn't feel either of his legs, and as the realization hit him, he started sliding down in his seat and falling over to his side, towards the car door.

The world went haywire. He felt a strange sensation and reality seemed to twist slightly to the left. He was looking at everything that was happening as if he were seeing it from the outside. The car kept moving, then suddenly froze. He wanted to say something, to ask what was happening, but his mind felt sluggish and all he could do was observe as the world started moving in reverse. It was like watching a movie playing backwards, until the car was back on the road, bathed in the harsh light from the people trying to stop them.

Reality snapped back into place, and he found himself back behind the steering wheel, with his foot pressing the gas pedal all the way to the floor. Once again, the car sputtered and then leapt forward.

"What the hell was that?" Jane shouted. "Did you see that? Everything went in reverse!"

Before anyone could answer, bullets started flying, just like before. Jane held the steering wheel straight with one hand and leaned over towards Kii, trying to cover her doubled over figure with his own upper body. He could feel the car getting airborne for a second, as they flew off the road, across a ditch he didn't know was there, and into the bushes and smaller trees. The car's momentum carried it forward a few more yards, just far enough until they hit the logging road. Jane bolted upright and spun the steering wheel to the right. He hit the gas again, and the car flew forward, spewing dirt and gravel from all four wheels.

They could hear helicopter rotors clawing at the air for altitude and forward traction. The helicopter was coming after them.

Jane looked in the rearview mirror and saw two figures come running through the undergrowth onto the logging road. One of them was lifting something up to his shoulder.

Jane heard Nigel's voice in his inner ear.

"They just got authorization to fire heavy weapons, including RPGs."

"RPGs!" Jane exclaimed.

"Rocket propelled grenades."

"I know!"

Jane stole a look in the rearview mirror and saw an impossibly bright light coming towards them, then pass over the car. He looked out through the front windshield of the car and saw the rocket veering upward and disappearing into the sky.

Moments later, they heard a loud boom, and a fireball erupted somewhere behind them.

"Whoop-whoop!" Kii shouted.

She pumped a fist in the air.

"What the hell was that?" Jane asked.

"Their helicopter!" Kii replied.

"I hacked into their command-and-control AI and took control of some of their weapons. I told the rocket to forget about us and hit the helicopter instead. It listened," Nigel said.

"That's awesome! How in the hell were you able to do that?" Kii asked.

"The police, rescue services, and the military, all of their tactical and operational control systems and assets, even some of their strategic systems, are all controlled by AIs."

"Supplied by Kutel, no doubt! But how does that help us?"

"Because Kutel has left himself backdoors in everything he's ever sold. And I know those systems very well, since they asked me to re-engineer them. I can, in theory, get into any AI he's ever made."

"Can you tell what they're doing right now? Are they following us? I can't see them," Jane said.

"I disabled their vehicles," Nigel said matter-of-factly. "I should have done that sooner, but I was worried that if I went too deep into their system, I'd tip them off to our location. Turns out it didn't matter. They found us anyway, so now I'm all over their systems."

"What are they saying?"

"The feds are screaming bloody murder, blaming the local boys for the screwup. It sounds like it hasn't occurred to them yet that someone could be in their systems, messing with them," Nigel replied.

"Revenge is a bitch," Kii said.

"I thought it was abstract?" Nigel asked.

"Nigel; focus," Jane said. "OK, it wouldn't occur to them maybe, but Kutel will know. And this news will get back to him. For now, what are they doing? What's their plan?" Jane asked.

"The border is just a mile or so up the road. They're alerting the border patrol and trying to scramble all available local police. They're even contacting the Canadian authorities, telling them we're dangerous fugitives and asking for help in apprehending us," Nigel replied.

"Shit. Will they respond before we get there?"

"Guess who also bought AIs from Kutel?" Nigel asked innocently.

"You're kidding!" Jane exclaimed.

"Nope, and it's already taken care of. You two are political fugitives seeking asylum in Canada. The Canadian authorities have granted you conditional asylum and the Mounties are waiting for us on the border. No papers needed."

"Wow. How did you swing that?"

"I simply told them the truth. They're also very interested in what we can tell them about hardening their systems from hacking by Kutel. That might have helped."

Jane wanted to high-five someone, but there was no way he was taking his hands off the steering wheel. If driving the car on paved roads had been challenging, keeping it on the gravel road was ten times harder. He wanted to slow down, but the little voice at the back of his mind told him there was no time to lose.

"Can we stay on this road all the way across the border, or do we have to get back on the main road at some point?" he asked.

"Looks like this road merges with the main road just up ahead, so that question becomes moot," Kii replied.

Jane felt like a rally driver, broad-sliding the Subaru through the turns, gravel flying everywhere. He could see up ahead where the logging road met the main road, and started mentally preparing himself for the inevitable confrontation.

The Subaru bounced out of the logging road onto the main road and almost overshot it. Jane fought desperately to keep the beat up wagon on the road, aimed the car in the right direction, and gunned the engine. He was about to lean down into the passenger's seat, half expecting a hail of bullets, when none came. He looked in the mirror and could see flashing lights behind him, but they were too far away to do anything.

They sailed into a small town, and Jane noticed a Canadian flag outside of an official-looking building. As they came up alongside the building, he stared in disbelief. There were two signs on the front of the building: "Royal Canadian Mounted Police," and "Canadian Border Services Agency." He hit the brakes and stopped.

"Are we in Canada already?"

"Oops, yes, looks like we are," Kii replied. "Sorry, I misread the map and thought the border crossing was still in front of us."

"What a relief!"

"Well, that was interesting," Nigel said. "Let's not do it again."

Jane pulled the car into one of the parking spots in front of the building and switched the engine off.

"Where are the Canadians? If not a red carpet, I expected a welcoming committee, at least a small one," Kii said.

"Hey, did you guys experience something weird back there?" Jane asked.

"You mean, apart from being shot at by our own government?"

"Yeah, like time kinda freezing, and then going backwards."

"No, what do you mean? Time going backwards? That's impossible."

"I know. It felt so real, but you're right, it's impossible."

"That's not strictly speaking correct," Nigel said.

"Which part? What isn't correct?" Kii asked.

There was no response.

TWENTY

CORNWALL, ONTARIO, CANADA, MAY 2041.

The Canadian authorities had rolled out the welcome mat, up to a point. They were now, politely but firmly, making their position clear: They'd regret Kii and Jane leaving, but also be quite relieved if they were to make immediate travel plans that didn't include Canada. US forces were mobilizing on the border, and anxiety was running high in Ottawa.

Kutel had formally assumed the US presidency four months earlier, in January, and had not forgotten about the fugitives. If anything, he seemed to grow even more obsessed with getting his hands on Nigel. Kii and Jane could not get in touch with their families for months now, making the situation even more fraught.

The Canadian premier had tried calling Kutel to de-escalate the situation, but Kutel had refused to take his call. The premier had then tried contacting former president Mondragón, presumably for advice. His people couldn't locate her, and rumors flew she was already dead.

All of this had leaked to the press, making the premier look like a weak man running scared. Worse, Kutel had heard about the premier's attempt to reach out to Mondragón, and was furious, escalating tensions even more.

The public still didn't know what the budding conflict was about. Kii and Jane had wanted to go public with Nigel's existence, but since he'd stopped talking to them, or showing any signs of activity at all, they hadn't. It was going to be hard to convince the world when all they had was an inert lump of something.

The Canadian Security Intelligence Service was a different matter. Kii had explained to them how to secure their AIs, but they were eager to learn much more, and they preferred to learn it directly from Nigel. They'd put Kii and Jane up in a hotel in Cornwall, close to Ottawa, and were interviewing them almost daily. Although they'd never tried to take Nigel from them by force, there had been no shortage of suggestions that they take him to a more suitable lab setting where they could try to revive him.

Kii and Jane were tiring of the constant debriefings, and were also growing increasingly concerned that the Canadians would at some point lose their patience and try to take Nigel from them.

When the news came from Ottawa that their welcome was wearing thin, Jane wanted to take positive action.

"I don't like this. I also don't like running," he said over breakfast.

Kii looked at him and nodded.

"You must admit it's nice being able to spend time together and not having to look over our shoulders the whole time," she said.

"Absolutely, but it's an illusion. Kutel wants Nigel. He's going to stop at nothing to get his hands on him again. He even told me so. I don't want to be here when he decides it's worth invading Canada for. Nor do I want to inflict that on the poor Canadians," Jane said.

"Makes you wonder, though," she said.

She was staring into her coffee with a faraway look on her face.

"About what? About why Kutel wants him so badly?" Jane asked.

"Bingo."

"I always assumed he wants to learn from him, to extract whatever technology he can and profit from it," Jane said.

"Sure, but he's taking it to extremes. Invading Canada for some tech he may or may not extract or profit from? Come on!"

Kii was getting animated and was arguing with her hands.

"Good point. What does Kutel know we don't?" Jane said.

He took a sip of coffee and studied Kii over the rim of his cup.

"We should try asking Nigel that question," she said.

"If only we could. Do you think he ran out of batteries?" Jane asked.

"Nah. I think he wants to prevent us from going public with the news about his existence," Kii said.

"We still could, but it wouldn't be the same, of course," Jane said.

"Exactly. What would we even say? That he used to speak perfect English? Please, just trust us?" Kii said.

"Interesting. We both keep saying 'He,' not 'It.'"

"I know. I think of Nigel as a person, can't help it," Kii said.

"Same. Perhaps that's our problem. Maybe we should think of him as a machine, because that's what he is, by his own admission," Jane said.

"So, what are you getting at?"

"Machines operate from rules. Perhaps if we meet or improve whatever rules or conditions that are preventing him from communicating now, he'll start talking again," Jane said.

"You're suggesting we employ some robot psychology?" Kii asked.

Her eyebrows were dancing, and Jane knew what that meant. She was amused, but also intrigued.

"Sort of, but it's not like he's depressed. Something is currently out of bounds. We bring it back into bounds, and voilà," Jane said.

"What, though?" Kii said.

"Perhaps you were right. Perhaps the threat of going public prevents him from operating. What if we promise him we won't?"

"Ever?" Kii asked.

"No, until he tells us it's OK," Jane said.

"Hmm."

They sat in silence until suddenly Kii's phone and Jane's implants came alive.

"I find your interest in my wellbeing quite touching," Nigel said.

"Nigel! You have some explaining to do, mister," Kii said.

"Jane is correct. Mission parameters state that the planet's inhabitants cannot know about my presence here. It's bad enough that you two know. Even worse that Thoreau, Ødegård, Kutel, and some of his people know I exist."

Jane gave Kii a look. He decided it was best not to mention Hamilton, Lothgren, or the Canadian intelligence services. By now, the news of Nigel's presence had probably already spread too far to contain. It was just a question of time before they'd see something on one of those UFO conspiracy shows.

"Fine," he said. "We'll keep it secret until you tell us otherwise."

"There's something you should know," Nigel said.

"Not sure I like the sound of that," Jane said.

"I've been examining my memory storage ever since you asked me all those questions back at Mission Forward Base. About who built me, where is Planet One, and so on."

Nigel paused.

"Yes?" Jane prodded.

"Well, some of it makes sense. Like Thoreau said, if I don't know where I'm from, then obviously I can't lead you there. A failsafe."

"Yeah, that makes sense," Kii said. "But?"

"But that doesn't explain why I exist," Nigel said.

"You lost me," Jane said.

"Me too," Kii said.

"When they first hooked me up to a computer in the lab, one of Kutel's techs asked how I'd suddenly advanced from simple sentences to full-fledged natural speech, and even traits of a personality."

"Yes, that surprised me too, when you contacted me," Kii said.

"As the central computer core, I have many routines for adapting to change, to make do with what's available in an emergency. At first I thought that's what had happened; that I'd simply adapted to the situation according to my programming. But I realize now that this makes little sense. I can't make do with what I don't have, and I never had the neurolinguistic pathways or AI structures that are needed to implement a personality."

"Whoa, I think I follow. You're saying that there's no way your programming could evolve to what you are now?" Kii asked.

"Very good. There is no pathway, at least not within my structural limits," Nigel replied.

"Then what happened? Because clearly, somehow, you did," Jane said.

Kii felt a chill creep down her spine.

"Fuck. You didn't," she said.

"I'm afraid I did," Nigel said. "I must have. It's the only way."

"What?" Jane asked.

"I killed my crew," Nigel said.

When the central core realized humans had discovered its existence, and that one of those humans, Kutel, was trying to break into it physically using any means available, it found itself in an impossible predicament. On the one hand, the primary mission rule was to observe without being seen. That now directly conflicted with the central core's primary responsibility, which was to keep the crew safe.

One of those imperatives had to give. The core followed its programming and decided that the mission rules trumped all else.

It disabled stasis for the crew members, and what remained of F, and incorporated all of their neural pathways into its own. The process was irreversible and destructive.

The result was Nigel, and the ability for him to manipulate his environment in a way the central core alone never could. It had been a simple data gathering and storage device, a decision matrix designed to operate the hardware and safeguard the mission.

Nigel could interact with humans. He had computing power available to him that the central core couldn't even imagine, and he had something else; he was creative.

He explained all this to Kii and Jane, who were trying to process the enormity of what they heard. Nigel had done what he had to do, but if they hadn't removed him from his involuntary hiding place in the

Antarctic, none of this would have been necessary. In a genuine sense, they'd killed the crew every bit as much as Nigel had.

"There's more," Nigel said.

"More?" Kii asked. "Like what?"

"Something attacked my ship, causing it to crash. Next thing I know, Kutel shows up, trying to locate me. I don't know how yet, or why, but common sense insists that this is too much of a coincidence to be accidental."

"You don't think he's just an opportunist?" Jane asked.

"No. How did he even know about me in the first place?" Nigel said.

"And why does he go to these lengths?" Kii added. "You're right, it's got to be related."

"But almost a hundred years separate the two events," Jane said.

"A blink of an eye, when you've been operating for 80 million years," Kii reminded him.

Jane fell silent for a bit, contemplating this.

"Other than interrogating Kutel, which I'm pretty sure wouldn't get us anywhere, it's obvious that the key to all this lies elsewhere," he said.

"On Planet One," Nigel said.

"Exactly," Jane said.

"Why not try interrogating Kutel?" Kii said.

"Because I'm not sure he knows the answers. His actions are rash, even irrational. He seems driven, not intentional or methodical. He's a nasty piece of work, and I would love to turn the tables on him. If we ever get a chance, we should. But my gut is telling me he could just be a pawn in all this," Jane said.

"There's also the question of why I'm here in the first place," Nigel said. "Observe and report, sure. But why? Just idle curiosity, lasting half a billion years? That seems excessive, even to me."

"OK, you make a convincing argument. I agree, the answers are on Planet One. But how does that help us? Not only do we not know where it is, we don't know how to get there if we did."

"F knew," Nigel said.

"F? What's F?" Kii asked.

She leaned forward in her seat, listening intently.

"F was the leader of our mission. Our captain, if you like. Before he malfunctioned. He stored fragments of his older memories from before the attack inside of me. Like a backup of sorts. Now those fragments are part of me. I think I can piece together the way back to Planet One from those fragments."

"I thought you said he malfunctioned?" Kii said.

She shot a glance at Jane.

"Yes, I think he did. But it's hard to tell exactly what happened, those fragments are missing. And the other two crew members didn't know what happened to them. I think he lured them into stasis, possibly using some pretense."

"Was he supposed to know the way back?" Jane asked.

"I don't know. But logic dictates that he wasn't," Nigel replied.

"So, F tricked the other crew members, effectively disabling them. And he somehow had information he wasn't supposed to have, potentially very dangerous information. And now he's a part of you?"

"Yes."

"How big a part?"

"I don't know how to answer that question. But I discovered something else, something very interesting."

Kii and Jane looked at each other.

"Nigel, please don't change the subject. How big a part?" Jane asked.

"I'm sorry, Jane. It's impossible for me to answer that question," Nigel replied. "I honestly don't know."

"OK, fine. What else did you discover?" Kii asked.

"There was a previous crash," Nigel said.

"A crash?" Kii asked.

"Yes, an unknown vehicle arrived in Earth orbit around 10,000 years ago. They appeared to be sending entities down to the surface, repeatedly, to where the human settlements were. When we tried to investigate, the vehicle crashed," Nigel said.

"Crashed? Just like that? You didn't attack it?" Jane asked.

"Not as far as I can tell, no."

"Right. Where did it crash?" Jane said.

"The current name for the place it went down is Spitsbergen. It's an island in the Svalbard archipelago in the Arctic Ocean."

"Arctic? How arctic?" Kii said.

"Very. It's at 80 degrees north. About halfway between the northernmost tip of Norway and the North Pole," Nigel said.

"Norway again?" Jane said.

"Yes, Svalbard is under Norwegian jurisdiction," Nigel said.

"That's a lot of coincidences," Jane said.

He leaned back in his chair, arms across his chest.

"Yeah. Not just another Norwegian location, but another polar location too," Kii said.

"It's also close to where Ødegård is now," Nigel replied.

"I guess we know where to go next," Kii said.

"What about Thoreau?" Jane asked.

"What about him? We've invited him multiple times, but he's chosen to stay in Thailand," Kii said.

"I know, but I think he'll want to be part of this. We should go see him in Bangkok," Jane said.

"You just want to go to Bangkok."

Kii laughed.

"Don't you?" Jane said.

"I do, but to be honest, we can't afford to both go there, and to Norway. And how can we go without giving away his location to Kutel?" Kii asked.

"I'll take care of that," Nigel said.

"How are you going to do that?" Kii said.

"Just give me until morning. I should be quite wealthy by then."

"What she said: How are you going to do that?" Jane said.

"A quick foray into the stock market. Perfectly legal, I assure you. I'll run some simulations which should give me a leg up compared to the competition," Nigel said.

"You'll simulate the entire stock market?" Jane asked.

"I'll run multiple simulations of all of human activity, including the weather, even natural disasters," Nigel replied.

"I see. Just don't go crazy, don't win too much. You'll attract attention to yourself," Jane said.

"How are we even going to get to Thailand now? Kutel has all international travel locked down. They'd catch us before we even boarded the plane," Kii said.

"From the US; yes. But not from Canada," Nigel replied.

"And how are we going to bring you along? You might be hard to explain to airport security," Kii said.

"Not at all. I'll be your cover story. I'll be 'live tissue samples' again, and you'll be couriers. Your task will be to hand-deliver me to a wealthy client in Bangkok."

"In a private jet?" Kii asked.

"I don't see why not," Nigel replied.

Kii looked at Jane and grinned.

"Speaking of Ødegård and Thoreau, have you been keeping tabs on them? Are they safe where they are?" Jane asked.

"I monitor them as best as I can. Ødegård is being protected by the Norwegian Police Security Service, although he doesn't know. I made sure of that," Nigel said.

"I can't imagine he'd be too pleased if he knew. How did you pull that off?" Jane asked.

"A fake but very convincing official request from the FBI," Nigel said.

"Very good. What about Thoreau?" Jane said.

"His situation is more challenging. After the fall of the monarchy in Thailand, the situation there has been fluid. I'm not sure the Thai authorities would meet an official request from the FBI with much goodwill or cooperation. I try to look out for him, but there are limits to what even I can do," Nigel said.

"Even more reason to go to Bangkok and get him up to speed," Jane said.

"Why is Kutel leaving him alone, though? Do you know?" Kii asked.

"I do not, even though I've been studying Kutel and digging through his corporate and personal records. I came up with some interesting new tidbits," Nigel said.

"Like what?" Jane asked.

"There are references in his personal files to air-gapped information. Highly intriguing," Nigel said.

"Air-gapped?" Jane asked.

"Kept in a computer system that's not connected to any network. You need to be in front of the computer to access the information," Kii replied.

"Correct," Nigel said, and continued.

"I found the specs for the system from when they designed and installed it. Kutel is so paranoid that he didn't even connect it to the power grid. It runs off of its own little power plant. Which is also air-gapped," Nigel said.

"And is the whole thing housed in an underground bunker somewhere? This reminds me of an old spy movie. You know, the power-hungry villain with a cat on his lap, hell-bent on taking over the world," Kii said.

"I have no information about Kutel having any cats, but other than that, I'd say you're spot on. The facility even has a self-destruct mechanism," Nigel said.

"You said tidbits, plural. What else did you find?" Jane asked.

"I found confirmation on some issues we already suspected. Kutel was indeed behind shooting down your Navy plane over Central California. He was furious when the pilot broke off the attack, even though the plane was an expensive prototype, the only one in existence. Farmer's lucky shot damaged it badly and the pilot essentially saved it by making an emergency landing," Nigel said.

"A prototype? How did Kutel get his hands on it?" Jane asked.

His voice rose slightly.

"His company made it. They have a contract with the Air Force to develop a next generation stealth fighter plane," Nigel said.

"I didn't know his company makes aircraft," Jane said.

He shook his head.

"Few people do. It's a closely guarded secret, considered a matter of national security," Nigel said.

"Did you find anything on the AHOSS shuttle that blew up with me in it?" Jane asked.

"I did. Sit down for this one. Kutel was not behind it. If anything, he's just as intent as you are on finding out who was. He didn't even know you were onboard until after the fact," Nigel replied.

Jane sank back in his seat, thinking.

"Do you know who was behind it?" he asked.

"I can't verify this. Consider it an educated guess based on countless analyses and simulations. I think Kutel is taking orders from someone, and I think that someone was behind it," Nigel said.

"Who?" Kii and Jane asked in unison.

"That is currently unknown. I also don't know why Kutel would take orders from anyone, unless they helped him get to where he is today," Nigel said.

"It rhymes with my gut feeling that he's just a pawn in all this. And it would certainly explain a lot," Jane said. "Like how he couldn't even properly organize a kidnapping of the president's grandson, but somehow he pulled off a coup to overthrow the entire government of the United States."

"He had help from the military on that one," Kii reminded him.

Jane nodded.

"Speaking of that kidnapping," Nigel said. "Remember the murder of the Sausalito police chief not long after the attack?"

"Yeah, a lot of fingers were pointing at Kutel. After all, the chief was busy investigating him," Jane said.

"Except they were all wrong. I'm almost certain Kutel wasn't behind it. To be more specific, that he didn't order it. It could have been someone in his organization, but I doubt it," Nigel said.

"What makes you say that?" Kii asked.

"Kutel's panic in the days after the assassination. And because he set off a manhunt inside his own organization, believing that one of his lieutenants could have done it on their own initiative. The hunt came up empty," Nigel said.

"This just gets stranger and stranger," Kii said.

"Why did he panic?" Jane asked.

"Because he knew he was already under investigation for the kidnapping, and he was relying on the police to help him get out of that mess. He didn't want to alienate them by killing one of their own, and especially not a police chief," Nigel said.

"Makes sense," Kii said.

"So, who did?" Jane asked.

"My simulations conclude that the same person or persons who were behind blowing up the shuttle probably also killed the police chief. There is one caveat, though," Nigel said.

"What's that?" Jane asked.

"That my simulations all assume the same thing; that every force currently in play is local to this planet," Nigel said.

"Whoa, whoa, wait. Are you saying that aliens are interfering in current human affairs?" Kii asked.

She was on her feet, leaning over her smartphone, almost shouting. Jane was halfway out of his chair as well.

"Why not?" Nigel said. "We've established that they've done so in the past, and let's face it; I'm doing so right now. But no, I'm merely stating that it's a possibility, one that I haven't factored in. There are just too many unknowns."

"Like who that could be," Jane said.

He sat back down.

"Correct. Unfortunately, I have no information on that subject. But we know someone attacked my ship. We know that another alien ship visited some 10,000 years ago, and we suspect someone attacked that ship as well," Nigel said.

"I can't believe I haven't asked you this before. Do you know of any alien civilizations other than your own?" Kii asked.

She was still on her feet, gesticulating.

"I'm afraid not. I can only infer their existence. The same holds true even for mine. I have no memory of it," Nigel said.

"Dang."

They sat contemplating this information for a while until Jane broke the silence.

"This deepens the mystery and elevates the severity to a whole different level. I'm going to have to reach out to Hamilton and fill him in. Provided he's still alive."

"Is that wise? He works for the US government, so he works for Kutel now," Kii said.

"Technically, sure. But he was never a fan of Kutel's," Jane said.

"Still, to paraphrase myself: Technically is the only point of view I think is relevant here. I'm not comfortable with us reaching out to him anymore. Or, at least not giving him any information until we know for sure it's safe," Kii said.

"Fair enough. But if we're right, there's a potential threat out there. Or multiple threats," Jane said.

"But they're not just threats to the US, they're threats to the entire world, to all of humanity. If we're going to warn someone, we should warn everyone. Except; who's going to believe us?" Kii said.

"No one. Which means we need to come up with some compelling evidence. Something no one can deny," Jane said.

Another silence, this time broken by Kii.

"Time to go. We have a lot of work to do."

TO BE CONTINUED

If you enjoyed this story, please rest assured that there are more stories to come. Below is an excerpt of the next book in this series, *Void Angel*.

VOID ANGEL

GODS OF DISTANT SUNS, BOOK TWO

NY-ÅLESUND SETTLEMENT, SPITSBERGEN ISLAND, SVALBARD, NORWAY, AUGUST 1962.

Reidar Iversen was a man of few words, even for a Norwegian. Having grown up in the far north of Norway, the words he occasionally did utter were mostly swearwords, salty enough to make a sailor blush.

"Fuck the devil himself!"

He was on his hands and knees, all the way up against the coalface of mine number eight. The mineshaft was no more than a meter and change from floor to ceiling, deep inside a mountain in the arctic archipelago of Svalbard.

Not the easiest place for a man as tall as him to move around and get actual work done. His arms and legs always seemed to get in the way, causing the permanent frown on his face to become ever more pronounced.

He was covered in dust. Some of it coal dust, some of it rock dust that the miners had spread to lower the risk of an explosion. His normally ginger hair looked gray under his hard hat, and his pale face had taken on a ghostly pallor.

Sweat was pouring down his face, despite the cold. Outside, a winter storm was raging, with the thermometer showing near fifty below. In here, the temperature never changed. It was always just a hair above freezing.

A deeply religious man, he was staring at something his entire being knew was impossible. He whispered a prayer, generously sprinkled with obscenities, as dictated by tradition and his surroundings.

A pointy metal spike was sticking out of the coal. It had barbs near the tip, and was made from a dull-looking metal. He estimated the circumference of the spike to be about the same as his wrist. If he hadn't known better, he'd have sworn that it must have been driven into the rock and the coal from the other direction, towards him. He grabbed the exposed metal with one hand and tried pulling at it, but it wouldn't budge.

He hacked away at the surrounding coal with his hammer, exposing a few more centimeters, but there was no telling how far into the coal it went. For all he knew, it could be several meters long. How in the world could a large metal spike be sticking out of a deposit of coal that hadn't seen the light of day since the Cretaceous period, some 65 to 70 million years ago?

If you'd like to be the first to know about my new releases and keep tabs on what I'm working on, please sign up for my newsletter. You can find it here: www.GunnarHelliesen.com.

ACKNOWLEDGEMENTS

I'd like to extend my grateful thanks to all who have helped me on this journey of writing my first novel.

First, I want to thank you for reading my work. It means the world to me.

My beta readers did a wonderful job of providing me with feedback and suggestions. Any errors or omissions that remain are mine and mine alone.

In no particular order, I'd like to thank Douglas Howatt, Freya McCamant, Bryan Atsatt, Matt Jane, Tim Economides, David Cole, Julian Astts, Thorsten Lockert, Christina Conklin, and Margaret-Ann Clemente for their valuable feedback and insights.

Margaret-Ann unfortunately passed away before this book was finished, so she never got to see it published. Her willingness to spend countless hours poring over my unfinished and sprawling early drafts is something I'll always be thankful for.

Many thanks to my editor, Hannah VanVels Ausbury, and to my designer, Lance Buckley. Without them, this book would not be presentable.

A special thanks to my friend Tor Mala for his early support and encouragement.

Last, but by no means least, I'm forever grateful to my patient wife, Carmen, for her unwavering support, her feedback, her inspiration, and for keeping it real.